The Angel of a Madman

Ricky Dragoni

Published by Ricky Dragoni, 2017.

THE ANGEL OF A MADMAN

First edition. June 18, 2017.

Written by Ricky Dragoni.

Also by Ricky Dragoni

Prime Infinity
Ripples
The Angel of a Madman

Dedication

There has always been a voice encouraging me no matter what path or adventure I have chosen in life. A rock holding me up even when life feels like it is falling apart. Words of wisdom and encouragement that have kept me going even when I wanted to give up. Throughout my life, there has been chaos and pain but you have always been there to soothe my pain and help me get up. I always say, "Everything good about me comes from you and everything bad I have figured out myself." It is because of you, that I am the man, the dad, and the person I am today and I will never be able to thank you enough. I live my life trying to honor the amazing person you are, live by the example you set for me, and always try to make you proud. This book and journey are possible because of you and belong to you as much as me. Rita Dragoni, thank you for being my mom, my friend, my counsel, my editor, my Sherpa, my example, and my hero.

Te quiero tanto, tanto, tanto, con todo mi corazón!

Ricky Dragoni

Bracket's Escape

My Codename is the Bracket and these are the tales of my missions and adventures.

We had made our escape from the detention center and were now being chased by four of the slimy guardians. In our escape we were able to elude them but we were still detected. My three partners and I had constructed the perfect escape plan. Unfortunately we hadn't accounted for the new guard not knowing his route and running into us in the hallway.

The detention facility, from where we had escaped, was a level 9 maximum facility. Someone within my organization had sold me out and I resided in the Super Max for the past 5 months. Using my extensive training, I was able to break out of what most would consider an inescapable prison. If we hadn't been detected by a rookie guard we would be well on our way to a clean getaway. Instead I could hear the wet footsteps and gargled breathing of the guards behind us.

We had cleared the fence, were quickly making our way out of the city and heading towards the train tracks. It was 3:00 AM and I could already hear the train whistling in the distance. We could not miss it, the train was our only way out of this hellhole. This was our one chance and I was sure not going to blow it.

We were outside the city now and I could see the train tracks out in the distance. Along with the rumbling of the approaching train, sirens were now filling the otherwise quiet night's air. The colorful flashes inundated the darkness, as their presence became imminent. In the panic Charlie stumbled and let out a loud yelp. I stopped and considered going back to help him. Before I could decide two of the green slimy guardians had enveloped him in their oozing saliva. I could hear Charlie scream as their acid drool burned and consumed his skin. Charlie was gone and the screaming of the train's engine mercifully drowned out his cries for help.

I continued as planned and made the last sprint towards the moving train with my two remaining partners. Paxson and Jaxson had passed me in my hesitation to save poor ol' Charlie. I picked up the pace and quickly passed the dangerous twins. I had recruited them for the escape but I knew the level of savagery they were capable of. I might have been betrayed into that prison but the twins had earned it. I knew I could not trust them long term but for now I didn't have any other options.

I could see the train barreling down the tracks, we were going to hit it just in time, hopefully. I dug deep and forced my already exhausted legs to move a little faster. The engine of the train quickly passed us, along with the first few cars. We were aiming for the rear cargo cars, the ones usually empty and just being moved around from train yard to train yard.

I was now running along the train trying to do my best to keep up. Even though the train had slowed down as it traversed through town, it was still moving faster than even my carefully trained legs could. We slowly started to approach the train as we ran alongside it, the wind created by the moving train forcefully blowing on our sweaty faces. I looked over my shoulder time and time again trying to spot the right train car to infiltrate. I could see the twins close behind me, their lungs burning with each stride and their faces showing the struggle. Not far behind them the monstrous green blobs kept pace with us, somehow moving their lumbering slimy bodies faster than they should.

I spotted the train car I had been looking for and made my move to attempt boarding it. I got dangerously close to the train as it whizzed by us and still I got closer. I would have one chance to jump, grab the railing and board the train car. Everything slowed down as my eyes fixated on the rusty piece of tubular railing that I was targeting. The noise of the train and the screeches and screams from our pursuers disappeared into the tranquility of the dark night. I extended my arm with my hand open and ready. I didn't so much catch the train; it was more like the train hooked me like a fish. I closed my hand around the beat up looking railing and hoped it could hold me. Mercifully the railing held. I pulled myself onto the steps and I was now moving with the train. Jaxson and Paxson somehow achieved the same feat on the other end of the car.

We moved inside and collapsed in the empty wooden vessel. We had made it. I felt bad for Charlie but such were the risks you had to endure when living this type of life. I had sprawled my body out on the old dusty floor and was considering giving in to slumber when the first side door of the car was violently ripped open. The guards were not accepting their defeat and still wanted to capture us.

I quickly sprung to my feet and scanned around for anything I could use or turn into a weapon. I was well trained and wouldn't need much but there was nothing to be found, not even a loose board. I readied my fists and got as far away from the now open door. The noise of the moving train thundered through the opening as the wet smacking sounds of the guards disturbed me.

One of the ugly creatures was desperately trying to board. The twins, fearless and psychotic, charged it. I had moved back to a safe distance, assessing the situation and waiting to capitalize on our pursuers' mistakes. I had been trained to handle situations like this. Paxson and Jaxson on the other hand, were quite unpredictable and enjoyed embracing violence. They engaged the slimy green creature and did their best to avoid their giant mandibles and slimy finger tentacles. The guard screamed in pain as the twins took turns swooping in, assaulting it then retreating to let the other twin have his turn.

The twins had almost knocked the beast off the car when the guard reached up with one tentacle filled hand and grabbed Paxson by the leg. The guard's grip broke off the car and both the disgusting creature and Paxson went flying out of the train. I could hear the deep gurgly laughter of success the creature made as it fell away with its prey. Jaxson screamed his brother's name and without a second of hesitation dove out of the train to rescue him.

I was left all by myself in the empty train car. I kept my attention on the open side panel, waiting for another guard to come after me but only the scenery flashed by in a dark blur. Before I knew it we were far out in the wilderness and nothing had tried to jump in the car with me. I had allowed myself to relax a little and slowly approached the open door. I quickly peaked out, jumping back as soon as my eyes had processed enough information. I felt a little foolish; after all my years of training, all my missions and I had jumped like a frightened cat. I shook the embarrassment aside and realized that I had successfully escaped.

There were no green slimy guards chasing anymore, I had lost my escape crew and the train car was missing one of its side panel doors. The original plan we had made was no longer going to work. I had to figure out what I needed to do next and fast. If I made it into the next populated area, I would quickly be spotted and the chase would be on once more. I needed to figure out how to stay safe and hidden as I made plans to escape this rock. This planet was a penal colony, the less time I had to spend on it, the better.

The night was peaceful but hot. I could feel the dry heat pressing down on my skin, drying my sweat before my skin could even release it. I stood by the large opening and contemplated my options. I had to do something and quick. In the distance I could see the lights of what looked like a small town. I knew from my reconnaissance this had to be Pecos, the only town before I hit the next big city. I knew the train was not going to stop at Pecos but I had to get off somehow.

I explored the train car, even visited a few others, trying to figure out how to get off the train but with no luck. The distant lights were becoming larger and if I didn't figure out something soon I was going to lose my chance. I returned to my train car, out of options and with time quickly running out. The train had already passed Pecos and the lights were shrinking as it moved away. As darkness kept rolling by outside the car I did the only thing I could do. I jumped off the train and hoped I didn't land on anything too hard or sharp.

I couldn't see where the ground was until it was too late. I had planned to hit the ground, roll to absorb the contact and be on my merry way. Instead, I hit the ground like a bug hitting a windshield and bounced like a ragdoll a couple of times for good measure. I was a tough and strong man but I lay on the ground whimpering and unable to move. My lungs slowly remembered how to breathe and several ribs protested at my expanding ribcage. Tears escaped my eyes no matter how hard I fought them back. I slowly began to move each extremity searching for damage; everything was sore but thankfully in working order.

I rested on the dry dirt and took in the beautiful stars up in the sky. I had never seen the stars from this angle and they were quite beautiful. A long white streak of the galaxy adorned the darkness like a beautiful scar. I forgot about the pain in my body for a while and collected myself while admiring such incredible beauty. I could see in the eastern sky the first signs of the approaching sun. Even if my body protested, I had to move and find somewhere to get shelter and hide.

It took a few painful attempts but I finally made it to my feet. I took shallow breaths to avoid upsetting my ribs any more than I had to, while I figured out my next move. The town was north and distant, there was no way I could make it there tonight and find shelter. To the south were some majestic mountains, their sandy colored soil peppered with a multitude of green trees and shrubs. It wasn't ideal; I didn't know the terrain, I didn't know what kind of animals I might find and shelter wasn't assured but it was my best option.

I dusted myself off and gingerly started my slow walk into the beautiful wall of earth that grew before me. The terrain was dusty and rocky. Small patches of short grass grew randomly in the valley and up the hillside while arid, mean looking trees hid where I was going. I weaved my way up the mountain until thankfully I spotted what looked like a small cave. I tried to pick up my pace but my ribs quickly overruled me. The sun was now starting to crest over the horizon and I knew the authorities would be looking for me for the next few days.

I made it to the cave and in reality it was more of a glorified rocky overhang. I was exhausted and the day was pressing on me, so the overhang was going to have to work. I used the walking stick I had procured on my hike to clear out the small opening for unknown and dangerous critters. Nothing lunged out at me and nothing attacked me. My body was throbbing in pain and my eyes were becoming heavy. I pulled down a couple of coniferous branches with my last few bits of strength, crawled into my new home and covered myself with them. The bushy branches would provide some shelter from the elements but more importantly hide me from any searching eyes. Beaten, bruised and tired I gave in to sleep, while keeping my eyes half open and my ears alert.

A persistent rattle brought me out of my slumber. It was a slow and painful awakening. My eyes creaked open and followed my ear to the origin of the rattling sound. Through the evergreen branches which were still concealing me there were three heads dancing in the air. It was a three headed snake but larger than anything I had seen in my life. The main body was as thick as my thigh and the three viperous heads danced rhythmically, and full of dangerous potential.

The snake seemed to be very interested in something in the direction of my feet. The two outer heads flanked out continuing their entrancing movements, while the middle and slightly larger head danced with its eyes completely focused. I felt the sudden urge to flee but thankfully my battered and tired body refused. I held back a whimper and continued to watch the strange creature.

As the outer heads continued their hypnotic dancing, the middle head struck the unseen prey faster and more viciously than any other viper that I had ever seen. I heard a small yelp come from near my petrified feet, which was quickly extinguished by the other two attacking heads. The beast slithered away carrying in its jaws an unrecognizable furry creature.

I exhaled a breath I hadn't realized I was holding once the creature was out of sight. I forced my body to move and it protested every step of the way. My ribs in particular would send sharp pains all the way into my core. Once I made it to my feet and once my vision stopped swimming, I was able to appreciate some of the carnage left behind by the three headed snake. A pool of bright red blood rested not a foot from where my feet had been. The trail of red blood decorated the tan rocks and disappeared into the shrubbery.

I felt partially responsible for the poor creature's death. I had stolen its burrow and it had perished on my account. I had to find better accommodations or I might be the snake's next meal. I gingerly started to stagger down the mountain in search of suitable shelter and resources. I desperately needed water; my lips were about as smooth as sandpaper and my head hurt so much it felt like it needed a hole to relieve the pressure.

Every step was excruciating and after many hours of searching for a better shelter without success, nightfall was quickly approaching. I did not want to be wandering around in the dark out here. The heat was oppressing and my already beaten body wasn't putting up much of a fight. My vision was becoming blurry and the dryness of my lips had spread all the way down my esophagus. I had to stop and use a hearty coniferous tree for support.

I could hear the terrifying howls and screams of predators welcoming the night. The sun had almost submerged itself into the horizon, leaving the mountain and countryside in a dance of fiery reds, pinks and oranges. While soaking in the beauty of it all I spotted what might be my salvation, a small cabin on the side of the mountain. Adrenaline or optimism coursed through my veins and gave life to my legs. I was almost trotting as I weaved my way to the cabin, trying to escape the darkness.

Closer to the structure I could see it wasn't much of one, just a simple wooden shack probably over a hundred years old. It might not have been a five star hotel but it was going to be home and safety for me tonight. The door devoid of a lock didn't fight my entrance into the shack. Inside I was welcomed by four bare walls and a wooden plank floor. Besides a few cobwebs there wasn't much of anything in the shack. I closed the door and hoped the thin piece of worn wood would keep the monsters out for the night.

Gabriel's Penance

My name is Gabriel Moreno and this is the story of how I die.

The air conditioner blared in the old Jeep as I made my way through the desert down the highway. The sun was beating down on the countryside and not even the desert willows dared move. It was a majestic view full of death and hidden life. My exit was coming up and not a moment too soon, I had been driving now for two days and needed some proper rest.

As I entered the small desert town, memories came flooding back to me. The streets were all familiar and I found my away around without any difficulty. It is funny, no matter how long you are gone, how far one travels or how hard one tries to forget you always remember your way around home. I stopped at the gas station to fill the old red monster and bought myself some drinks and food for the house. My walk in and out of the gas station was filled with familiar yet unrecognizable faces. It was nice to be home but I still felt out of place.

Back in the Jeep I finally headed to my childhood home. Anxiety, sadness and excitement filled my stomach as I made my way through the very familiar streets. It didn't take more than five minutes before I had left all the businesses and most of the houses in my rear view mirror. On the southern outskirts of town was a small, but full of memories, house. The short drive down the long driveway stirred more emotions than I could contain, causing tears to stream down my face.

I parked in front of the house and squeezed the steering wheel as hard as I could as I tried to compose myself. I hadn't seen the house in almost fifteen years let alone set a foot in it. I grabbed the bags from the gas station and started to make my way to the old ranch house.

It was a humble house, but even without anyone attending it you could see the pride that had gone into it. My father had built most of it; I had lived most of my early childhood years in a construction zone. As I grew older my dad always involved me in the projects and had even gotten me my own little tool belt. I was his little helper in much simpler and happier times. I made it to the front door and my hand refused to reach for the knob. I wanted to call

8

and scream "Mamí, Papá llegué!" but I knew there was no one there to greet me or respond.

Instead, I hauled my bag down the covered front porch and found a seat in my favorite rocking chair. My "Abuelo" had built this one and it had truly withstood the test of time. I sat in it and both my body and the chair recognized each other. It was a simple wooden rocking chair but not even the fanciest and most expensive chair in the world could provide a tenth of the comfort. I gently started swaying back and forth in the chair, taking in the beautiful explosion of color on the Cerro de Escobas mountains. The last of the setting sun always made such a spectacle of the red hills. I reached into my plastic bag, found one of the cold beers and began to drink.

The sun had long set and 12 empty cans of beer littered the wooden porch. The chill of the night was moving in so I felt forced to find refuge inside the old house. I used the momentum of the rocking chair to help me up and I grossly miscalculated. Instead of standing, I stumbled forward off the porch and felt flat on my face onto the hard dirt. I let out a drunken grunt as I landed and found myself laughing at my clumsiness. I tried to stand up and it took a few attempts. The beer was playing tricks with my equilibrium and giving me a fit of the giggles. Once on my feet, I walked up the two porch steps once more and ungracefully made my way to the door.

The key kept refusing to go into the door lock and I found myself having a conversation with the key, trying to convince it to just go in. My little pep-talk worked and the key slid right into the doorknob. I threw my hands in the air in celebration and let out a wolfish howl of excitement. I turned the key, opened the door and turned on the light. It had been many years but the house still looked just as I remembered it. Every piece of furniture was still there and everything still in its rightful place.

Once I was done wrestling the keys out of the doorknob, I shut the door and looked for a place to crash. I knew very well where my room was, but the beers made it seem like it was so far away. After a brief and intense negotiation with myself, I settled on the couch. I stumbled my way to the couch and collapsed on it. I started to put my feet up on the couch and I could vividly remember my mom scream "get your shoes off the furniture!"

"Sí Mamá!" I answered into the empty house and slid off my shoes before putting my feet on the couch. The living room was starting to spin on me so I clutched onto the pillow, closed my eyes and went to sleep.

I woke up the next morning thankfully not as hung over as I had expected to be. I did have an immediate and desperate need to go pee. I got up from the couch, leaving the drooled pillow behind and made haste to the bathroom. After what must have been the longest pee in human history I washed up and headed back into the living room.

The room was just as I remembered it from the previous night and just as it had always been, but it felt empty. My stomach grumbled so I headed into the kitchen. I opened the fridge and it was bare. That was the first time I had ever seen that fridge empty of food and it broke my heart. So many memories of my mother cooking and my father attempting to cook flashed before my eyes. We had spent so much time in that small room, cooking on that tiny stove and eating the most delicious food I have ever tasted. Food that at one time I deemed common and boring, food I had rejected in search of other culinary adventures, and food I wished I could taste just one more time.

I slammed the fridge door harder than I expected and went out to search for my gas station provisions. I walked out on the porch just to find my bags ravaged and torn. Some lucky skunk or porcupine had greatly benefited from my drunken shenanigans. They had made an easy meal out of groceries and now I was hungry and pissed. I had no one but myself to be pissed at but I still wanted to bitch and moan at the damn critters. I picked up the mess left after the feasting and found that my can of peanuts had survived the ordeal. The critter had tried to get into it from the teeth marks but for some reason had quit before it found its bounty.

I threw away all the torn bags in the garbage, filled a cup with cold tap water and sat down at the tiny kitchen table to enjoy my breakfast of dry roasted salted peanuts. Once done with my breakfast of champions I decided to unload the Jeep and settle into my old room.

I passed my parents' bedroom door several times as I hauled bags of clothes and what few personal items I had brought with me. I could see the door in my peripheral vision but I didn't even want to look at it. I wasn't ready to open that door just yet; I would keep the band aid on for just a bit longer before I had to completely and painfully rip it off.

Mom had done an amazing job preserving my room. I felt like a time traveler going back about three decades. The same posters of angry bands and sexy women still adorned my walls. Men who were probably now bald and women whose external beauty had been overran by their internal ugliness by now. The bed looked smaller than I remembered it but it was still perfectly made, waiting for me to mess it up.

My study desk was still where I had last seen it. It looked more like a drafting desk with its own built in lamp and a secret compartment under the writing surface. It had been made by the strong hands of my father. I had spent so much time sitting at that desk, reading about the world, planning all the adventures I wanted to take and learning everything I could that existed outside my speck of dust tiny town. My feet had led me next to the desk and as I lifted the writing surface all my old National Geographic's were still neatly stacked inside of it. Those ugly yellow magazines were my only window into the world as a child. But the universe has its way, after all this time, after all the wasted years running to something, my path lead me right back to where it all started.

I'd had enough of memory lane and my stomach was complaining. I left the house behind for a while, got in the Jeep and headed into town. I picked up some fast food and then headed into the Dollar General for a few things. I filled my little cart and headed for the registers. There was only one register with two people in line. My eyes followed the short line until they rested on a vision from the past. I quickly panicked and did the only thing I could think of and hid back in the aisles pretending to still be shopping.

She still looked so beautiful and I looked like total hell. The years might have been fun but they certainly were not kind to me. To say that I was overweight was an understatement; I was as round and fluffy as a summer cloud, my hair had thinned and although I still had my beautiful smile, my eyes looked as tired as my soul. I hid for as long as I could but I knew I had to man up and face the music.

I headed towards the register after filling myself with fake valor. The moment I saw her, my heart fluttered as it had so many times and my face was instantly decorated with a big smile. The lane was now empty and she was keeping herself busy organizing the candy and gum. Her hair was as black as crow's feathers and her eyes the most amazing shade of green. They were a light shade of green, almost olive, and they sparkled and shone with specks of gold. Her hair was put up in a messy bun which just highlighted her sexy neck and jawline. And unlike my fat ass, she looked just like she did in high school.

"I can help you here Sir." Monica said without even looking at me. She turned away from her wall of colorful treats, walked around the checkout lane and started to scan the items I was putting on the belt.

"And how are you today?" She asked smiling and finally making eye contact with me.

"I'm good; how about yourself?" I kept unloading my tiny cart as fast as I could, hoping she would not recognize me. Such wasn't my luck. After cheerfully replying that she was good as well, she did one of those cartoons double takes and stared at me like a deer in headlights. She didn't say a word. She just looked at me, letting her brain catch up with what her eyes were seeing. It was the same look I saw when I professed my love for her so many years ago. Needless to say she hadn't felt the same, she saw me only as a friend and even used the dreaded phrase "I love you like a brother".

It had been our senior year when I finally worked up the courage to tell her. We had been friends, well most of our lives. My foolish teenage heart was convinced she was the one and that we would have a long life together. As I said, my heart was very foolish. I must admit that at the time I was devastated, but time and space heals all wounds, right? That devastation was the last nail in the coffin for me leaving this tiny town. I went as far as I could, met so many people and enjoyed the company of many women. I thought all those years and all those miles had made me forget about her, but there truly is nothing like a first love. So I stood there not being able to say anything, feeling as insecure, anxious and uncomfortable as I did all those years ago.

The items on the belt were starting to fall off the belt and broke both of us out of our respective trances. "GABRIEL!" She screamed and screeched, making me jump. She was talking so fast asking question after question as she came around the lane again and gave me a huge hug. I melted into the hug but quickly composed myself. The embrace broke and she grabbed my face with both her hands, she kept talking and talking but I just stared into her eyes and enjoyed the moment. She hugged me once more and I could finally process some of the questions she was asking.

"What are you doing here? How have you been? Oh my god it has been so long Gabriel!" Her smile gently dissipated and her face held a nurturing pouty look to it. "I am sorry, how rude of me. I heard about your Mom, I'm so sorry Gabriel."

My Mom had been my rock. She was tough, stubborn, and independent but always there for me. Even after my dad died, she refused to leave the house he built for her. I was her youngest, her baby and we had a very special relationship. I was traveling in Europe when she had fallen ill. Cancer, and by the time the doctors found it, it was in the final stages. Like I said, she was tough and stubborn and never got it checked out. My brother and sister had forced her to go to the doctor. From diagnosis to the moment she passed, it was only one month.

My sister called me and finally gave me the news once Mom had passed. I begged and pleaded for them to allow me to return before the funeral but to no avail. I made it back in three days; the funeral was two days after she passed. I wasn't very popular amongst my siblings and the will didn't help my case. My mom had left me the house. My brother and sister were irate over it and repaid me cruelly.

Monica was hugging me once more without me even being aware of it. I said the only thing you can say in that moment. "Thank you." We didn't say much after that, she finished checking me out, I grabbed my bags and started to head for the exit.

"Gabriel." I stopped my pilgrimage with hands full of grocery bags and turned to face Monica once more. "When you have the time and if you want, we should catch up Gabriel."

I couldn't help but smile even as I was holding back tears. "That sounds good Monica."

"I'm here every day, eight to five and I take my lunch at eleven, stop by some time and we can go grab something to eat and talk." She smiled and waved at me as I turned, walked out of the store and entered the overbearing heat of the Pecos.

With every step on the hot pavement beads of sweat formed on my head. Once they had reached critical mass they plunged down my forehead. Most just streamed down my face but a select few would invade my eyes, making them burn as my hands were held hostage by the grocery bags. I finally made it to the Jeep, threw the bags in the back and turned on the air conditioning as high and cold as I could. I was finally able to wipe the sweat off my brow and rub my eyes to try to provide them relief.

While I drove quietly back to the house my Mom had left me I could still smell Monica's perfume on me. It had been great to see her but it just made me more numb. I had some cereal and decided to call it an early night. I was emotionally and mentally exhausted and a little tired from the night before. My body was kind enough not to fight me, I settled into my childhood bed and went to sleep.

Hunger in the Desert
(Bracket)

It had been a couple of days and the small cabin had provided great shelter. My ribs were still sore but upon further observation I think they were just bruised and not broken. I had found a small ravine which provided me with my needed water but hunger was overwhelming and I needed to find something of substance. I had laid a few traps but had struck out with all of them. Trying to hunt in this wilderness was not only foolish but also dangerous. I was both hunter and prey out here. It was unbecoming of an agent as well trained as me, but survival does make us do unbecoming things. I was going to have to venture into the strange town to the North and try to procure some provisions without being detected.

I wanted to enter the town during the cover of the night but did not want to walk there during it. I waited as long as I could and with the dying rays of the sun I started my march through the orange and pink soil. I had to painfully sprint the last half mile to escape the approaching darkness, but I made it.

My first order of business was procuring some new clothing. The uniform from the Super Max was tattered and filthy, plus it would give me away if someone spotted me. I carefully and stealthily navigated myself through the yards of the small square houses. I finally came across a shelter where the local beings used the warm breeze to dry their clothes. What I found didn't fit me perfectly, but it was a good upgrade. With new clothing acquired I was now ready to search for a good food source.

After weaving and searching the town for hours I finally came across a building with "market" in its name. I was hoping it still meant the same here. The building was closed and I didn't have any of my gear to be able to break in undetected. I would have to wait until it opened and figure out another way of procuring some food. The cramps in my stomach kept intensifying and the grumbling noises gave away my position. I found some decent cover within the bushes and trees and settled in for the night.

Daylight hadn't come when two bright and moving lights awoke me from my half slumber. The vehicle came to a spot closer to me than I had hoped. The door of the long brown metallic transport opened and a giant stepped out of it. Seeing him standing and stretching in all of his glory, I was confounded in how he fit into the vehicle. The creature had to stand at least ten feet tall. His shoulders were wide and muscled; his hands large with long threatening fingers and his head so large no hat could ever fit it.

My stomach made a loud grumble and the giant turned his attention in my direction. His eyes pierced through the darkness, searching for the origin of the strange sound. His face was decorated with a full, almost black beard which made him look even more menacing. After a few tense seconds and having not spotted me, he turned and started walking towards the market. He carefully unlocked the door, hunched through the opening and disappeared into the building.

This definitely didn't look promising but it was my only option to get food. I was going to have to carefully consider how to go about this venture. I was starting to run extremely low on energy so I could not keep waiting much longer to find food. On the other hand, if the giant apprehended me while I was trying to steal his merchandise he would undoubtedly crush my skull with his immense and strong hands.

After much consideration and thinking, I knew I had but only one option and I wasn't happy about it. Using my invisibility ability was dangerous, draining and exhausting. I could not leave empty handed from the giant's market or the drain from going invisible, on top of my current exhausted state, might actually lead to my death. Any other day I would have been at peace with dying. It is after all a very possible reality for agents like me. But I refused to die right now, not until I discovered who betrayed me and sent me to the Super Max.

Even with the loud protest of my stomach, I did the prudent thing and used the whole day to do reconnaissance on the place. A flow of odd and strange creatures visited the giant's market throughout the day. Some were human like me while others, well, the others I didn't recognize or identify. The sun had gone down before the giant finally exited the building, locked the door and walked back to his car.

The night's air had a chill to it tonight and in my weakened state I was desperate for any food. Throughout the day I had seen many items put into the round bin right outside the door of the market. I waited a few minutes after the giant had driven away in his carriage and I made a mad dash for the grey round bin. The top of the bin had a small swinging door so I tried to look through it and reach inside but could not make heads or tails of what I was feeling. I removed the cube top, gathered the edges of the bag, pulled it out and took it back with me to my temporary shelter.

The bag was heavier than its size and it sloshed and made wet sounds as I ran with it. I carefully opened it and a very strong smell came out of the plastic bag. I started to carefully pull things out one item at a time and asses the viability for consumption. The first item I deemed safe was a plastic bottle with a little bit of brown liquid inside. I was extremely parched and I remembered seeing a human take a drink before disposing of the bottle. I knew it was safe but did not know what it was. I slowly untwisted the blue cap and once open, I took a quick whiff of the liquid inside. The brown liquid smelled sweet. I should have done more due diligence before drinking it but my body overruled my brain. I tipped the bottle back and the little bit of liquid inside of it met my lips. The liquid was warm but it tasted even sweeter than what it smelled like. My tongue exploded in excitement as it met the brown substance and an instant rush shot down my spine and through my body.

Energized by my sweet find I kept digging through the bag. I found a few more bottles with small amounts of sweet liquids in them. Food on the other hand was a little harder to come by. In all of the immensity of the bag I was only able to find one peanut who had stealthily hidden in its bag, avoiding being eaten by its purchaser. I slowly consumed the crunchy morsel and sipped on my bottles of liquid sugar.

The night was long and cold but if what I found in the garbage was any insight to what was inside the giants market, my wait was going to be greatly rewarded. From the day's observations I knew my optimal time to strike would be midmorning. Once the early morning traffic dissipated I could slip in, grab some provision then exit while the giant prepared for the midday rush.

I tried to sleep but the cold air made my rest intermittent at best. Mercifully, the sun finally came out and the desert air quickly began to warm. The giant had arrived under the cover of the night as the day before and was already in his market taking care of the parade of morning customers. I knew my one and only chance was quickly approaching.

The morning rush had thinned out and only two cars besides the giant's sat in the parking lot. It was time. I disrobed and once naked, I focused my energy and focused on becoming invisible. I felt the energy concentrate deep in my stomach and once ready, disperse throughout my body like a bolt of lightning. I instantly started to feel the drain in my already depleted energy reserves. With no time to lose I walked across the parking lot towards the entrance door. I took one more second to focus my energy before I opened the door on which my hand already rested.

I quietly pried the door open and snuck in. As I suspected the place looked empty. I made a quick scan of the few aisles and settled on my targets. I was quietly grabbing bags of peanuts when one of the remaining patrons appeared in front of me on the other side of the aisle. From first appearances it was a normal looking human and I instantly relaxed since I knew he could not detect me. He looked in my direction but as I expected didn't see me. I waited for him to walk away and resumed collecting my provisions.

I had one more spot to hit before I fled the giant's store. I stealthily arrived in front of the candy bars without being detected. The high sugar content of these snacks would prove great out in the desert, plus they did taste delicious. I was grabbing the last few candy bars when I heard the oh so dreaded words.

"What the hell is that guy doing? Griego come here, you got to see this!" I looked over to see a humanoid being with the head of some sort of insect. The two giant black compound eyes staring right at me. Obviously they must have seen in infrared and the man-bug could see me. I stood there paralyzed, contemplating what to do next.

The giant stormed from the back exploding through the door by the counter. He was angry before he saw me, and once the bug-man pointed me out he became furious. I had but one recourse and I didn't like it. Still holding onto my bounty I darted to the door and out of the store. I didn't have time to stop for my clothing as the giant, the man-bug and the human patron were hot on my trail.

I held tight to all the bags and bars clutched in my arms and decided to make a run for the mountains. I ran as fast as I could as the giant wasn't giving up on his chase. I had hoped that after a while they would find the chase futile and return to the store but their persistence surprised me. I dashed through yards and backstreets until I was weaving through bushes and trees. A few of the items I so zealously clutched fell as I ran but I dare not stop to gather them. I would have to just consider them casualties of war; sweet, salty and delicious casualties of war.

I was growing tired and my ribs were beginning to ache once more. The man-bug kept guiding the giant on my trail and as with all giants I had previously encountered, they would not be satisfied until they recovered all of their treasure. My pace was starting to slow and they were starting to gain on me. Ahead I saw what might be my only option to escape the mob chasing me. I could see a small patch of trees up ahead. If I climbed one of them and hid properly my heat signature would be broken up and I could disappear, even from the man-bug creature's eyes.

I knew that having to climb a tree would mean having to let go of all the goodies I had gathered. I did the only prudent thing and started throwing them in multiple directions as I ran. I hoped that once the chase concluded I would trace back my steps and collect all the hidden treasures. By the time I had reached the small cluster of trees I had but one candy bar left in my hands. I quickly placed it in my mouth, its plastic wrapper protecting it from my teeth and started to climb.

I made it to my desired hiding point by the time my pursuers caught up to me. I could see all three of them scanning through the trees hoping to find me. Thankfully after some very tense moments it was obvious they could not see me. They picked up some of my dispersed bounty as they walked and eventually the giant, in his deep voice, gave the word to start heading back.

I didn't dare move a muscle as they kept looking back while they headed back into town. I could feel the sweat gliding into all the small scratches and cuts climbing the tree had caused. However, I focused to block out the pain and remained still while their silhouettes grew smaller and smaller in the distance. It wasn't until I could not differentiate the giant from the bushes that I was able to relax.

My momentary relaxation was abruptly broken when surprising words startled me and almost made me fall out of the tree in which I had perched myself. "What are you doing up there buddy?"

I quickly turned my head to see a round, brown corpulent man looking in my direction. I stayed still and used what felt like the last of my energy to strengthen my invisibility. I quickly moved to another branch in hopes of losing the preying eyes of the hefty man. He was but a human so I knew I had lost him. Or so I thought.

"Hey buddy, what was that all about? What are you doing up there?"

The man had kind brown eyes and they were fixated on me. Somehow he was able to see through my invisibility cloak. He looked like a normal human being, a rather chunky one, but normal. I had no idea how he was able to see me, he shouldn't be able. Knowing my cover was blown I decided to reply to the man.

"You can see me?" I asked him and an immediate look of confusion flooded the man's face. Again I asked him to ensure he understood me. "You can see me Sir? How are you able to see me? You are but a human."

The look of confusion painfully intensified in the round bearded face of the man. After a brief moment the man replied. "Of course I can see you! Get down from there buddy, you are bleeding pretty badly, let's take a look at your leg back at the house."

I saw a few cuts and scrapes but nothing I hadn't experienced before. I think the man was extending a peace offering and maybe I had just made an ally in this planet. He didn't seem threatening and his kind eyes showed honesty, so I decided to trust him and allow him to cure and serve me. I carefully climbed down the tree with my candy bar securely held between my teeth. Once down on ground level, the man kept his head down to show servitude and asked me to follow him.

The round man led me back to an old house which apparently was his shelter. It didn't look like much but it was much better compared to where I had been staying the past few nights. He provided me with a towel and some strange clothing and asked me to please clean up, so he could tend to my wounds. I embraced the opportunity to have a hot shower and entered the small bathroom. I let the hot water beat down on me, slowly taking off layer after layer of desert dirt that had accumulated on my skin. The droplets of water searched my body for every cut and made me aware of them with an intense stinging sensation. The clear water turned red, tinted with a mixture of dirt and blood. I guess one of the cuts was more severe than what I had assessed.

My left thigh had a three inch gash which didn't want to stop bleeding. It had opened like a mouth revealing the fat and tissue underneath it. I cleaned it with the water as best as I could but the bleeding persisted. I finished in the shower, put on the clothes the kind man had given me and exited the bathroom. I held the shorts above the cut to not get them bloody while the red liquid kept oozing out of the wound and running down my leg.

The man was standing right outside the bathroom with a small plastic case in his hands. His brown eyes instantly went to my cut and he ushered me to a chair so he could tend to me. As I sat on the chair, he knelt in front of me and tended to the gash on my thigh.

"I need to take you to the hospital buddy, you need stiches here." The man made a whistling sound and his eyes opened wide as he inspected the wound. I had been through so much and fought so hard to escape the Super Max, there was no way I was going to a hospital and reveal my location. Without hesitation and with great animosity I replied to the man.

"NO! No hospital! Just do what you can but I am not going to any hospital!" Even to me the words sounded loud and desperate. The man studied my face, looking deep into my eyes searching for the answer to my reaction. He looked at me with his kind brown eyes, which became piercing and inquisitive.

"Fine buddy, no hospital." The moment he said it my body relaxed and I started to feel lightheaded. I was hungry, dehydrated and had just lost a fair amount of blood. The room momentarily swam on me; my forehead felt cold and sweat started to bead on my face.

"You don't look too good there buddy, here keep pressure on it." He placed my hands on the rag he had covering my wound and quickly disappeared into another room. Seeing the large man walk fast made me chuckle, even in my debilitated state. He quickly returned with a clear glass of water. He handed it to me and his hands went back to tending my wound. I chugged every last drop of water and I could feel it being instantly absorbed into my body. The room stopped moving and I did feel a tad better.

"Ok if you won't go the hospital I am going to have to stitch you up. What's your name buddy? I'm Gabriel."

Stitch me up? What was he planning on doing to my leg? I stared him down and it was my turn to dig and prod in his eyes for the truth. I could see from his kind, almost childlike, eyes that he was telling the truth and did have my best interests in mind. I felt reluctant to give him my name but at this point it would have been rude not to give to him.

"You may call me Bracket. And how are you planning to stitch me up Gabriel?"

Gabriel smirked as I told him my name; I wondered if he had heard of my exploits. He explained he would have to use a needle and thread to close up my cut. I was a tough agent but I was pretty sure this was going to hurt. We discussed methods to anesthetize the region before the procedure but settled on me drinking a lot of tequila and biting down on a leather belt during the stitching.

As dehydrated as I was, it didn't take much tequila to make me feel like I was on top of the world. Pain evaporated and liquid courage came pouring out of me. Gabriel had tightly placed a belt on my leg to slow down the bleeding as he stitched me up. The other belt was folded and ready for me to bite down on once the needle met my flesh.

"This is one of my Mom's leather needles, if anything is going to work, this is it." Between his meaty sausage fingers Gabriel held a quite large needle. He had already threaded some sort of string through it and was now running the needle through the open flame of a lighter. I took one last long swig out of the bottle of tequila and to my surprise, so did he. I put the folded belt between my teeth and hunkered down for what was about to come.

Gabriel's hands were trembling so he decided to take one more swig out of the now almost empty bottle of tequila. He took a deep breath and started to move the needle towards the soft flesh of my wounded thigh. I spit the black leather belt out of my mouth and interrupted his approach. "Have you ever done this Gabriel?"

The large man sat there giving me wide eyes, unable to give me a response. I could feel the full effects of the alcohol hitting me so I just sat there, swayed and waited for him to answer. Gabriel lowered the needle and the movement seemed to snap him out of whatever trance he was in. "No."

His monosyllabic response was not what I was hoping for. I wasn't going to a hospital so this was my only option. I took one more swig out of the bottle, bit down on the belt, and mumbled through it; "Do it!"

Gabriel nodded and his fingers once more approached the wound holding the thick and sharp needle. The first stitch was the worst. His trembling hands dug the needle through my flesh, unsure and hesitant. I bit down on the belt and could feel my teeth almost gnawing through it. One the first suture was done, either endorphins kicked in, the tequila overran my senses or my training took over, but I could no longer feel the pain. I watched my ally finish up the stitches. Once the job was done; I thanked him, found somewhere to lay down and decided to finally get some quality and comfortable rest.

Gabriel left a glass of water on the coffee table next to the couch that I had found and he excused himself. I laid on the soft couch, grateful for meeting such a caring ally in such a strange place. I think Gabriel underestimates his true potential, after all, no mere human had ever been able to spot me while invisible, yet somehow he had. I gently drifted into sleep thinking about how I could repay him for his kindness, as well as how our newly formed partnership might grow into something truly special.

Naked Coffee
(Gabriel)

That humiliating run in with Monica was the cherry bomb on top of what seemed like a never ending shit-storm. All the angst and emotions I thought I had outgrown as an adult came rushing back. Maybe I was just too raw or maybe it just took one smile from her to break down all the walls I had built over the years. Broken, sad and defeated I decided to self-indulge in a binger of spectacular proportion.

I had stocked up with tequila, beer, vodka, wine, more tequila and even more beer, on my way back to the house. I had decided I was going to test the limits of my liver and see how many brain cells I could kill. After all, what did I have to lose?

My father had taught me how to be strong but my mother had always been there when I was weak. She had been my rock even when I had moved away. Letters, post cards and phone calls kept us in contact. I even got her to video chat me once; she just hated it so we stuck to regular phone calls. She sat there frozen half the time staring at the camera, it was hilarious but it was also nice to see her face. I remembered thinking how old she looked on the video but I never doubted she would be there whenever I decided to come back. How wrong I had been.

The next two days were a blur of memories, uncontrollable sobbing, drinking and frozen pizzas. I relived thousands of happy memories, all which ended up with guilt, regret and more tears. I drank more than I ever had and I had been part of some crazy parties in my day. After the first night of drinking, some hair of the dog took care of the hangover. I drank the whole day, while doing a pretty good job of making the immaculate house a total mess.

I resented the house, it felt like an empty prison now. All my fellow prisoners had left and it was just me, locked in it, alone with nowhere to go and no one to share my misery. In desperation I called my siblings but after the first few slurred insults they hung up and refused to pick up any other of my calls. I vaguely remember tossing my cell phone across the room in anger.

By the end of the night I was so drunk that walking was impossible. I ungracefully tossed myself off the couch to the hardwood floor. I was crawling towards my bedroom as I held back the pepperoni and tequila percolating in my stomach. As I approached my Mom's room tears just started to sprout out of my eyes. I wasn't crying but tears just uncontrollably flowed and fell to the floor as I crawled. I missed her so much. I would have given anything for one more day with her. The overwhelming guilt made my stomach and chest feel like they were caving in.

Desperate to be close to her, I clumsily grabbed on to the door handle to her room and opened. The moment the door swung inwards her smell filled my nostrils, speeding up the flow of tears from my eyes. Her room was still pristine, unlike the mess I had made out of the rest of the house, better yet it smelled and felt of her. I whimpered my way to her bed on my knees and somehow managed to climb onto it. Nausea and grief quickly had me in the fetal position. My head resting on one of her pillows, while I clutched and spooned the other one, letting its scent and memories lull me to sleep.

A strong gust of the cold desert night woke me from my slumber. I was lying on top of the sheets and maneuvering to get under while on top of them proved impossible. Incapable of the impossible feat, I gave up and stumbled my way to the window. I hope closing it would not require much dexterity, as I possessed none at that moment. I walked with my hands extended forward in hoped of not slamming face first into the wall. Instead I succeeded in severely jamming my right index finger on the closed window.

I opened my blurry and confused eyes to find the window completely shut. Confused about how the cold desert night had invaded the room, I did a quick scan of the room for any other open windows. I knew there were no other windows in my Mom's room, but I still searched.

That is when I saw the unmistakable figure sitting at the foot of the bed. She looked younger than what she was and reminded me of her when I was kid. Her soft supportive smile and loving eyes were directed at me. She wore a colorful sun dress, covered with yellow flowers in a blue background. I stood paralyzed, unable to process the vision before me. Her smile widened and her melodic voice broke the silence.

"Come here Mijo." Her right arm extended towards me, while her left hand gently patted the bed inviting me to sit next to her. I didn't know whether to run to her, jump out of the window in fear or do what she said. As always I listened to my Mom, walked over to her bed and sat beside her. I sat there trembling, eyes wide as saucers, not knowing what to say or ask first. As always she knew exactly what to say and do.

Her hand started to gently caress the top of my head and she hushed me to tranquility. Her eyes searched and inspected me and a look of sadness engulfed her face. Her eyes remained loving but I could see the concern in the creases of her face.

"You are not taking care of yourself Mijo." Every word she emoted warmed my heart and her caressing hand sent electricity down my spine.

"I am Mami, it's... it has just been a rough couple of months." My half-truth was instantly replied to with a scowling and disapproving face and I could not help but to smile in return. She was not a large and imposing woman, calling her petite would be calling her big. She was dainty and delicate but even with her small stature I can admit I was terrified of her when she reprimanded me. My smile was part happiness, part seeing how cute she was but mostly it was nervous fear.

Her scowl softened as she continued. "You have to promise me to take care of yourself. I worry about you Mijo. Please promise me you will." Her small hands were wrapped around my right hand as it rested on her lap. I slowly shook my head in agreement while avoiding her insistent and concerned eyes. The bony fingers of her left hand gently guided my chin until we were making eye contact. "Promise me."

Her words held a gentle authority that I could not defy. "Si Mami." I said it and meant it. Her loving smile flooded back into her face and she hugged me. My head rested on her shoulder and she held and petted me while gently rocking me. I wanted to say so many things to her, I had so much to apologize for but all I wanted in that instant was to enjoy being in her loving embrace.

While still gently holding me she spoke once more. "I need you to promise me one more thing Gabriel." My body tensed at what her request might be and she instantly made shushing sounds like you would to a newborn. The reassuring noise made me close my eyes and my body relaxed once more as she continued.

"I need you to promise me to be happy. I raised you to be a good man; I want to see that good and proud man come out and for you to allow him to be happy." Even in her most gentle voice the words stung as I heard them. My Dad had made sure I was a strong man but my Mom always, always, always stressed that I needed to be a caring, noble and good man. So many lessons and litanies flooded out of my subconscious and into my mind. "Be good and be happy", echoed inside of my head, said and thought in so many ways. That is all that she had ever wanted for and from me.

I lifted my head and tears were streaming down my face as I once more looked at my mother's beautiful face. "I am sorry Mami." Her face softened at my words and she repeated her request. "Yes, I promise you, I'll be good, noble and happy." The concern she held on her brow disappeared as I uttered the words. Happiness and joy exuded out of her face and deep into my soul. She grabbed me once more and brought me in close to her.

She squeezed me so hard and she felt so real, I wanted to live that moment for the rest of my days. I sobbed while she held, caressed and comforted me. She leaned into my ear and whispered the last words I would ever hear said in her voice; "I love you my little bear."

I woke up replying into the empty room "I love you too Mami." The words echoed in the empty room as the darkness enveloped me. I sat on the bed clutching her pillow tight to my chest and face. I took in her scent and cried for what seemed like hours. The merciful rays of the sun leaked in through the window and her words echoed through my head; "Be good, be noble, be happy." My eyes, almost empty of tears, burned as I soaked in the explosion of colors outside the window. The sun had set the desert on fire and the impossibly warm colors gave me hope.

I got out of the bed and made sure it was perfectly made before I exited the room. My eyes felt swollen and my throat and chest were hoarse and sore from the night's meltdown. I walked through the house, ashamed of what I had done to it while my head throbbed in excruciating pain. I needed to clean the place up but first things first; I needed some coffee so that I could function.

I had to pitch quite a few beer cans just so I could reach and operate the coffee maker. It wasn't anything fancy but it made the most delicious and soothing cups of coffee that I had tasted anywhere in the world. I opened the cabinet, placed the filter in the coffee maker, filled it with coffee and water, hit the start button and waited for the smell to fill the kitchen. I sat at the table and tried to explain what I had lived or dreamt the night before.

The machine made its gurgling noises and soon I was enveloped in a delicious aroma. I decided to stop trying to figure out what had happened and just be grateful and happy for it. I filled my cup with the delicious dark nectar, along with some sugar and the smallest splash of milk. I didn't want to stare at the cemetery of cans, bottles and paper plates at the moment so I took my coffee to the front porch. I sat on the old rocking chair, sipped on the hot elixir while I enjoyed the last few cool gust of the desert air before the oppressing heat of the day took over.

I gently rocked while holding the cup with both hands. I was almost half way done with the coffee and just about a quarter awake, when an even more confounding vision caught my attention out of the corner of my eye. I looked at what was developing in front of me, looked away refusing to believe it and then observed it unfold. A gaunt looking, bearded and naked man was running across the fields as if someone were chasing him. His arms were folded over his chest clutching a multitude of shiny looking bags and objects.

He kept running as fast as the coarse terrain would allow his feet to go. He kept frantically looking over his shoulder as his nakedness swung through the morning air. I looked in the direction he was fleeing from and finally spotted his pursuers. There were three of them, two of them who I didn't know and the third who looked very familiar. He was a tall man with broad shoulders. He looked a little long in the tooth but still seemed to move well as he chased the naked man. I took another sip of my coffee while I took in and enjoyed the ridiculous and hilarious scene developing in front of me.

I looked back and forth between the naked man and the three men chasing him. It finally dawned on me where I knew the tall guy from. He was the owner of one of the markets in town. He had lost a lot of his hair and what little he had was almost white. It had been years since I saw him but even from afar I could tell it was him. Not many people of that size in this little town. I took another sip and I tortured myself trying to remember his name.

Ha! The Greek, El Griego, that's what people called him. I felt foolish not being able to remember, considering that was the name of his store after all. I shrugged and continued to enjoy the naked slow speed chase I was witnessing. I was giggling at the insanity of it all until the skinny naked man changed his course. He spotted the small patch of tall pines about two hundred yards from the house. Mom always said they felt Christmassy so they never got cut and cleared out.

The Griego and his posse were starting to gain on the naked man. I found myself quietly cheering for him and his escape. As he turned and made a bee line for the pines I started to shake my head and quietly repeat "No" over and over. The posse changed their heading also but it looked like they had the angle to chase him down.

The naked man hurried his pace as he started to throw and heave the items he had once clutched so tight in his arms. My coffee was now gone but I did not dare leave to go get another cup. There were no commercials and this spectacle was too good to walk away from. I held on to the empty cup and watched as the naked man, arms now empty, placed one of the shiny objects in his mouth and began to climb the tallest pine of the bunch. Seeing a naked man climb a tree like a scared monkey was not something I ever thought I would witness, but here it was unfolding right in front of me.

Closer to the house now, I could see more details from the naked man's body than I really wanted to see. I could also see that his leg was painted with blood. He climbed half way up the 50 foot pine, then sat motionless perched on a branch. The small, shiny object was still secured in his mouth as he closed his eyes and froze. I thought it could not get any weirder but apparently it could.

The Griego's posse picked up the dropped and thrown items as they approached the pines. They huddled at the base of the trees and had an animated discussion. I broke out in laughter, as it looked as if the Three Stooges has been chasing a naked man. Once up close it didn't look like they wanted to deal with him anymore. They turned around, their hands and arms toting what the naked man once held and started to walk away.

The man in the tree sat motionless through all of it with his eyes closed. I was hysterically laughing as the animated chase came to an anticlimactic completion. I needed a good laugh after everything I had recently been through and the hilarious and ridiculous events that had just unfolded provided the perfect outlet. I laughed deeply and completely it wasn't just a laugher of joy but a cathartic one. I embraced it and healed a little with every burst of laughter.

The words from my mom once more echoed inside of me and the laughter dissipated. The man's leg grew redder by the minute and I knew I had to do something to help him. I wasn't excited about approaching a strange, naked man but I knew it was the right thing to do. I set the coffee cup down on the porch and started to trek across the field towards the pines.

Once I reached the pine I could see the bloodied leg and a pair of hairy lemons I wished I hadn't seen. The man's eyes were still closed so I had to call out to him several times before he would acknowledge me.

"What are you doing up there buddy?" His body tensed at my words, making his hairy lemons jiggle. I tried to avert my eyes from them but it was like trying not to look at a car crash while on the highway, simply impossible. I focused my attention on his leg which looked pretty beat up and in need of some serious medical attention. I shouted out to the naked man on the tree once more.

"What are you doing there buddy?" His eyes finally opened as he seemed to be studying me. I waited patiently but the heat of the rising sun was starting to make me impatient. I shouted up one last time.

"Hey buddy, what was that all about? What are you doing up there?" The tension on his body released as he looked somewhat defeated. He finally decided to verbally acknowledge me and his response was as confounding as the whole situation.

"You can see me?" He asked completely serious. The question caught me off guard and made me wonder if I was still sleeping. I shook my head and gently pinched my left arm as he asked again. "You can see me Sir? How are you able to see me? You are but a human."

The ridiculous statement not only confused me but infuriated me. I considered turning around and leaving the naked crazy man alone in his tree. I repeated over and over to myself in my head "Be a good man, be a good man." I thought I was calmed but as I spoke once more it sounded angry even to me.

"Of course I can see you! Get down from there buddy, you are bleeding pretty badly, let's take a look at your leg back at the house." I really didn't want this guy passing out from blood loss and me having to carry his naked ass back to the house. Thankfully sensing the urgency in my words the naked man started to climb down the pine tree.

Unfortunately for me this meant getting an even more private and intimate look at the man's naked body. With the descent down every branch things dangled, dark regions were visible and body hair covered him like a skinny, tall ape. I averted my eyes but once more I was the bug and his dangling hairy lemons were the light.

Once on the ground my attention went to his wounds. I did a quick scan and he was covered in scratches and small cuts. The one that really worried me was the on one his leg, it was about three inches long and I could see way too deep into his thigh muscle for comfort. As he approached me his stench overwhelmed my nose and made me start to walk. I had smelled pigs being slaughtered that smelled better than this guy. I did my best to walk fast enough to take in the least of his musk as possible while making sure he was still following behind. Once at the house I knew I needed to tend to the gash on his thigh but there was no way I would work on it while he was naked and smelling that rancid. I found him some clothes and a towel and directed him to the shower. Thankfully he didn't protest and went right in.

Once the naked man was in the bathroom I started to look for Mom's first aid kit. I knew she had one somewhere but I just couldn't remember exactly where. I looked in her bedroom but with no luck. As I walked past the bathroom door on my way to the kitchen I could hear the man whimpering and complaining probably as the water found his wounds. I hurried, I didn't know if I could patch him up and I wanted him conscious in case I had to drive him to the hospital.

I finally found the white box under the kitchen sink. I grabbed it and went back to wait for the man outside the bathroom door. The water had stopped so I was counting the seconds until he came out. The door opened and the thin man stood there, a little surprised by me. Thankfully he was wearing the clothes I had given him and he no longer smelled like the missing link.

I guided him to the dining table, had him sit down and started to inspect the wound. I first used some gauze to dry it so I could see the extent of the cut. Once the bleeding had slowed down a little bit I was able to use my thumb and index finger to gently spread the wound. A whistle of amazement escaped me as my eyes opened wide. The cut was deep, like over an inch deep. There were not enough butterfly stitches and Band-Aids in the first aid kit to patch this together. I needed to take him to the hospital before he bled to death.

"I need to take you to the hospital buddy, you need stiches here." I broke the news to my patient. He instantly panicked and anger started to escape him. I had dealt with people who were horrified of hospitals like my father was. As he would say, "People only go to hospitals to die, not to get well." The thin man's reaction was much more than that. I could not quite figure out what his reaction meant, but he made his wishes known very clearly.

"NO! No hospital! Just do what you can but I am not going to any hospital!" I saw concern and terror in his eyes so I assured him I would not take him to the hospital. I should have forced him to but against my better judgment I decided to mend him myself. As he relaxed over the news of no hospital I started to stress on how I was going to sew him up. He was starting to look pale; I knew I had to hurry. I instructed him to keep pressure on the wound and I grabbed him a cup of water. He had to be dehydrated from the blood loss and the desert. The man giggled as I hurried away and I fear he was starting to reach a delirious stage.

We introduced ourselves to each other; I guess it is the least we could do considering the circumstances. He said his name was "Bracket" which seemed a ridiculous name. Who would name their kid that? Who would want to call themselves that? It wasn't the time for that conversation so I chucked the disbelief aside and proceeded to assess the situation with him.

I explained to him he needed stiches, he attentively looked at me and listened to every word I had to say. He was pretty fair skinned but he was becoming paler by the second. His lips were turning a light shade of blue and the dark circles under his eyes were intensifying. I grabbed one of the bottles of tequila I hadn't finished and told him to start chugging. I left him there drinking and complaining about the burning spirit and went to my Mom's room to search through her sewing supplies.

It didn't take long to find some of her sewing needles. The problem was which one to pick. There were small, large, medium, straight and curved needles. I wasn't sure which one to go for so I picked the most heavy duty curved one. I remembered the doctors using curved ones when I got stitches. I gathered some string and grabbed a couple of belts on my way out of the room.

By the time I got back he had drank what was left of the bottle of tequila. Half a bottle down and Bracket was still somehow sitting. I opened another bottle of tequila and handed it to him. I tied one of the belts around his thigh creating a tourniquet. I didn't know what I might hit while sewing him up and the last thing I wanted was his blood to spray all over my face. I handed him the other belt and he looked at me perplexed.

"You are probably going to want to bite down on that while I'm stitching you up." He raised his eyebrows and nodded his head in acknowledgement. I used my lighter to sanitize the needle; well at least I think I did. That's what they always show in the movies. I could feel myself trembling so I grabbed the bottle of tequila away from Bracket and took one long flowing chug out of it. The familiar burning down my esophagus relaxed me a bit and I focused my attention back on the wound. As my fingers approached the open laceration Bracket spoke, breaking the tense silence and startling me.

"Have you ever done this Gabriel?" His voice had startled me and the answer to the question had me pondering if I should really be doing this. I could see him swaying on the chair and I knew consciousness would be fleeting for him. I gave him the short and honest answer.

"No."

Bracket looked at me with great concern and didn't seem quite pleased with my answer. I wasn't going to lie to the man, not now. He looked around the room, took one more swig from the bottle and shouted his form of approval before biting down on the belt. "Do It!"

There was no more time to be wasted, I carefully plunged the needle into his soft flesh and it went through a lot easier than I had expected, pulling it out the other side proved a little bit more difficult. Every time I pushed on the needle his thick hide would bulge up preventing the needle from breaking the skin. Bracket grunted with every failed attempt of me pulling the needle through, as he forcefully bit down on the leather belt. I carefully placed my two fingers on each side of where I expected the sharp needle to pop through. While pressing down with my fingers, I pushed on the needle once more. Mercifully for Bracket and luckily for me, the needle finally broke through the skin, missing both of my fingers. I tied the first knot and repeated the process.

By the time I was done with the thirteen stitches, Bracket was slumped over on the chair barely able to move. I helped the exhausted man to the couch, covered him with a blanket and left him with a full glass of water. He was going to need it once he woke up. He kept mumbling as I moved him, I think he was trying to thank me but his words were slurred and tired. I hoped he still wanted to thank me once he woke up. I left him, took what was left of the bottle of tequila and went out to the porch. I dumped out what little coffee still resided in my cup, I filled it with tequila and tried to process what just had happened. I was resolute on making my mother proud and being a good man but I think I should get some extra credit for that one.

Promises to Keep
(Gabriel)

I finished the bottle of tequila while taking in another spectacular summer sunset. I had a million questions for the stranger sleeping on my couch but he was still in no condition to answer. I checked to make sure he was still breathing on my way to bed. I watched him carefully to see if his chest was moving up and down as he inhaled and exhaled. The problem was that my vision was too blurry from all the tequila and I could not really differentiate between him moving and the room swaying.

I grew a bit worried so decided to go in closer to check. I put my ear close to his face and tried to listen to him breath. Bracket was lying face down on the couch, head turned outwards with his mouth open. Again I failed to figure out whether he was breathing or not. I didn't want to wake up the next morning to a dead stranger on my couch. The effects of the tequila were intensifying with every second that passed and with no other option I went for the most rudimentary method to check if he was alive. I clumsily rubbed my hand on his face. Bracket made some protesting unintelligible sounds, turned his face inwards to the couch and continued to sleep. I guess he was alive and breathing after all. Satisfied with my inquiry I headed to bed.

I lay in bed trying to figure out what I was to do with the wounded stranger in the house. Drunk logic combined with what had been the most unique and intense experiences of my life guided me to one simple conclusion. Bracket was my opportunity to do right to the promise I made my Mom. I didn't know where he had come from or where this adventure would lead, but I was determined to see it through with every breath I had left. I found such comfort in my resolute conclusion that relaxing sleep took me under. I awoke the next morning determined, recharged and ready to take on the day. I cleaned up in the bathroom and went straight to check on Bracket. He was still passed out looking exactly how I left him the night before, except the drool spot on the couch had grown I had cleaned the wound as good as I could but the possibility of infection still worried me. I wanted to keep him out of the hospitals as he had requested but I wasn't equipped to deal with an infection. I gently placed the back of my hand on his forehead and his temperature felt just right. Luckily, it seemed a trip to the hospital would not be in Bracket's future.

The place was a landfill of empty cans and dirty paper plates. I had company now and this was no way to show off my Mom's house to him. I started the coffee pot and as the smell of java filled the house I started to clean up. Once the machine had finished percolating, I served myself a cup, sat on the chair opposite of the couch and just watched Bracket sleep. The hot delicious fuel filled my body and kick started my brain.

Who was Bracket? Why was he being chased? Where did he come from? He is definitely not a local. There was something off with him; but what? Why did he think he was invisible? Where were his clothes? What kind of name is Bracket?

My brain, finally awake after days of drunkenness, kicked into overdrive and continued to flood with more questions. However, the empty coffee cup signaled the end of my break and pondering. I went back into the kitchen, refilled it and continued with the cleaning. By the time I was done there were 4 large bags full of garbage sitting out on the front porch. The litter was gone from inside the house but all the surfaces felt sticky and the smell wasn't quite right. I dusted, wiped and cleaned all day long. I stopped several times to eat or just take a break and every time I parked myself on the chair across from the couch and mused about the origins of my new friend.

Night came and I was exhausted but the house looked as it did when I first walked in a few days back. Bracket had slept the whole day and wasn't showing any signs of getting up. He had muddled gibberish a couple of times and once started talking in his sleep. I had stopped mopping the floors and stood there attentively to find what he might reveal during his sleep talking, but I could not make asses or elbows out of it. Bracket apparently would keep his secrets for one more day. I changed the water in his still full glass and went to bed.

I hadn't worked that hard in quite a while so I was truly exhausted. I don't even remember my head hitting the pillow and before I knew it was morning again. I opened my eyes and for once my head wasn't throbbing. It felt quite pleasant. I was sore but it was a good sore. The kind of sore you only get from self-accomplishment and hard work. I stretched and rested in bed with a surprising smile on my face. My self-congratulatory party was interrupted by the unmistakable sound of the toilet flushing.

I quickly sprang to my feet and set an intercept course to Bracket. He was taking his first couple of imping steps out of the bathroom and into the hallway when I caught up to him. He heard my heavy footsteps coming, stopped and turned to greet me. He looked a little pale but otherwise well. That was until he started talking and made me concerned at how much blood he had actually lost.

"Good evening Gabriel, I hope I haven't inconvenienced you over the last couple of hours while I recharged my energy matrix. I should only require one or two more hours. I appreciate all you have done but I must embark on my next quest and find the traitors."

Every word sounded crazier than the last. Bracket was looking at me but was having difficulties making eye contact. He swayed a bit as he spoke and if I didn't know better, I would have sworn he was drunk. I listened, agreed then carefully ushered him back to the couch. I insisted he drink all of the water in the glass. He chugged every drop quite loudly and disturbingly. I wanted to scream "Manners" to him the whole time as he sounded like some sort of wild animal trying to gulp down his prey whole. I took the glass to the kitchen to refill it and by the time I had returned Bracket was once more cuddled in the couch and asleep. I tried waking him but the Sandman had clearly claimed him.

I kept busy and let Bracket rest. His activity was negligible except a few loud gas releases he was so kind to share with me. They were mortifying but still hilarious. I guess farts just never stop being funny. I had quietly finished unpacking and was getting ready to start dinner when there was a knock on the door. It was loud and authoritative and startled me to high heaven. I hurried to the door as my mystery visitor decided to knock again. I wanted to yell out but didn't want to wake up the sleeping man. I walked by the couch and he was still restfully sleeping, even with the loud knocking.

I arrived at the door, turned the knob and swung the door in to open it. The old wooden door creaked and protested at being forced to move. Outside the door I was greeted by the very familiar but exasperated face, Jose my older brother and Pecos' sheriff. He was wearing his tan uniform, gun holstered at his side, shiny gold badge on his chest, while his patrol Jeep sat next to mine.

He looked around my head and over my shoulders into the house searching for something or someone. He refused to look at me as he spoke while all I wanted to do was give my brother, who I idolize, a big hug.

"Excuse me Sir; Mister Vassallo has filed a complaint about a man who robbed his store while naked. He said he chased him to this vicinity before the man got away. Have you seen such man?" My desire to hug him was quickly replaced by the desire of punching him in the head. Why was he talking to me like that? Old habits and muscle memory took over and before I knew it my fist had forcefully made impact with his left shoulder.

Jose finally looked me in the eye and he was furious. His cheeks turned beat red and I could see his jaws muscles trying to grind his teeth together into dust. "I should arrest you for assaulting an officer Gabriel!" He forced his words through his clenched jaw, while his right hand rested on his pistol and his left was made into an angry fist.

"What?! What are you going to do? Shoot me? Go ahead pendejo! Shoot me!" My chest was puffed out and my head tilted back, I had squared up to him as I had done a thousand times before. He hadn't been a Sherriff then but he had pissed me off like only a brother can. "What do you want "Officer"?" I had been so happy to see him, now I could not wait for him to go away, so I said "officer" with as much contempt and condescension as I could muster.

Jose's head shook as it hung from his neck. The hand that had rested on his gun was now pinching the bridge of his nose. "Welcome back Gabriel." He said and I almost believed him. "This guy, the naked guy, he robbed Griego's Market, he didn't make it out with much just some food but Mr. Vassallo won't give it a rest. Did you see what happened? Have you seen the guy?"

He had turned down the asshole volume so I followed suit. "What happened with calling me Sir? I kind of liked it." He couldn't hold back the smile; I could always make him smile. I turned my body and looked in the direction of the couch where Bracket was resting. Jose followed my eyes and nodded in understanding when he saw him. "Let's talk outside" Jose agreed and I joined him on the front porch. He led the way to the rocking chairs and the expanse of his back reminded me how I had always been his little brother, both in stature and name.

Jose has always been a large strong man, even as a kid. When kids were hanging from the monkey bars, he was doing pull ups and by the time he was nine he could beat my Dad in a push up contest. He had been captain of the football team, basketball team and baseball team back in High School. He was a physical specimen and to my surprise had aged incredibly well. I had looked up to him figuratively and literally all my life. I tried very hard to be like him but I got the runt end of the genes. He had been a good big brother; no one ever messed with me, even though my weight and awkwardness was tailor made for being bullied. I had always lived in his shadow of protection, which can be a double edge sword. Even years after he had graduated I was known as "Jose's little brother". I wasn't Gabriel until I left and got to meet new people. I remember accidentally introducing myself to people as Jose's little brother and people looking at me as if I were an alien. Out in the rest of the world I was finally able to be me and step out of his comforting shadow.

Oh how I wished he could protect me and fix things now, but even mighty Jose could not fix me now. We sat on the rocking chairs and I told him the insane spectacle I had witnessed a couple of days back. He looked at me in painful disbelief as I told him the play by play. By the time I reached the end of the strange tale, we both were laughing our asses off together like in the good old days.

I convinced Jose that Bracket was harmless and more than anything needed a helping hand. He agreed with me but we both knew something had to be done to appease Mr. Vassallo.

"I will swing by tomorrow and square things up with Mr. Vassallo, ok Jose?" He was still in a good mood after the ridiculous story so he promptly agreed. I thanked him and offered him my hand as he was getting ready to leave. Jose stepped in and hugged me. He had to be about six inches taller than me and just as wide, but in his case it was muscle. The embrace was as comforting as I remembered. It must have been what being hugged by a bear must feel like, if the bear wasn't trying to rip your soft underbelly open so he could eat it. His strong arms were comforting and made me feel safe. We might not be as close as we once were but he was still my big brother, I was still Jose's little brother and I loved him. He got back in his Jeep and left me standing on the porch waving at him like a little kid.

My heart was revitalized and warmed by his visit even if he hadn't been there to visit me initially. I went back into the house to find Bracket trying to stand up from the couch.

"Where are you going buddy?" Without hesitation or elaboration Bracket replied that he was going to the bathroom. I didn't think much of it until moments later I heard all sorts of ruckus coming from behind the closed door of the bathroom.

I rushed to the door and tried to open it but it was locked. "Are you ok in there?" I pounded on the door but no reply came back. I could still hear him stirring around like a raccoon in the night from behind the door. I recognized the distinct sound of the window being opened and slamming right back down. If you didn't know the tricks of how to open and secure the windows you could lose a finger. I didn't hear Bracket yell in agony so I guess he had escaped the wrath of the slamming aperture.

I didn't bother anymore with the door and decided to go around the outside and wait for Bracket to attempt to make his grand escape. By the time I had made around the house Bracket's feet and legs were perilously dangling from the bathroom window. He was trying to shimmy down carefully but was being incredibly ungraceful. The shorts I had given him were ridding up on him, distinctly highlighting the boniness of his ass. I shook my head and soaked in the second ridiculous and hilarious scene Bracket had provided me in the past days.

He continued to struggle and slowly tried to escape the hold the window had on him. His final thrust had him temporarily land on his feet, stumble a few steps back and awkwardly landed on his bonny ass. I chuckled but my amusement was soon replaced by concern as I saw his leg once more covered in blood. I rushed over to Bracket and he instantly started to scramble back while still on his backside.

"What are you doing Bracket?" He continued his backward shimmy and refused to answer until I asked him again.

"You are going to turn me in, I saw the golden knight, and he convinced you to turn me into the giant." I frowned as my brain hurt trying to process what he had just told me.

"What in the world are you talking about?!" My screaming question brought Bracket's backside escape to a halt. He had stirred up a small cloud of dust which was quickly starting to stick on the goopy liquid and blood seep-ing out of his stitched wound. He looked at me in total despair and tried to explain.

"The man, the knight with the golden armor, who came to visit us. I saw you stand up to him but only for him to lead you out onto the porch. He convinced you to turn me into the giant didn't he? Bracket sat there looking pathetic and desperate. I think I had deciphered what he was trying to say but his senseless ramblings and his dilapidated state made me feel such pity for the man.

"I talked to him yes, but I arranged to take care of your debt. I am not turning you in to any giant. Now let's go back in the house, we need to clean your leg before it gets infected." I spoke to him as I would have spoken to a child and it seemed to work. I extended my hand out to Bracket, he took it and I helped him to his feet. With every step I could see in how much pain he was and felt only worse for the guy. It was slow going but I finally managed to help him back into the house.

Once inside we made it to the table and I started to inspect the wound. The liquid coming out was either clear or blood. It had started to scab over but appeared that during Bracket's bumbling escape he had scratched part of the scab off. I used some alcohol, rubbing alcohol this time, which made Bracket scream bloody murder. I couldn't help but to tease him and chuckle at his high pitched whines. I finished up with some antibiotic ointment and covered the stiches with gauze and tape. I found some ibuprofen and gave it to Bracket, along with more water. I helped him back to the couch and asked if he wanted something to eat. The man had to be starving. His request, as everything else about him so far, was incredibly peculiar. Bracket wanted crackers with butter. I wasn't quite sure what he was asking for at first but he explained he wanted saltines with some butter on them. Very simple, but quite a bizarre request.

I went into the kitchen and luckily had all the ingredients for Bracket's gourmet meal. I cut little slabs of butter and placed them on about ten saltine crackers. I had to try one for myself, so I made an extra one and had it be-fore I returned to the living room. The combination of the salty cracker and the sweet butter was actually quite pleasant. I delivered the plate filled with square saltines with square pads of butter on them and Bracket's eyes just lit up. He quickly took possession of the plate and started to loudly devour his simple snack.

He had to eventually take a break to breath and decided to address me while at it. "Gabriel, these are delicious." I nodded and smiled. He was very grateful as if I had made the crackers from scratch and had just gotten done churning the butter. I took the compliment as he continued. "Are you really going to settle my debt with the giant? You would do that for me?"

I could see in Bracket's sad eyes that he didn't have many, if any, friends. I could see the loneliness and sorrow he held deep in his soul. I also finally figured who the giant was, Mr. Vassallo. He was a tall man but by no means a giant, but I could see where he came up with it.

"Yes Bracket I will settle things with Mr. Vassallo and your debt will be paid. You can rest easy buddy." He gave me a puzzled look and I corrected myself: "I meant the giant." A smile quickly replaced his puzzled and sad look as he leaned over on the couch and gave me a hug. I hadn't expected him to hug me yet once in the embrace I decided, what the hell, and I hugged him back.

As I hugged him he held on to me like a drowning man holds on to lifesaver. He broke the embrace while still holding me by my shoulders. He smiled and gave me a compliment, I think. "You might not look like much Gabriel but you are a valiant man. I am pleased that you have pledged your allegiance to me. I appreciate you settling the score with the giant for me. You have made a good choice my friend; you will not be disappointed with our arrangement." He smiled and joyously slapped me on the arm. Bracket mumbled incoherent gibberish and chuckled as he lay back down on the couch. I sat there perplexed at what the man had just said as he settled in for some more rest.

New Alliances
(Bracket)

I was exhausted after being stitched up but knew I had to recover quickly. Gabriel had proved a great resource but I still couldn't trust him fully, honestly I didn't know who I could trust anymore. By my internal clock I had only been out a couple of hours before I had the need to empty my bladder. I held it for as long as I could but defeated by my biology I made my way to the small bathroom. There was still sunlight coming in through the small window above the toilet. It made me wonder what the duration of the days on this planet must be, since it should be night by now.

Filed that tidbit of information and started to wash my hands. I could hear what sounded like an approaching elephant outside the door. I opened the door, ready to defend myself and to my surprise it was only Gabriel standing on the other side of the door's threshold. He was smiling from ear to ear, eager like a dog when his master returns home.

He followed me like a good servant as I slowly made my way back to the couch. My leg felt swollen and stiff. The pain had become intense but it wasn't anything I hadn't felt or had been trained for. The wound was throbbing, with the surrounding area feeling painfully numb. As I moved, the skin tugged on the stiches and sent burning pain up and down the leg. The urge to pee had brought me to the bathroom, overriding the pain in my leg. The call of Nature abandoning and left to my own devices, the long painful walk back to the couch proved difficult.

Once on the couch, I quickly chugged the full glass of water and with it some of the pain. I knew I needed some more rest; I informed Gabriel and settled back in for a couple more hours of recovery.

I must have been out for another couple of hours before the rattling wooden door awoke me. The pounding on the door was threatening and forceful. I didn't need to know who it was on the other side of the door to decipher those knocks were not friendly. I was about to hurry off the couch to make my escape when Gabriel scurried by on his way to answer the door.

Unable to escape undetected I decided to maintain my position, learn as much as I could about who was on the other side of the door and wait for the right moment to make my escape. The door opened and a golden paladin filled the void the door once occupied. He was about three feet taller than Gabriel and wider than the door. His armor was immaculate and fitted perfectly to the being inside. Layer upon layer of golden metal formed a fully articulating armor with no weak points that I could detect.

The golden paladin spoke, his voice deep and strong, filling the house with its velvety echo. He was looking for me, the giant had sent him. I wanted to flee but in my debilitated state I knew I would not be able to avoid him, cunning and stealth would be my weapons.

To my surprise, Gabriel forcefully stood his ground, even challenging the golden paladin. The stocky man kept surprising me at every turn. He might be more than a servant; he might actually be a worthy partner. My high hopes for Gabriel were quickly squashed when he gave up my position to the golden paladin. My eyes were the slightest bit open and I could see his betrayal without unequivocal doubt. Having betrayed me he and the paladin joked before heading out on the porch together, probably to plan how to dispatch of me.

Disappointed, hurt and in pain, once alone I knew it was my only chance to escape and save my life. I remembered the small window in the bathroom and hobbled my way towards it as fast as my leg would allow. I heard the front door open and I quickly shut and locked myself in the bathroom. I could hear the giant footsteps thundering through the house as the paladin approached to claim my head with his golden sword.

Straddling the toilet I attempted to open the window but it proved more difficult than its simple looking design implied. After struggling and successfully opening the window, the house's defenses attacked me. The window slammed down and it was only my quick reflexes that prevented it from crushing my hand. Aware of the defenses, I carefully approached the window again but this time ready to foil its crushing plans.

The door shook as Gabriel and the golden paladin tried to kick it open in their pursuit of me. I opened the window once more and stuck the wooden plunger handle to keep it open. I pushed the screen out and started to climb out the window as the pounding on the door stopped. I had but a matter of seconds before the paladin blasted the door open and beheaded me. Of course I had made it easier for him since I had gone feet first out the window. The fall didn't look like much but I was learning that this house had it secrets.

I didn't want to plunge head first down to my death. I could deal with a broken leg; even with my healing powers I could not survive a broken neck.

I carefully lowered myself to the dry soil but my leg gave out. I ungracefully fell and tried my best to quickly get up. I had a lot of running to do if I wanted to be able to get away from the golden paladin. Five simple words paralyzed me as my attempts to flee were obviously foiled, "Where are you going buddy?"

Gabriel's friendly and inquisitive tone broke the silence of my stealthy escape. How had he found me? I didn't have much choice but confront the man about what had just happened. After a heated exchange, Gabriel explained to me how he had convinced the paladin to leave as he had taken ownership of my debt with the giant. I felt foolish and grateful towards the large man. I didn't understand why he would do such a thing for me. We had barely met and if it weren't for him I would probably be well on my way to a slow and painful death.

He helped me back into the house and cleaned up my wound, which had gotten reinjured while exiting through the window and was now bleeding again. Gabriel explained to me what he had arranged with the paladin and I was both grateful and in disbelief. He disappeared into the kitchen and I was left alone to wonder if he was being honest or if I would be betrayed again. He had no reason to betray, but he didn't have a reason to vouch for my debts and serve me. I jumped from one thought to another faster than the speed of light, as if the thoughts were meteorites hurtling through space. I jumped from one rock to another, thoughts running away from me, trying to chase an unknown idea. My mind wondered away from Gabriel and the golden paladin and forced me to try to remember who had betrayed me.

I could almost remember her name when Gabriel came back into the living room carrying a plate with my most favorite snack, saltine crackers with little thin pads of butter on them. I wasn't sure if he somehow knew I love those or if I had requested them. I would ponder that later since my brain shut down and my stomach and tongue took over. The delicious mix of crisp salty cracker and sweet creamy butter exploded in my mouth. My tongue wanted me to slow down and take my time to savor every little morsel but my stomach overruled it and I ate them as fast as I could.

I had to ask Gabriel "Why would you do that for me?" He simply said it was something he needed to do. The man's will and resolution surprised me and I had to let him know. Waves of exhaustion started to flow through my body. I decided to trust the large man with the kind eyes and got some more rest.

I woke up once again on the couch. I had expected it to finally be nighttime, instead I could see the sun starting its blazing rise. It was morning and the hours were not adding up. I could hear Gabriel stealthfully moving around in the kitchen like a mouse hunting for scraps. The smell of fresh brewed coffee filled the air and a swarm of memories invaded my head. I knew them to be lies, false memories implanted by someone so I brushed them aside and went in search of my own breakfast morsels.

As I stood, intense pain exploded around the wound. I could feel how my movements were ripping some of the healing that had occurred as I rested. I walked trying to keep my leg stiff and as gingerly as possible. I held onto the couch, then the wall for support until I finally broke the opening into the kitchen. "Good morning!" Gabriel was too cheery and to awake for whatever time it was.

"You want some coffee? Toast?" I nodded in agreement at his offers and took a seat in my now familiar spot at the table. Gabriel buzzed around the kitchen like a happy honey bee. A cup of warm coffee appeared before me and with it a jug of milk and a container of sugar. I doctored my coffee how I liked it, three sugars and a splash of milk. I took the first sip and its warmth revived my still exhausted body.

The toaster recoiled and startled me as I held onto the warm cup in my hands. Before I knew it, a small paper plate appeared before me with two pieces of slightly brown bread. Alongside of it Gabriel delivered a small jar of strawberry preserves and a dish with a solid stick of butter. I kept holding onto the comforting cup and instructed Gabriel of what I wanted. "One with butter and one with the preserves."

Gabriel had just sat down and the scowl on his face reminded me of my rudeness. "I apologize; where are my manners? Please." His right hand went towards his face, covering his right eye, two fingers holding onto his nose while the tip of the other two rested on his forehead. The large man shook his head and audibly sighed. After a few seconds, he finally proceeded and prepared my toast as I had instructed. I made a note of his sensitivity towards manners and continued to enjoy my breakfast.

"I pulled some other clothes out for you, once you are done eating, try them out. We need to head into town and square things away with El Griego." He kept calling him by different names but I knew very clearly who he was talking about, the giant. As he had explained, the golden paladin had given us until today to square things away with the giant before he had to come back. It sounded like it could all be diplomatically remedied but the butterflies fluttering inside my stomach begged to differ. I nodded to acknowledge Gabriel while I hid behind the safety of a warm sip of coffee.

Gabriel left me to myself and soon I heard the shower kick on inside the bathroom. Having finished my toast and coffee, I decided to go in search of the clothing he spoke of. On the chair across from the couch, which had become my bed, lay a small pile of shirts and pants. I looked through them and all of them were way too big for my slender frame. I found the ones I swam in the least and put them on.

Gabriel soon rejoined me in the living room and a deep rolling laughter quickly exploded out of his barreled chest. I slowly stood, pain still enveloping my thigh. I had to quickly grab onto my pants, which being too big, were trying to slide off and leave my nether regions exposed. Gabriel's laugh intensified as he doubled over while repeatedly striking his own leg. Tears were running down his face and his stomach jiggled a bit with each boisterous howl.

"We need to stop and get you some clothes buddy." As soon as he said it his joyous demeanor changed. I could see the large man clenching his jaw and anxiety take over his eyes. I wasn't completely sure why me getting some clothes that fit would cause that in him, but I had to admit my curiosity was sparked. He gave me a belt which helped cinch up the pants so they would not fall. We got into his transport, which looked like a box with wheels, and he turned the key to start it and after a quick roar from the engine we were off.

As he drove I recognized a few of the streets we traveled. I hadn't spent much time in the town but it was small and its streets few. After a few turns, which I made notes of in case I had to find my way back, we pulled into the parking lot of some sort of store. The yellow sign decorated the façade of the building, with big black letters to contrast the ugly yellow of it.

We entered and Gabriel quickly avoided the registers and was lost down the aisle. Unable to keep up with my injured leg I did my best to follow his footsteps in hopes of reuniting with him. I didn't understand his hurried pace and after eventually catching up with him I knew he wasn't trying to get away from me. We shopped around and settled on a t-shirt with a howling wolf and some grey sweatpants. I felt ridiculous in them but at least my pants were not going to possibly fall off anymore.

We were ready to leave but Gabriel kept approaching the registers and darting back into the aisle. He would look at items, grab them, inspect them, just to put them back where they once sat. We did this game for approximately fifteen minutes. The pain in my leg made my patience evaporate and I finally snapped at Gabriel that is was time to go.

"I know, I know" the big man replied and with a big sigh we headed over to the registers. Only the light on register three was on so I hobbled my way over to it. Instead of leading me Gabriel was following me for once. There was no one in line and the beautiful girl behind the register greeted me with a friendly and kind smile. She looked at my hands, which were holding on to the counter for support, and I looked back to see where my companion was with my new garments. I did not see Gabriel so I hollered for him.

"Gabriel! My clothes." I looked back at the girl and her cheeks had turned red. Gabriel stepped out of the shelter of the end cap with a sheepish smile on his face, blushing as well.

"Hi Gabriel, nice to see you again" the girl greeted the large man. Obviously they knew each other. Gabriel greeted her as well and placed my new clothes on the counter so that she could check us out. There was some small talk but more than anything there were a multitude of nervous smiles.

"It's $25.33" the girl smiled as her melodic voice requested money.

"Do you have any money?" Gabriel queried of me and all I could do was give him an annoyed look. "Of course you don't". He shook his head as he pulled out his wallet from his back pocket. He rifled through the black leather wallet for what seemed like an eternity and finally his fingers produced two $20 bills. He handed the girl the money and she promptly returned the changed. They exchanged awkward goodbyes and we headed out of the store and back into the heat of the day.

"Who is she?" I asked Gabriel once outside. He promptly lied and said it was just an old classmate from high school. Not believing him I said the only thing I could. "Oh bullshit!" His once happy blushed cheeks now turned red in anger and he shoved the bag of clothing forcefully into my stomach. I doubled over and tried to catch my breath as he stomped his way to the car.

Able to breathe again, I made my way next to the car. I rested the bag on the hood of the car and removed my clothing. I could hear Gabriel screaming at me from inside the car but the closed window muffled what he was trying to say. I put on my new sweatpants and wolf t-shirt and used the bag to carry the oversized clothes I had borrowed.

"What the hell are you doing?!" I was rudely greeted once I entered the car.

"Changing, what did it look like?" Gabriel rolled his eyes, put the car into reverse and shook his head as he carefully pulled out.

He slammed on the breaks and my eyes darted around looking for the eminent danger that caused such an abrupt stop, but there was nothing. I looked at my companion, his jaw was clenched, his cheeks red and his eyes open a little too wide. "You have to stop getting naked in public places. Do you understand Bracket?"

I didn't understand what I was doing wrong but decided to listen to him. I put my hands up, raised my eyebrows apologetically and agreed. Gabriel seemed to calm a bit at my response, he put the Jeep in first gear and off we went to see the giant. Even though I didn't trust him completely yet, I needed to listen to him and his guidance. He knew this place much better than me and he was genuinely trying to keep me safe and out of trouble. The road moved too fast under the Jeep's oversized tires as we kept hurtling forward towards the giant's store. I knew we were getting close as I started to recognize the streets. I was taking a huge leap of faith coming here with Gabriel and I hoped he would not betray me.

We pulled into the store's parking lot and Gabriel found a spot. "Ready?" he asked me and I lied with a "Yes". All of a sudden, I was filled with anxiety and apprehension of entering the store, just like what I had seen Gabriel go to through moments earlier. The walk towards the front door was painful and full of terrifying anticipation. I had tried so hard not to be detected by the menacing giant and now I was just willingly walking in. Gabriel was my only companion and defender, I truly hoped he knew what he was doing and that his negotiating skills were more imposing than his physique.

Gabriel opened the door and the store welcomed us with the ringing of bells. Apparently the giant had upgraded his security and detection systems since I last had been there. The two brass bells made their melodic sound along with a horrific clanking sound as they banged against the glass door. It wasn't but a few seconds and the giant appeared to greet what he thought were customers. Instead, Gabriel and I stood there receiving the full intensity of his gaze.

The large hand extruded one finger which was menacingly pointed at me. "You!" His voice was even deeper than I had imagined and the anger in his eyes made me incredibly uncomfortable. I looked down and waited for Gabriel to intercede.

"Mr. Vassallo there is no need for that." Gabriel sounded confident and diplomatic. The gaze of the giant switched to him and he somehow met his stare. The giant let out a low grunt and lowered his hand as his attention was now fully settled on my companion.

"Your brother said you would stop by." The giant's tone had calmed quite a few notches but what he had said truly intrigued me. The golden paladin was Gabriel's brother? They had looked nothing alike, even with the paladin wearing his full armor. Maybe Gabriel was a bastard son, but the certain words of the giant assured they were somehow related. I filed that for later scrutiny and conversation, I needed to worry about now or there might not be a later.

"Yes Mr. Vassallo, as Jose must have told you I am here to take care of whatever my friend here owes you." Gabriel responded to the giant and I could almost swear that with every word the giant shrunk a tiny bit. The anger in the large man was starting to dissipate and with it, his size.

"Stay here." Gabriel gently whispered to me and took off to the counter with the shrinking giant. I could hear them talking from where I stood near the entrance but I could not make out exactly what they were saying. I was left to interpret their conversation with what their bodies and tones told me. They seemed to be looking at some sort of list, probably of the items I took.

After a short but heated exchange they both seemed to have settled on some amount. Gabriel pulled out his wallet from his trusty back pocket and from it several green bills. The giant took the bills in his large hand and somehow stuffed them into the tiny register.

They both started to walk back in my direction and I felt the tension I thought had gone, rush back into me. I stood stiff but somewhat perplexed. By the time Gabriel and the giant had joined me the giant had greatly decreased in size. He was still a tall and large man but he was a man. I don't know what kind of Hulk-like powers he possessed but the man before me was not the same giant that had been pointing a meaty finger at me just a few minutes ago.

Gabriel cleared his throat and with it my fascinated staring at the man was broken. "Time to go buddy." I nodded in agreement and turned to head to the exit door. From behind us the giant sent us off with a few parting words.

"His debt is paid but he is still banned from my store. You understand?" Gabriel and I turned and nodded in unison to answer the large man. We exited the store and before I could ask Gabriel any questions he quickly shushed me and picked up his pace to the car. I could hear him mumbling ahead of me as I tried to keep up with my still injured leg.

"Two hundred? Is he crazy?! Aggravating, what the hell? Big baby!" I hadn't seen my friend this angry before and I had to admit it made him look like a furious cherub. He got in the Jeep, slammed his door and continued his rant while he abused the innocent steering wheel. I finally made it into the car and after ungracefully plopping down on my seat my unconscious smile made Gabriel really loose it.

His language changed to Spanish, the speed of his mouth increased exponentially and his voice was starting to reach a pitch only castratos should ever reach. Although I was extremely amused at his tantrum, I was also very grateful. As a blossoming partnership, I needed to make sure he knew I appreciated him. "Thank you Gabriel."

The three simple words completely took the winds of anger away from his sails. He held on to the steering wheel instead of abusing it, hung his head and after a few deep breaths he finally answered me. "You are welcome Bracket. Please, just please, don't pull another stunt like that, those are nearly two hundred dollars I am never getting back."

I thanked him once more but this time I put my left hand on his shoulder, which coaxed a small smile out of him. He started the car and although loud, the air conditioning was a welcome relief to the hot, dry, air. He didn't talk any more on the drive back so I honored his silence. It was the least I could do for the man who had already helped me so much. Besides a quick stop at the liquor store the short drive was pretty uneventful. The sun was starting to set and the mountains were completely ablaze by the time we got back to the house.

The sound of pressurized gas being released broke my trance of the flaming sunset. Gabriel handed me a dark brown bottle and signaled me to the rocking chairs with a simple nod. I hobbled over and was surprised how the wooden chairs were more comfortable than I could have imagined. I sunk into the warm embrace of the wood and the gentle swaying of the rocker. I sipped the cold beer as Gabriel and I sat in a very comfortable silence, enjoying the site of the desert set on fire by the dying rays of the sun.

A night of beers and revelations (Gabriel)

I had woken up in a surprising good mood. I had never been a morning person but I caught myself whistling as I prepared breakfast. The knowledge of my purpose had lifted the dark gloomy cloud that had hung over me for years. Bracket would most probably figure to be a huge pain in the ass but I was glad to have found him. I served myself a cup of coffee as my new friend gingerly walked into the kitchen. I offered him coffee and toast and he agreed to both.

He meddled with his cup as if it were a science experiment. He kept adding the milk almost drop by drop and the sugar grain by grain. He kept fussing with his cup and to prevent myself from bursting out in laughter I offered him toast, to which he promptly accepted. I turned my back to him as he kept messing with the poor cup of coffee. The crusty bread burst out of the toaster and for some reason I decided to offer Bracket options of what to put on it. He opted for both butter and preserves. I brought everything to the table and sat down with my own cup of coffee.

Bracket kept sipping and trying the cup of coffee and after each taste he would add either more sugar or milk by the most miniscule amounts. I kept holding back my laughter as he instructed me how to prepare his toast. I stared at him with a furrow in my brow and a look of "no fucking way buddy", which caused him to say "Please".

I think pain in the ass was going to be an understatement for him. After a few moments of frustration and disbelief I decided to let it go and dressed the toast for him. To my surprise, he ate them without altering them or protesting. Yay, for me I guess.

I had found the smallest change of clothes I had and laid it out for him. I knew they were going to be big but hopefully it would get him by for a while. I needed to shower; someone was really starting to stink and although I wanted to blame it on Bracket, I was pretty sure it was me. I left him in the kitchen eating his toast and still fiddling with his coffee and decided to upgrade my current smell. The water felt wonderful as it hit the back of my neck. It was almost scolding hot water; I had always loved taking hot showers. The small bathroom quickly became a cloud and water began to condensate on its cold walls.

It was going to be an interesting day so I really wanted to enjoy the warm embrace of the sprinkling water. I had to keep adjusting the cold and hot knobs to keep the right temperature. I kept adjusting the knobs as the hot water slowly ran out, eventually leaving me with only cold water. I could hear my dad scream "Don't use all the damn hot water!" as I hurried to finish rinsing off. How many times Jose and I did that to him on purpose, poor guy, he would go into the shower to bathe and have about two minutes of hot water. Let's just say we did a lot of extra chores those days.

Clean and no longer smelling like a sweaty armpit, I got dressed and headed out to check on Bracket. The moment I saw the poor man I died laughing. I thought the clothes might work but he looked like a little kid wearing his dad's clothes. I had to embrace the laughter so I didn't start crying about how out of shape I truly was. It was a deep belly laughter and full of pain.

We had to stop and get Bracket some clothes that fit him. We got in the Jeep and headed into town. There was only one place to get him some clothes and I didn't know how I felt about seeing Monica again so soon. She might start thinking I was stalking her.

I devised what I figure would be the perfect plan to get in and out without her noticing me. I must have looked like an idiot as I tried to secretly enter and move throughout the store. At least that is what Bracket's annoyed stares told me. We found the poor guy some clothes that would fit him much better and headed to the register.

As we approached the register only one of the lights was on. I caught a quick glimpse of Monica and she looked even more beautiful today than she had looked last time. I cowered back into the aisle with Bracket's inquisitive eyes fixed on me. He wouldn't say a word, just stared at me like some bird of prey and cocked his head randomly to add to his weirdness.

He didn't have to say a word; I knew he was right. I needed to man up and head to the register. I took a deep breath and let my feet guide me where the rest of my body was terrified to go. I made it all the way to the register just to dart and hide behind the large display of gossip magazines and candy.

I tried my best to play hide and seek until Bracket yelled out for me. I had forgotten I was carrying his new clothes so my plans to hide were foiled.

I reluctantly exited and found myself instantly smiling at Monica. She was kind and returned the smile as we exchanged greetings. The checkout went smooth, unlike me. I grabbed the bag and quickly exited the store with my face still uncontrollably grinning as my cheeks were starting to hurt. Outside Bracket caught up to me and questioned who she was. I told him the truth and he called me a liar. Well, I told him part of the truth. Irritated, I shoved the bag of clothes at his stomach, got in the car and left him to catch his breath.

I sat in the car and memory after memory flooded my brain. How many times I came so close to telling Monica how I truly felt but never quite getting it out. I remembered supporting her through breakups and giving her advice to help her relationships even as it tore me apart inside. Even though it was just a high school "crush", it was love. It was a love intense and pure, the kind of love they write about in books.

I had been gone for my semester at college when I went back home for Christmas break. I knew I would see her since we had stayed in contact throughout the Fall. I was eager to see my family but truly excited to see her. A few months away on my own had given me the confidence and valor to finally tell Monica how I felt. I was a man now, no longer a boy in high school and I was going to flaunt my newly found manhood to her and tell her she was going to be mine.

I had barely been home, seen my mom and dad, and had dinner before I got into my old shitty Mazda and went in search of Monica. I pulled up to her house and she was sitting on her porch waiting for me to arrive. She hadn't come back from anywhere like me. She had taken a year off after high school to explore her options. I got out of the little car and started towards her; she exited the porch and met me half way. She hugged me and I melted into her. The hug held so much emotion that it made me get my hopes up and gave me the last little bit of courage to tell her how I felt. Maybe after some time apart she had realized she loved me too.

We walked back onto her porch and we started talking. Well, it was more me talking and her listening. I told her about all my adventures and exploits at college, even some that I should have probably kept to myself. She attentively listened, her olive eyes giving me every ounce of her attention. She had her turn but her list of things to tell me was much shorter. She had planned to travel and see the world, but instead her dad had forced her to get a job until she decided what to do.

New stories told, we sat and reminisced on the good old days. I kept waiting for the right moment to tell her how I truly felt. She was talking about prom and how glad she was we went together. Her other prospects were no one she wanted to go with. We had gone as friends but it meant so much more to me than that. My mouth began to open to tell her when she interrupted me with a heart breaking sentence.

"You know I love you like a brother, again thank you so much for making prom so much fun for me." With that my mouth closed and my heart shattered. Heart broken and with nothing to lose I suggested maybe we could be more than that. Her reaction was like a punch to the gut.

"Ewww, that would just be gross, it would be like being with my brother." She laughed and I laughed with her. I kept up the same charade I had kept up most of my life with her, but inside I cried and sobbed. That is all I did the rest of that trip, eat, sleep and cry by myself in my room.

After that my visits home were shorter and less frequent until they finally stopped. There was no longer anything there for me anymore so I didn't see the point of going back. Not until now. I sat in the car looking through the window at the only woman I had ever truly loved and felt sad for her. She had never left as she had planned, instead she was still stuck in this small town working a shitty job and just getting by. I would have loved to see the world with her.

My trip down melancholy way was abruptly interrupted by the naked man outside my car. Bracket had decided to make the parking lot his changing room. It was obvious the man didn't mind his own nudity considering the way we met but most other people would. He calmly stripped and changed into his new clothes. I didn't want to scream and honk and bring more attention towards him so I just resigned myself to sit there until he was done.

He entered the car and I welcomed him with an animated query. "What the hell are you doing?" He calmly responded that he was changing. I could see in his eyes that there was no maliciousness to his actions. Bracket walks to the beat of his own drum and his drummer is drunk apparently. I started to pull out of the parking lot and I had to try to get through to him once more. I slammed on the brakes and addressed him once more. "You have to stop getting naked in public places. Do you understand Bracket?"

He looked at me with innocent eyes and defensive hands. I don't think he understood what he was doing wrong but he agreed to stop doing it. I put the car into drive and started to head to El Griego's market to take care of unpaid debts.

We walked into the store and the familiar bells clanked against the glass door. I still remembered them from decades ago. The store was pretty empty and Bracket kept very close and just behind me. I could see the fear in his eyes and as soon as Mr. Vassallo came out from the back Bracket's eyes became white saucers. He tried to stand strong but couldn't really manage it hiding behind me.

El Griego, as usual, loved to intimidate with his size, he was now an old man and I had seen all his tricks as a kid. I wasn't impressed and told him to stop. As big and bad as he might think he was, I was there because of my brother and everyone respected him in this little town. I could feel the tension emanating from poor Bracket standing behind me so I took Mr. Vassallo away with me to talk business. Bracket was left there petrified like a kid on his first day of school.

I walked away with the large man and we talked money. He claimed he was owed $700. I quickly called his bullshit and offered to call my brother to straighten things out. We kept haggling and his next offer was $300 which was just as outrageous. Knowing I would not budge and that the law was on my side we settled on two hundred dollars. Mr. Vassallo wasn't thrilled but he knew it was fair. As we walked back I could see Bracket had calmed down quite a bit; that was until he was banned from the store. We left the store and got in the Jeep without a word being said.

On our way back I remembered I was out of adult beverages so decided to restock. Too bad for Mr. Vassallo that he had banned Bracket otherwise I would have bought it there, but fuck him. We made it back and settled in the rocking chairs, with some beers and enjoyed the glorious sunset. I had forgotten how truly and uniquely beautiful they were out here. Nature still owned this place and was kind enough to let us live and enjoy its beauty.

The last wispy clouds held on to the dying fire of the sun for as long as they could, but the relentless night eventually overtook the skies. The stars slowly started to explode in the infinite darkness of the night, until the sky became a field of twinkly glitter. Bracket and I had sat in silence this whole time. Now that all pressing matters and debts had been settled, I had quite a few questions for my new companion. I don't think the answers would sway how I felt about Bracket but I still wanted to know.

I turned to Bracket and our mouths moved in unison

"Where did you come from buddy?"

"Why are you helping me Gabriel?"

I couldn't help but to laugh but Bracket remained serious and stoic. My giggles turned into a serious look which he thankfully interpreted correctly. I wanted my answer first. He looked to his left then his right as if to make sure no one was close enough to hear, then proceeded to answer my question.

"What I am about to tell you Gabriel is highly classified. I am only telling you because I have been betrayed from within my organization and after today you have proven to me that I can trust you." He once more looked around making sure we were alone before continuing with his story.

"I was one of the top agents for a global organization. I won't tell you the name, it is better and safer for you that way. I had been working on one of the most delicate and important missions the agency had ever had. I was close to succeeding when it all started to unravel." Bracket kept looking around and spoke in a hushed voice as he told me his fantastical story. I had been around the block enough times to know something in what he was telling me didn't add up. But if I were to go just by the conviction in his eyes I would have believed every word he told me.

"I don't know how and I will find out, but I was burned. My true identity was revealed by someone from inside the agency. Once I had been exposed, I was left out in the cold. We all knew when we signed up that if we ever got caught we were on our own and no one would claim us, but when it really happened it was an immensely lonely and desperate feeling. In my case my cover hadn't been blown, I was too good for that, someone inside had betrayed me and that stung even more, especially after all my years of loyal and dedicated service."

"I had put my failsafe plans in place in case my cover was ever blown, so I quickly changed my focus to them. I would figure out who the traitor was at a later time. I retreated from my mission and went back to my partner. She and I had started as business associates, she was my tech specialist. As the years passed our relationship grew deeper and more complicated. I knew if I had been exposed she was in danger as well and being that I was in love with her I needed to protect her."

Bracket paused for what seemed an eternity, I could see the agony in his eyes for what he was about to tell me. I allowed him his time and waited patiently. His gaze came back from being lost in the stars and he continued with his story. "By the time I got to her it was too late. I went back to our safe house and somehow they had found that too. As I entered the house I could hear her screams coming from the bedroom. I rushed to her and slammed through the door, forgetting all my training and throwing caution to the wind for her sake. She was naked on the bed and he had been torturing her for information. I could see she was barely hanging on to consciousness and life as he continued to assault her."

"The crashing of the door turned his attention to me and what he had been looking for all along. He rushed me, trying to collect his bounty from whoever hired him. He was a skilled hand to hand fighter, but I was better. Decades of training took over, fueled by the rage of what he had done to my love. I eventually gained the upper hand and beat him mercilessly. I was on the brink of finally dispatching him when his cohorts showed up to stop me. I was blinded with rage but they were able to surprise me and rendered me unconscious."

Bracket's fists were tightly clinched on the arms of the rocking chair. The wood protested as he squeezed it tighter and tighter. I worried about the well-being of my grandfather's rocking chair, but it had survived worse. Bracket's sadness had turned into anger and he continued to squeeze words through his clenched jaw.

"I woke up in a Super Max black site prison not far from here. It is the kind of place they take the scariest people in the world to scare and break them. I knew no one would ever come for me and I would die of old age there, if I could survive the almost daily attempts on my life from the other inmates. After doing a few dirty favors of my own I was able to get a few allies in that hellhole. We carefully crafted our escape, each of us driven by different reasons. These were the kind of people I had fought so long to capture and in most cases kill. Now they were my only option and allies"

"Once we had refined our plan to the nano-second we waited for the perfect moment and executed it. I guess, fortunately, I was the only one to escape the monstrosities they call guards. I can't tell you the specifics Gabriel, but genetic modification and alien allies are real beyond anyone's imagination. The kind of shit I have seen and dealt with makes Area 51 seem like a kids show."

Bracket waited for some sort of response from me. I gave him my best wow, I am amazed look, satisfied he continued. "I was able to make it to the train and escape the supermax; that is how I ended up here. I had found shelter out there in the mountains but eventually the lack of provision drew me into the town." He pointed to the Cerros de Escobas as he mentioned the wilderness and I had to say I was impressed and surprised he actually survived out there for any period of time. Although beautiful that place can be ruthless, and don't even get me started on the snakes.

"I don't know how the giant's customer spotted me, besides that he is some sort of hybrid with infrared vision. There is no way he should have spotted me. I will admit my plan was put together hastily and out of desperation. I had been without food for days and been drinking what was probably contaminated water. I didn't infiltrate the giant's store out of malice; I was just a very hungry and desperate man. I must thank you for squaring that business for me, I am in your debt Gabriel. But why are you helping me? I am very grateful yet I don't understand why you are going out of your way to help me."

I thought of how to answer the man. His eyes were hungry for what I had to say but if I told him the true story it would sound even more fantastical than the tale that he had just told me. I knew somewhere in his story there were some grains of truth but I didn't know exactly what they were. My story was completely true and would have sounded just as ridiculous. I contemplated how to answer him, I did owe him some sort of explanation or he was going to start thinking I was just some creep that was going to lock him in the basement.

I told him the truth, well at least a version of it. "I made a promise to someone very important to me a long time ago. This is my last chance to make good on that promise, so it is my pleasure to help you Bracket." He looked at me, just looked at me. His eyes dug through mine and I could feel him digging inside my brain for what that meant. I felt petrified and was unwilling to break the gaze. He dug in my soul and my heart and I just let him. I wasn't going to tell him more but I was going to tell him the truth.

His penetrating stare seemed to last forever. Content from whatever he saw deep inside of me, he smiled and nodded in approval. "Please thank whoever it was you made this promise too. I am more than pleased to have you as my helper." I should have been offended as he referred to me as his helper but how he said it, the honor the word held for him and the reality of the circumstances made me proudly accept my role.

Our attention was pulled in the direction of the howling of a pack of coyotes talking to each other under the stars. Before I knew, I was standing and already heading to the door to get inside the house. The night was still gorgeous but it now belonged to beasts with teeth, fangs and a hunger that wouldn't make them hesitate making me their meal. Thankfully Bracket followed suit and was gingerly hobbling after me.

Although I knew the creepy crawlers were far away, I felt a great sense of relief as I locked the door once Bracket was in the house. We had forgotten the last of the beers outside and I wasn't brave enough to go get them. I felt bad as I saw Bracket starting to settle into the couch with his injured leg. I couldn't in good conscience let the man spend another night on it. The couch was old and although my mom took great care of it, I honestly couldn't ever remember having a different couch but that one.

I took him to my room and he gladly accepted the bed. I could see relief and a joy in his eyes as he lovingly looked at my old bed. He hastened his pace and quickly made it to the bed. He sat and took a moment to soak in the softness of the mattress. He rubbed his palms on the bed smiling like a young kid. He looked back at me and with a huge smile said "Thank you Gabriel". I nodded and smiled back at him and left him to frolic on my old bed.

I walked the short few steps to my mom's room and entered without hesitation but with a stomach full of butterflies. Seeing it was just a room and not a portal into another dimension, I let out a breath I didn't know I was holding. I tucked myself in to my mom's bed and took in her scent deep in my lungs. I kept staring at the window waiting for it to open or knock. Anything that might trigger or signal a visit from her, but nothing.

I don't know for how long I stared into that window. I fought the ever increasing weight of my eyelids for as long as I could but eventually they won. I didn't dream, at least nothing I could remember, I just slept. That was until I was awoken by frantic and panicked screams coming from outside my door.

Bugs and the first quest
(Gabriel)

I woke up in a stupor and ran into the hallway. I could hear Bracket screaming incomprehensible grunts and shrieks with "Get it out!" mixed in it. I rushed to where I had left him the night before but the room was empty. I wasn't awake yet and probably still a little drunk. I took a second holding on to the doorframe and dizziness overtook me. I snapped out of the unwanted visual gyration and figured the screams were coming from the bathroom.

As I approached the bathroom door I could hear Bracket not only screaming but throwing and tossing god knows what all over the bathroom. I carefully opened the door as a toothbrush holder came flying in my direction. I quickly ducked and the peach colored ceramic cup shattered on the wall. I looked back just in time to see the shards ungracefully fall onto the hallway floor. "Get it out!" Bracket's screams brought my attention back into the chaotic bathroom.

The floor was littered with everything from the hand soap, to the towel, to medicines and creams which had been strategically hidden in the medicine cabinet. Bracket was quickly pacing back and forth in the small bathroom, adrenaline and rage having made him forget about his injured leg. His hands were over his head and he just kept repeating the same phrase over and over, only interrupted by panicked screams.

He spotted me and started to head in my direction by the door. My brain was still refusing to work at full capacity, so it took me a moment to process what the crimson coloring was adorning the right side of his body. I followed the trail back to its source and found a shiny metal object held in Bracket's hands, as he kept thrusting it into his now red ear. His left arm was draped over his head while his hand probed and guided the tweezers that his right hand was brutalizing his ear with.

My brain, finally having caught on to what was going in front of me, launched my body towards Bracket, my hands ready to take the sharp tweezers away from his. His eyes where shinny with unshed tears and his look of complete panic and anguish scared me. I valiantly continued advancing on him, hoping to stop him before he ended up looking like a mangled version of Van Gogh.

"Please get it out! Gabriel you need to get it out! Please get it out! You need to get it out!" His eyes showed too much white as Bracket screamed over and over for me to help him, as he continued to jab the tweezers in and out of his ear. I didn't know what he was talking about but his panic and the blood had more than compelled me to help. My hands finally wrapped around his bloody and slippery fingers and stopped him from brutalizing himself even more. I had to almost pry the tweezers away from him and his screams were becoming desperate pleas.

"Calm down, please calm down. What do you need me to take out? Just tell me and I will buddy, but you have to calm down and tell me." Bracket lowered his voice but just kept repeating himself over and over. His whispers and pleas for help were heartbreaking as the man sobbed, only to periodically recoil to his left and away from whatever was terrorizing to his right. He was trying to calm himself but he was beyond words.

With his horrified jumps to his left and his bloody right ear, it didn't take Sherlock to conclude there was something inside his right ear. My first look was obstructed by the thick blood now covering the poor appendage. I looked around and grabbed one of the hand towels that now rested on the floor next to us. I ran it under some warm water and tried to clean up his ear as best and as fast as I could.

As I cleaned the area, the scratches Bracket had inflicted on himself were a bit horrifying. On the upper part of the ear he had clearly poked a jagged hole through his cartilage, it was the most brutal and grotesque attempt at a piercing that I had ever seen. I knew he wasn't attempting to pierce his ear, like a rebellious teenager in his bathroom, but it was the only way for me to process and keep myself from vomiting as I cleaned him up.

The bleeding wasn't stopping but I had cleaned him up enough to try to figure out what he was digging for. He continued to sob, his body now gently rocking and he continued to plead for me to, "Get it out." The scratches on his ear all seemed to concentrate around his ear canal opening. I had to close my eyes for a second before I ventured to look at what he had done to himself in there. I tried to look but thankfully the light in the bathroom didn't allow me to see much further in.

His pleads were now becoming screams as he felt my efforts were not progressing. I didn't want to see but I had to figure out how to look in his ear and help the panicked man.

"I'll be right back buddy; I'm going to get a flashlight." He stopped pleading as I spoke to him and frantically started to nod at the idea of the flashlight. I ran out of the bathroom, now sober from adrenaline and the site of blood, and ran to the Jeep to get my flashlight out of the glove box. There had to be a couple inside the house but I wasn't in the mood, nor had the time to go hunting for one.

I pulled the front door open and slammed the screen door as I ran to my box on wheels. The rocks and pebbles dug into the soles of my feet as I tried to run across the driveway. It changed my running from a manly stride to squeamish hops. I reached the passenger door as my feet were screaming at me. I opened, reached in and grabbed my trusty Maglite. I turned it on and off to make sure it worked and the bright blue light of the LED bulbs quickly assured me of its functionality.

The run back to the house was a lot slower and much more painful. I welcomed the feel of the cold wood planks of the steps on the front porch. I was going to have to check my feet for imbedded pebbles and cactus thorns but that would have to wait. Bracket's sobs were once more full on screams that could be heard coming out of the front door. I hurried to the bathroom and seeing me calmed him down some.

His ear was covered in blood again so I had to clean it up once more before I could try to look down the probably mangled ear canal. I directed the bright LED light into his ear, waiting to see a crime scene. I was pleasantly surprised when I found little or no damage to his ear canal. He had a couple of scratches near the opening of his ear but it was like Bracket could not find the ear hole. There wasn't even any blood down his ear. I carefully inspected his ear but could not see whatever he was so desperate to have removed from inside of it.

Unable to find anything, I had to ask Bracket what I was looking for. He was able to calm himself down enough to tell me "The Bug!" Even more confused with the whole spectacle I tried looking down his ear once more. The wounds and holes around and on his ear were starting to sprout again with fresh bright red blood. I ignored them for now and stretched his ear in all directions trying to look as far in as I could. He whimpered and complained as I handled his mangled ear, but besides needing a desperate ear hair trimming I could not see any bug of any kind.

Bracket kept mumbling, "Get it out, get it out", his desperation was contagious and I had to try real hard to stay calm. I grabbed the frantic man's face, my hands flanking his cheeks and gently but firmly holding him. My hands and direct eyes demanded his attention and after a few moments the mumbling stopped and he looked right back at me.

"Bracket I can't see any bug of any kind inside your ear. There's nothing there."

He started to shake his head in disagreement but I steadied his face, preventing him from freaking out once more. "It is in there. I feel it crawling around. It is trying to get out so it can broadcast my location. I need to get it out and squash it before it can." The conviction in his eyes made his insane ramblings seem almost plausible. It didn't matter how I tried to understand it, it just didn't make sense.

I took a deep breath and tried to figure how to diffuse the increasingly bloody situation. "Ok buddy, I can't see it but you can feel it. You are going to have to guide me and once you know I have it I can yank it out and kill it." He must have approved, because he started to nod in agreement and his demeanor changed from hopeless to determined.

I grabbed the tweezers and was instantly repulsed by the wet sticky blood covering it. I quickly wiped them down on the towel and carefully started to insert them into his ear. I used my left hand to steady the flashlight and try to look at what I was trying to grab. Bracket kept guiding me but so far his instructions were to keep going in deeper into his ear. I still couldn't see anything and now the tweezers were starting to obstruct my view. I was getting closer and he announced that apparently I was there. I clamped down on the tweezers and he assured me I had the critter trapped. I started to pull and to my surprise felt quite a bit of resistance on the other side of the metal tool. I kept pulling but something was preventing me from pulling the tweezers out.

Maybe he wasn't crazy after all; maybe he did have some sort of critter burrowing in his ear. How in the hell a bug would broadcast any signal, and to who, well, yea that still sounded crazy. I squeezed as hard as I could to make sure whatever had holding on to his ear didn't escape and I yanked the tweezers out. Bracket began to scream, squish it squish it. I put the tweezers on the counter still squeezing them as hard as I could and slammed my fist down on it. It was all so quick and sudden I didn't even take a moment to see what I had usurped out of his ear.

I slowly lifted my fist, anxiously waiting to see what creature I had just pulled out of a man's ear and killed with my bare hands. As my hand moved away from the counter I saw the culprit. It was about three inches long, skinny and black. It was covered in ear wax and it wasn't moving or trying to broadcast anything. I had never seen an ear hair that long. It curled on itself a few times then straightened out like some kind of disgusting ear waxed covered curly fry. I stared at it for a few seconds and was interrupted by Brackets demanding updates on the creature's condition. I assured him it was well dead and still holding it by the tweezers; I walked the long black ear hair to the garbage can.

I patched Brackets' ear with my new stock of gauze and first aid supplies. He of course had refused to go to the hospital so I did my best to clean his mangled ear and stop the bleeding. I knew he obviously had some issues but the behavior tonight; well it truly scared and worried me. Bracket was a severely disturbed individual and for the first time I was worried I was in over my head. I heard the words of my father echo through my head "If it's easy it is not worth it." Bracket was definitely not going to be easy to deal with so I guess it was worth it. Still, I needed to know what I was dealing with. After Bracket was tucked back in bed for a midmorning nap I called the only person that could help me, Jose the Sherriff, my brother.

I carefully cracked the door to make sure Bracket was still asleep as I dialed the Sherriff's office number in my cellphone. Satisfied that my call would not be interrupted, I carefully walked down the hallway, through the living room and out of the house. It was just past noon and the sun was mercilessly blazing down on dry dirt. Even the birds had stopped flying and were resting in shady branches rather than defying the burning star. But there I stood, holding a small plastic case full of high tech electronics to my ear as sweat started to instantly bead on my forehead.

The phone rang four times before someone finally decided to pick up. I guess it was a good thing I wasn't calling for a real emergency. The voice on the other side was, formal, rough and very familiar. "This is Sherriff Moreno, how can I help you?" Hearing him be so official made me snicker, he didn't seem to approve of it. "How can I help you?!" His tone went from gruff and professional to angry and insulted in a matter of seconds. I considered messing with him for a while but being that I was calling to ask for his help, I decided otherwise.

I paced back and forth under the hot sun explaining to my brother some of the events that had happened. Sweat was making my shirt stick to me and I could feel the salty droplets running down my back. Once I was done Jose kindly said "What do you want me to do, arrest him?" Black and white, always black and white when it came to him. I had no doubt he was a great policeman, ever since I could remember he had always been preoccupied with the rules. He had been a great athlete but only because of his physical gifts. I don't think he ever broke a rule or even tried to bend it. He was a mother's dream. Obsessed with determining what was right and what was wrong and always trying to be on the holy path. Me on the other hand, well I liked to live in the gray and there were few rules I didn't try to bend.

After passing on the offer for Jose to arrest Bracket, I asked what I truly wanted help with. "I just want to know what I am dealing with. He has no I.D. and all he will give me is his "code name", I just want to know more about him. Who he is, where he came from and if he just got dropped off by aliens or not. Can you help me? .... Please." Jose waited until I said please to reply, and as any good big brother and law man would do, he agreed to help. I said thank you and before I could say bye he had already hung up the phone. Mission at hand, he had no time to waste.

Beers remembered and ears forgotten (Bracket)

I woke up in a strange bed in an oddly decorated bedroom. The right side of my head was violently throbbing in pain while the rest of my head dully ached. I reached my hand to my right ear just to find it covered in bandages. I sat on the edge of the bed for quite a few moments and swallowed back the previous night's beer and nausea came at me in merciless waves. I poked and prodded my right ear under the bandages but the slightest touch made the already excruciating pain flare up into even stronger agony.

I sat there trying to figure out how I had gotten there and what had happened to me. I remembered drinking with Gabriel the previous night but I didn't think I had drunk enough to wake up in this egregious state. I used my training and focused on finding the first solid memory I had from the night before. From there I slowly started to reconstruct what had happened. I remembered the porch, the beers and the conversation. Panic instantly coursed through my veins as I worried of having divulged too much to Gabriel. I pushed those fears aside for the moment and tried to remember more about the previous night.

Nothing, I could not remember anything else. It was all but a blank from then on until now. The pain on the right side of my head made it impossible to try to keep concentrating, so I gave up. I gathered myself and worked my way to my feet. My leg still hurt but it dulled in comparison to whatever the bandage hid. I carefully shuffled out of the strange room and into the familiar hallway. There was no sign of Gabriel anywhere. I passed the bathroom and I considered going in to vomit before I continued to search for Gabriel. My stomach had somewhat settled, so I carried on down the hallway.

The living room welcomed me and still there was no sign of the large man. I reached the kitchen opening and peeked in and still my companion eluded me. I stopped and looked around making sure he wasn't hiding in plain sight when I could vaguely hear the familiar tone of his voice out in the distance. I followed the voice and it led me to the front door and out into the porch. I could see him pacing back and forth out in the dirt driveway. His shirt was stained with sweat down his back, under his armpits and a cross pattern on his chest.

The wind carried his voice to and fro making it impossible to tell what he was talking about or with whom. I hung on to the pillar on the porch for support and waited for him to be done. I needed to know how much I had told him and what in the world had happened to my throbbing ear. The look on his face as he turned and spotted me concerned me. He hadn't expected to see me and his eyes told me I had caught him doing something he shouldn't have been doing.

He shoved his phone in his pocket and quickly made his way to me. "What are you doing up? You need to get back to bed buddy, you need to recover." I could see the honest concern in his eyes but the tension in his jaw gave away his guilt.

"What happened to me?" It stopped him from trying to usher me into the house and he took pause.

"Let's get you in the house and we can go over it Bracket." I carefully studied his micro-expressions as he spoke and I could tell he was being honest in his concern. I let go of the pillar and held onto his arm for support as I made the slow and painful walk back to the familiar couch. Once inside and next to the familiar furniture, I ungracefully plopped down. It was a horrible idea. Pain shot everywhere and anywhere where my body had been harmed over the past week. I could only see a bright light as my eyes stopped functioning because of the overwhelming pain. I concentrated on breathing, trying to collect myself but it proved more difficult than usual. The room began to swim on me and sweat spouted on my icy cold forehead. I gripped the couch urgently with my hands trying not to fall into the sky.

In the distance I could hear muffled sounds but could not make out what they were. I focused on them, and as if I were coming up from being under water, Gabriel's voice focused into clarity. "Bracket, are you ok? Can you hear me buddy? Bracket?" He repeated himself over and over, intensely looking at me while holding onto both my shoulders with his meaty fingers.

His face painfully came into focus and his words too loud to bear. "Yes, yes, I am fine, just get me some water." I needed him to stop shouting at me and my mouth and tongue felt unusually dry. After a few seconds he returned holding a clear glass with sloshing liquid inside of it. The water hit my lips and they felt like sponges rehydrating after being left out to dry in the sun. The precious liquid flowed over my tongue, making it tingle in joy, and down my throat bringing it back to life. I chugged the whole glass and didn't care that some of it spilled down the side of my face and onto my shirt. I don't think the water made it to my stomach. I could feel my body absorbing it as it swam down my esophagus and spreading out to my extremities. The hairs down my back stood at attention and a surge or energy coursed through all of my body.

I lowered the glass and found myself smiling with joy. Who would have thought a simple glass of H2O could ever bring me so much pleasure. Gabriel grabbed the fragile vessel from my shaky hands and set it on the coffee table. He sat down across from me wide eyed and filled with concerned. "You ok there buddy?"

"Yes, I think so, but what happened to me?" I raised my right hand to my ear and gently touched it. Even that slightest touch made me wince with pain. Gabriel's brow furrowed and he bit his lower lip. I could see his eyes searching for the words to try to explain to me what had happened.

After a few moments of intense silence Gabriel began to tell me the events that had led to my bandaged ear. I listened attentively but they sounded too fantastical I almost didn't believe the man. I could see in his face he wasn't lying but it still didn't make sense to me. What bug is he talking about? I would never hurt myself like that. There had to be a rational explanation for what happened to my ear and I suspected Gabriel's recollections were affected by alcohol and lack of sleep. What he was saying was true to him but it wasn't the truth.

I stopped his fantastical jabbering and demanded he help me go inspect the wounds. He sighed but agreed to help. We made our way to the bathroom and stood in front of the medicine cabinet mirror. I gave him a mean look and pointed to my ear. I wasn't in there to look at my handsome reflection, I was there to see the injuries he claimed I had inflicted on my ear. Gabriel tentatively approached my right ear and started to carefully remove the bandage. I noticed that the white bandage had soaked through with blood and was mostly red even on the outside.

The gauze made wet ripping noises as it was carefully but forcefully pulled away from my ear. Gabriel finished removing the bandage as my jaw was clinched and my eyes were closed. I hadn't closed them in fear of seeing but to steady myself from the overwhelming pain. Once I felt I could breathe I opened my eyes and tilted my head to my left.

The lighting in the small bathroom wasn't the greatest and I was still having a little bit of trouble focusing, but all I could see was red. There was a cacophony of shades of red, from bright to dark almost brown reds. Under all that fresh and partially clumped dried blood was my ear. I rapidly turned my head to the right, inspecting my left ear then went back to examining my right one. I was well aware that there is no true symmetry in the human body but my right ear looked like it came from another body, a body that had been gnawed at by coyotes and had started to decay.

I reached up with my fingers and gently tried to move and touch my ear but I instantly recoiled away from the pain. "You need to clean it; I need to see the damage." Gabriel sprang into action and started to pull out small square packets out of a first aid kit. He ripped the square packages and unfolded delicate moist sheets from within them. He gently cleaned the blood off my ear as I bitched and moaned about every single touch. He was truly a patient soul. Once Gabriel was done, I got to truly soak in the brutal damage to my ear. There were cuts and scratches all over it as if some beast with fangs had repeatedly struck at it. There were holes where no hole should have been and I could see through the large cartilage of my ear.

There were two large holes to be exact and the picture became clear. "It was a snake." I had to share my revelation with my partner and clarify his erroneous recollections. It was clear from the wounds that sometime the night before, probably while we were very intoxicated outside, I had been attacked by some form of viper. The several scratches on my ear reminded me of the three headed snake I had barely escaped while in the desert. It looked as if two of the heads had only been able to cut and scratch me while the third plunged its large fangs through my ear. Whatever small amount of venom it was able to plunge into me also explained my lack of recollection of what happened.

The more I looked at it the more it made sense. I looked back at Gabriel chuckling "Metal tweezers, how crazy do you think I am? It was obviously one of the desert's three headed vipers Gabriel, I am certain you must have seen one at some point in your life while living out here."

Gabriel's bewildered and confused look seemed to be causing him physical pain. He looked back between me and my ear and although his eyes asked me a million unspoken questions, his lips never allowed one to escape. He attempted to say something several times but was never able to get it out. Instead, looking defeated he asked me if he could dress my wound again. I accepted his kindness and care and sat as still as possible while he sprayed some antibiotic and covered the ear with gauze and tape once more.

My stomach protested its lack of food and being that my questions had been answered I could now focus on more mundane necessities. Once patched up, we headed out of the bathroom and into the kitchen at my stomach's requests. Gabriel offered item after item and I declined each and every single one of them. Many of them did sound quite delicious but I had an ulterior motive to decline them. Gabriel had been a loyal companion and a great caretaker. It was time I repaid some of his kindness. Once he was done offering and me declining I requested we head into town in search of more savory morsels.

He didn't seem very enthused about the drive for other food, considering he had a fridge full of options but knew I would not be satisfied otherwise. With his help I made it to the Jeep and painfully climbed into it. The large tires of the boxy vehicle looked great and I was pretty sure they would be very handy on rough terrain, but they certainly made it difficult to climb in and out of the beast. The top of the Jeep was down and the breeze felt heavenly blowing around my face. Gabriel kept offering options of where to buy food and every time, like at the house, I said no.

There were only two places he hadn't queried me on so far. Reluctant to say it, at last he asked about El Griego's, the giant's market. We both got a good chuckle out of that and it felt good to finally laugh without my ribs hurting. After I declined that location too, he was left only with Family Dollar, where Monica was hard at work this time of the afternoon. I finally agreed to search there for something more delicious to eat and my plan to repay my partner was set in motion.

We pulled up in the parking lot and the large red and orange letters once again greeted us. There was a spot right next to the entrance and Gabriel secured it for us. I opened my door and exited into the dry afternoon air and started to walk towards the door while using the Jeep for support. My ears didn't hear the echo of Gabriel's closing door so I turned to see what was going on. The vehicle remained running and Gabriel within. I waved at him, trying to get his attention but he did his best to pretend he didn't see me. I was already to the front of the Jeep so I kept following the contours of it until I was standing next to the driver's window.

I waved and motioned to Gabriel but now all of the sudden his neck could only turn to his right and was unable to see me to his left. I started to grow frustrated at his childish behavior and at his foiling of my plans. I knocked on his window and still no reaction. I kept knocking, slowly increasing the violence of my fist on the glass window until he finally conceded defeat, looked at me and rolled down the glass.

"What?!" I couldn't help but to smile, he looked like a pouty kid. He seemed crabby and his full cheeks and full lips gave him the appearance of a tired whiny baby.

"Aren't you coming in with me?" Gabriel huffed and puffed inside the vehicle looking around the seats and floor for an excuse he didn't have. Unable to find it he just gave me a simple and grouchy "No" as a response. "Well I am going to need some of your currency." He rolled his eyes and proceeded to wiggle and struggle, trying to get his wallet out of his front pocket. He kept trying to lean back as his fingers ungracefully searched for the pocket's opening. Once his chubby fingers disappeared down the front of his pants he started to shift left and right as his hand clinched on the prize and slowly pulled it out. The wallet finally escaped the jail of his pants, as his hand flew violently upwards, as if all the kinetic energy of the struggle was finally released.

Gabriel was breathing heavily as he thumbed through the slits of the black leather wallet searching for what bills to give me. The ordeal had left him looking a little tired and winded and I worried for the man's health. He handed me a twenty dollar bill and I just stared at the green piece of paper having expected more. He didn't get or want to get that I needed more money, so I had to divert my eyes from the single bill to his sweaty face.

I raised my left eyebrow, clearly questioning the small amount he had given me and after a couple of exasperated sighs he handed me a couple more twenties. I thanked him and gracefully made my way into the store. Gabriel might have altered my original plan but by the time the cool air conditioned inside had welcomed me, I had devised a different strategy.

I walked in and Monica cheerfully welcomed me into the store. We exchanged quick pleasantries and off I went using a small grocery cart to collect my future bounty and as walking support. I searched and searched and finally decided on a ham, a big fancy spiral cut ham. It sounded appetizing and perfect for the plan I had come up with. I made my way to Monica's lane and placed my single item on the conveyor belt. The shiny gold wrapping of the ham made crinkling noises as it wiggled on its way to be scanned.

Monica picked up the large ham and looked at me perplexed. "You guys having company?" I smiled as the poor girl fell right into my trap.

"Well yes we are. Tonight. You." It took her a second to process it but her happy demeanor and smile let me know instantly she was interested in coming over. "Gabriel would love to have you over for dinner tonight. He is sitting in the car out there, he is just too shy to ask himself." I pointed to Gabriel sitting in the car and he looked at me suspiciously as he could not hear what Monica and I were talking about. She waved at him and his semblance changed immediately from angry to that of a happy cherub.

"Oh I don't want to impose on your guys." I assured her it was no bother or imposition and that we expected her at 7pm sharp. She hemmed and hawed a bit more but could not keep resisting my incessant invites. Once she finally agreed, I let it slip that Gabriel would be very pleased to have his high school crush come over for dinner. Her face turned as red as the tomatoes I had walked by earlier. We said our goodbyes as she tried to compose herself but failed.

I must say I was surprised by both of their behavior. They both had to be in their thirties but were acting like love-struck teenagers. I was also pleased I could tell Gabriel needed the company of a good woman and I was almost certain Monica would be his first choice. I grabbed my ham and made sure not to drop it on the hot pavement on my way to the Jeep. I climbed aboard the beast and just sat there and grinned.

"Ham? Really a ham?" Gabriel's frustration leaked out in his words but I just smiled and nodded as we drove back to the house.

Gabriel turned on the radio in the Jeep and sound and rhythm surrounded us. The drums, the horns and the guitar echoes made parts deep inside of me wiggle a dance. I refused the temptation and decided to study this new but excellent music I was hearing. A voice interrupted the melodic rhythms, full of pain and bravado. It was a sad voice but full of strength and determination, it glided over the beat and it all tied together into musical art.

Another voice, not as beautiful and far less in tune slowly grew from my left. Gabriel's body had succumbed to the beat of the drums and his head was bobbing back and forth. His lips were moving but barely any noise was coming out. By the time the song had been playing for a minute or so, his painfully out of tune voice was competing with the beautiful melody emanating from the speakers. The rest of his body gave in as well to the percussion and was moving and dancing as much as anyone could while still driving and keeping the Jeep on the road, most of the time at least. The large man had very good driving dancing moves, which partially made up for his horrible singing.

The song ended and I hadn't reacted so he must have thought I wasn't looking. When the next song started the wheels fell off Gabriel's cabaret show. The rhythms and instruments were a bit different but I could tell it was still the same band playing. It was a much happier song from what I could make out from the lyrics and the inspirational music. Gabriel was singing at the top of his lungs while beating on the steering wheel, pretending to play the drums. His dancing had become spastic twitches and his hips and arms could not seem to agree who was in control.

He beat and squeezed his hands on the steering wheel, while his singing became almost shouts. I could see the goose bumps form on his forearms as he fought tears back while he sang. A few tears escaped and he didn't even bother whipping them. He was having a cathartic and desperate experience being part of that particular song. The song ended and he quickly hit the rewind button on the console. The song started over again, the now familiar spastic guitar and pain-filled voice caressing the inside of my ear. This happened two more times before we finally reached the house.

Gabriel kept singing from the bottom of his heart, trying to believe the upbeat and hopeful lyrics. There was such a deep pain in his eyes and I hadn't figured out why. As he parked the Jeep on the dirt driveway I was very glad I had enacted my plan to reward him for his loyalty.

"Who was that?" Starting to grow fond of the melody, I was curious as to who it was.

"Ozomatli, Brighter." He sniffled as he said it and quickly tried to inconspicuously wipe away his tears. I had understood the name of the song, but the name of the band perplexed me.

"Oso...what?" I had to ask for help with saying the confusing name. Gabriel explained, well tried to explain the name to me several times. As I repeated the name, I thought I had it a couple of times but he kept correcting me. He tried spelling the name but it just confused me more. Frustrated, he got out of the Jeep slamming the door and cursing in Spanish as he made his way to the house. I had eventually understood him but seeing him get so worked up made me keep playing dumb for a few more times, until he majestically snapped. It was hilarious how red his face was and I didn't know he could talk that fast until he started to spit word after word in Spanish, every new one sounding more angry and vile.

Having left me behind, I negotiated my way back into the house while carrying the prized ham. I had to stop a couple of times to catch my breath; the whole excursion had worn me out. I needed to recharge once more but before I did I had to make sure Gabriel got the ham and the house ready for our impending company.

Once I made it into the house Gabriel had already found his way to the fridge, cracked open a beer and was lounging on the couch. He wasn't being really helpful right now and it was starting to annoy me. I needed to lie down and didn't have the energy to make the detour to the kitchen to drop off the ham. Instead as I passed by the couch, I deliberately and violently dropped the ham on Gabriel's lap as close to the sensitive parts as I could.

"What the fuck?!" He yelped as he recoiled, the ham having found his eggs. He dropped the beer he had been holding in his hand, the bottle making a dull echoing sound as it hit the rug and started to spill. I kept walking away from the angry man fumbling to get a handle on the ham and trying to pick up his spilling beer. As I reached the hallway on my way to the comfortable bed, I informed him of the news.

"You might want to clean that up and start cooking that ham. Monica is going to be here at 7PM sharp for dinner. Didn't figure you and I could eat that ham all by ourselves." I smiled and kept walking. The obscenities began to fly both in English and Spanish, some of them even sounded like a made up language. I reached the door to the room as Gabriel entered the hallway.

"Are you serious? She is coming over?" He asked and his voice sounded hopeful but yet terrified. I had messed with him enough for one afternoon so I told him the truth.

"Yes, yes she is Gabriel. She will be here at seven. I am exhausted; I am going to take a nap so that I can be ready for dinner. Please wake me up around 6:30pm." I closed the door, found my way to the bed and my eyes quickly started to fail me. I didn't hear any more questions or screaming coming from outside the room. Instead I could hear hurried, panicked and forceful steps scattering all over the house as the large man began to clean up and get ready for our visit. Satisfied with my good deed, I let slumber take me and I left the conscious world with a smile and a happy heart.

Hopelessness and Ham
(Gabriel)

I hung up the phone and was startled to see Bracket leaning on the doorway as I made my way back to the house. He looked like death warmed over and I was horrified to see him walking around. I don't know how much blood you can lose from an ear but he was looking drained and a little vampirish.

He looked at me with accusatory and confused eyes as I had to convince him to go back into the house. I helped him to the couch and as he sat down, somehow he went even paler, his eyes rolled into the back of his head and he started to convulse. His body broke out in spasms and tensed as he made heavy breathing noises. His muscles contracted further and further until he was a rigid mass of trembling extremities. I kept calling out his name while looking at him but there weren't any pupils to be found to look into.

It must have been but ten or twenty seconds but it felt like an eternity waiting for him to come back to. Eventually the violent shaking of his body ceased and he gently sunk into the soft couch. His eyes opened and looked at me as if he had been teleported to a strange planet and was just now getting the first look at it. He insisted on sitting up and in the process he discovered his injured ear. The pain washed away the temporary confusion and made him focus on finding the answers to what had happened to his ear.

He was oblivious about the seizure he just had and kept demanding I explain what happened to his ear. He kept touching it, every time his fingers recoiling away from the shooting pain he must have been causing to himself. As I was learning with Bracket, I just played along and answered his queries about his mutilated ear. I could see the smile slowly growing on his face as I told him about the bug incident. By the time I was done he was laughing at what he thought was a preposterous story.

He wasn't satisfied so decided to stand up to go inspect the wounds in the bathroom mirror. He had drank all the water I had brought him and seemed in better spirits, looking much better than he had a few moments ago during his seizure. Color had flushed back into his face and the glassy shine had disappeared from his eyes. The moment he stood up it was clear that he wasn't well yet. He swayed in every direction as he stared into oblivion. I quickly reached him and helped him steady his balance.

Unshaken or unaware by his gyroscopic misalignment, I helped the stubborn man to the bathroom. I tried to carefully remove the bandages but even my gentlest touch solicited whines and complaints from Bracket. Finally done, the inexpertly pierced and maimed ear was left out in all of its bloody and gory glory. I didn't want to admire it anymore since it was making my stomach churn, so I focused on Bracket's reaction. He slowly moved his head, trying to see the ear from as many angles as the mirror over the sink would allow. His hands were firmly gripping the white pedestal sink, until he raised his arm to try to touch the ear.

His fingers pulled away from his ear as if they had been struck by electricity. To my surprise, besides a couple of pained looks, Bracket studied his ear carefully. I could see the wheels turning as he rationalized and came up with his explanation of what had destroyed his poor ear. The light bulb moment was almost comical, he did a small hop, his eyes widened and an accomplished smile adorned his face. His piercing blue eyes turned their attention to me as he clearly explained the cause of the damage.

I stood there and listened wanting to break into uncontrollable laughter. But the amazement of his story and the conviction in which he told it helped me keep my composure. Bracket spoke of three headed snakes, nights in the desert and how only he could have survived this most recent encounter with the beast. It was like listening to a kid tell you about their imaginary friend but with the knowledge and intelligence of a very smart man. I didn't know whether to be impressed at his imagination or feel sorry about his delusions. I let him finish while I nodded in agreement and then I redressed his ear and helped him back to the couch.

I insisted he rest but he was ravenous for some food. I could eat a little myself so I started offering everything I had at the house. He declined every single item, from his crackers with butter to a ten year old jar of homemade pickled beef my mom had left in the cupboards for some reason. Nothing, "I'll pass, no thank you" over and over. At least he was courteous. Now hungry myself and out of options, we ventured into town to hopefully find something to suit Bracket's palate.

It didn't take long to go through the few options in town for food and after much avoidance we ended up at the Family Dollar. I was tired and smelled of sweat so I didn't really want to let Monica see me like this. Even though I felt guilty, I sent Bracket in all by himself. After all, he was the one looking to satisfy a specific and impossible craving. I grimaced as he hobbled his way in, all patched up and injured but even with the guilt mounting I would not leave the cool comfort of the car.

Bracket disappeared into the store and left me alone to my thoughts. I wondered if my brother had found out anything about Bracket but my phone had no text or messages. By reflex my hand went towards the radio knob but Bracket's friendly conversation with whom I could only assume was Monica stopped me. I could see him smiling and chatting but the display obscured her. Soon after, he exited the store holding a large ham between his arms. He struggled his way back into the car and sat holding onto the ham like a kid would hold on to a stuffed animal.

"Ham? Really a ham?" I started driving and he just sat there smiling, clutching his smoked porcine butt. As I turned into the street my hands, driven once more by muscle memory, turned on the radio. "Cumbia de los muertos" began to play and the rhythms made my blood pump faster and my hips to sway in the seat of the Jeep. I had been listening to a couple of songs on repeat on my drive back to Pecos. This one reminded me of my mom and gave me a little peace.

I gave in and started to sing and dance as I tapped the steering wheel, losing myself in the song. I found comfort in the words and it made my nightly encounter with my mom's ghost even more concrete. It was a short song and the next one soon started playing after a short silent pause. It was also by Ozomatli and it was a cathartic song of hope for me. The reggae guitar echoed inside the car. I turned up the volume in anticipation of the chorus which I had sung to myself so many times.

"Weight's gonna get much lighter
World's gonna look much brighter
Though the heat's gonna carry on
We'll make it through the night..."

I knew every word by heart; I had after all sung them hundreds of times. My hands gripped the steering wheel tightly as my lips shouted the words and my mind wandered. I remembered sitting in my doctor's office as he delivered the crushing news. "There is nothing more we can do for you Gabriel, I am sorry. We just have to figure out how to manage it." The words made my body recoil then and made me sing louder now.

I had been gone from home a couple of years to college. I didn't know what to study but a broken heart will make you leave in search of new horizons. I had managed to keep myself in good standing with the University as I figured out what I wanted to do with my life. I had just gotten back from visiting my parents during spring break. Most kids went to exciting and exotic places, I went to Pecos to get lectured by my dad and babied by my mom. It could have been worse I guess, some poor students couldn't go anywhere at all and got to patrol through the empty campus like lost souls. It was also the last time I went home for many years. I had left and didn't want to burden anyone with my problems.

The doctor had explained the tumor was in an inoperable part of my brain. Trying to take it out would cause severe permanent damage, so it wasn't an option. He took me off the migraine medicines since they weren't working anyway and he set me up for Chemotherapy and radiation to try to shrink the tumor. I had to drop out of school and survive. I should have gone home but fear, shame, guilt, I honestly don't know exactly what, kept me away.

For a while I was a shell of who I had been. Once the treatments were done the weight really started coming on. Between the pain pills and the comfort eating I got to where I am today. Doctors gave me the good news, bad news speech. The tumor hadn't shrunken but it was a slow growing cancer. I was supposed to look at the bright side of life but I didn't see it from the darkness and gloom that surrounded me.

I felt let down and betrayed by the doctors. They put me through hell physically and for nothing. I wanted answers, needed answers and options; that is when I left. My dad was furious, my mom broken hearted and my siblings I think jealous. Everyone thought I was leaving just to globe trot the world and live on vacation. I wanted to tell them the truth and almost did. Only almost, I'd rather have my mom disappointed at me than worried that her baby was going to die.

I traveled through Asia, Europe, South America and Australia, all in search of alternative medicine and miracles for my tumor. I tried so many herbs, prayed to so many gods and was cleansed and "cured" in so many ceremonies. Nothing worked, the tumor grew slowly, but it did grow. Alcohol and pain killers were my only salvation and companions. Numb the pain, make it through another night and hope the next miracle cure was actually real. I had tried so hard to keep my ailment away from my mother; it took me away from her. We always talked and I wrote her religiously. She always wanted me to come back; she missed me but wanted me to be happy above all.

She died never knowing my condition. My fears of her finding out were for nothing, and all it did is take precious time away from her and my family. I had nieces and nephews I had never met. I wasn't there for her when she needed me and couldn't even make it back in time for the funeral.

I sang louder as every hair on my body stood at attention. Tears were running down my face and I didn't care if Bracket noticed or not. My eyes were so flooded with the tears that I could barely see the road but I managed. It wasn't the first time and probably wouldn't be the last that I broke down while driving. The familiar but almost forgotten mountains framed the house as we started to approach it. I pulled in, stormed inside and found my first beer. I was hurting but it wasn't my head. My eyes tried to cry tears from my soul. I repeated the lyrics over and over in my head, "we'll make it through the night...", I wanted to believe, needed to believe it. I had wasted so much in search of a miracle and was now left with nothing.

Bracket's silhouette broke the brightness shining through the open doorway. As he entered the room and I could finally see his face, I spotted the same cheesy grin he had as he walked out of the store earlier. He threw the ham on my lap making me spill my beer. Before I could get pissed at him he informed me of our impending visitor. He kept walking towards the bedroom and I had to chase after him. I asked once more, my stomach filled with anxiety and panic. I didn't know whether to punch him in the face or hug him. Monica was coming over for dinner and the house was a shithole of empty alcohol bottles and I needed to cook a ten pound ham, something I had never done before.

Bracket closed the door and I was left alone in the hallway holding the ham in my arms. I scrambled to the kitchen and started to read the instructions on how to cook the big hunk of meat. I ranted and raved in Spanish trying to figure out how get it ready. I pulled mom's cast iron pans out of the oven and started to pre-heat it as the package indicated. I left the oven to do its thing as I grabbed a new garbage bag from under the sink and started to run around the house picking up all the garbage I had indiscriminately tossed. What little progress I had done cleaning the place up had disappeared. It was back to looking like a frat house after a New Year's party and also smelled like one.

I started to open windows, trying to air the place out of the stench of beer, alcohol and even darker and nastier odors. I had filled the first trash bag and was on my way to the kitchen to grab another one when the oven dinged and startled me. I jumped back as if the stove had shot me. My reaction made me start to laugh; the laughter grew and became uncontrollable. I threw the ham in a roasting pan and shoved it in the oven as I giggled. Tears of laughter, this time, began to run down my cheeks as I left the kitchen with a brand new empty trash bag in search of more litter. I felt like a teenager again full of angst and anticipation of seeing Monica. I laughed out of nerves and relief. I picked up cans and bottles off the floor, along with empty food wrappers and I honestly could say I felt happy. For the first time in a long time I truly had something to look forward to besides more disappointment and pain. I didn't know what possessed Bracket to invite her over but I was glad the crazy bastard did.

I walked around talking to myself in Spanish and cursing the mess we had made. It was almost six and I had but one more hour before Monica was to show up. The place looked as good as it was going to get. I had lit some vanilla candles, between them and the ever increasing aroma of the ham I think I had the smell of the house taken care of. Now I needed to do something about my personal smell. I had worked up quite a sweat and the vodka was seeping out through my pores. I headed to the bathroom just to find the door locked and I could hear the shower running inside. Mierda! Bracket!

I pounded on the door and all the response I would get from inside was the same horribly vocalized song. "I like to move it, move it..." Over and over again. I shouted and banged on the door so hard it rattled, but the painful singing never stopped. I went into the bedroom and tried to figure out if I could get ready without taking a shower. The moment I took my shirt off and raised my arms, I knew that was an impossibility.

I returned to the bathroom door and before I could start pounding on it again the water stopped, along with the incessant singing. I could hear Bracket stirring around inside the bathroom; finally his footsteps seemed to be approaching the door. I stepped back, not wanting to startle the bathroom tenor and finally the door opened. He wasn't startled but surprised to see me standing there with no shirt. I had been trying to get into the bathroom now for half an hour and still he blocked my access to it.

"You might want to hurry up and get ready Gabriel, Monica should be here pretty soon." Bracket spoke to me with a concerned brow while holding the towel to keep it from falling to the ground. He once more gave me that devilish smile and started to hobble down the hallway, leaving a trail of water droplets behind him. I ranted and raved some more but quickly entered the bathroom.

I finished undressing and quickly jumped in the shower. I turned both knobs as I had done a million times before but only cold water came out. I shrieked and screamed like an excited school girl as I tried to catch my breath from the frozen water hitting my skin. I violently turned my body trying to protect my more sensitive areas from the freezing rain falling from the show-erhead. I retreated as far back as I could in the tub and waited for the water to warm up as I was starting to tremble.

The hot water never came. I slowly braved limb after limb into the frigid waters until I was completely submerged. I got wet as fast as possible and re-treated once more into the far corner of the tub seeking refuge. I needed to start washing myself but had left the soap on the other side of the tub. The waterfall of ice divided us and I was still trying to catch my breath from my previous plunge. I peeked out of the shower and checked my cellphone and it was 6:40PM. Panic shot through my body. If I didn't hurry Monica was going to catch me walking out of the bathroom in nothing but a towel.

I set the phone down and without hesitation defied the frigid falls and snatched the soap. I lathered up, returned the soap and repeated the process with the shampoo. I stood there, a mess of bubbles as I got myself mentally ready once more to take the polar plunge. I took a deep breath and ventured into the freezing cold water. I scrubbed and rinsed all the soap off my body as I shivered uncontrollably. Feeling clean and somewhat shrunken I shut off the water and quickly started looking for my towel. Then I remembered it comfortably wrapped around Bracket's waist.

I scanned the bathroom and my only option was the small hand towel hanging next to the sink. I plodded over, careful not to slip on the tiles and grabbed the little towel. It was better than nothing but it wasn't much. I rubbed the two by one foot rectangle of cloth all over my body, trying to soak up all the drops of cold water still clinging onto my skin. I was as dry as I was going to get and I proceeded to brush my teeth. The last thing I wanted to do is have dragon's breath while trying to be suave with Monica. Wait, why did I have to be suave with her?

I kept brushing my ivories vigorously as I tried to figure out what I expected out of this dinner. It was just a dinner with old friends catching up. Right? Then why I was so nervous and anxious. It wasn't a date, it is not like I asked her over, for all I knew she was interested in Bracket. Thoughts of conquest and excruciating defeat kept flooding my brain as I mindlessly rubbed the toothbrush upon my teeth. I stopped torturing myself as I decided it was time to rinse. I quickly gargled the minty mouthwash and headed to the door with my loin cloth of a towel. I reached for the doorknob just to hear the front door open and two very familiar voices greet each other.

I could hear Bracket and Monica chatting it up just a few yards outside the bathroom door. They had settled into the living room and were getting to know each other. I checked my cellphone and it was 6:50PM, she was early. My heart was sinking with every passing second as my brain frantically and unsuccessfully tried to figure out a solution for my quandary. I paced back and forth, naked in the bathroom with the small towel clenched in my right hand and my phone in my left. I watched as minute after minute changed the last digit on my phone's display. I had but one option and I was seriously considering spending the night in the bathroom instead of acting on it.

I had to make a dash for the bedroom and hope Monica was sitting with her back to me on the right couch. I had a 50/50 chance that she would either be oblivious as I ran naked to my room or she was about to get one hell of a show right before dinner. I covered as much as I could with the small towel, focusing my efforts on my front and my dignity. I took one last big slow breath and I went for it.

I could have cracked the door and taken a peek but panic made me swing the door wide open. I started to scurry towards my bedroom like a mouse running for cover in a house. I looked back toward the couches and to my complete embarrassment I saw Monica's eyes widen enough that they looked as if they might burst out of her head. It was too late to stop or retreat, so onwards I went. I held on to the towel for dear life but as I scampered down the hallway I knew my butt was completely exposed. There wasn't enough fabric to cover it and not much I could do about it. I quickly reached my room and quickly locked the door behind me.

I dropped the towel to the floor and leaned on the door as if a zombie might push its way through if I moved. I could feel my heart racing, beating loudly inside my chest. Drops of sweat started to form on my forehead and I was finally no longer cold. I didn't know if I could go out and face her now, she had gotten one glorious and giggle filled view of my backside. But first things first, I was in desperate need of some clothing. I rifled through my suitcase that I still hadn't unpacked and found some decent items to hide my nakedness and shame.

It was 7:15PM and I was still locked in my room. Bracket had come over and knocked a couple of times already, letting me know our visitor had arrived. Each time I said it would only be a minute but the minutes kept accumulating. I leaned on the door, listening to them talk as I tried to figure out how to face Monica now. That is when my nose brought me back to the simple reality of life.

Something was burning and the only thing cooking was the ham, the ham Bracket had bought with my money and Monica was here to eat. Shit! I left the room without hesitation and rushed into the kitchen. Smoke was seeping out of the oven and ruining the delicious smell that had once filled the kitchen. I opened the oven door and the sweet and bitter smell overwhelmed my nostrils. I reached in to pull out the roasting pain and my fingers quickly and painfully recoiled away as the met the excruciatingly hot metal.

I jumped around clinching my fist and using every curse word in every language I had ever learned. Both thumbs, index and middle fingers throbbed as the skin slowly died after its brutal thermal encounter. The smoke kept pouring out of the open oven so I pushed the pain aside for the moment, found a couple of dish towels and placed the hot pan on top of the stove.

The delicious drippings that once had kept the ham nice and moist had now turned into black and brown smoldering goo.

The kitchen smelled of a smokehouse which had gone up in flames and not the least bit appetizing. Bracket and Monica stood at the entrance to the kitchen watching me struggle to save some part of the deceased ham. I tried to pick it up with a couple of serving forks but it was stuck to the burnt pan. I tugged as hard as my injured fingers would allow me, but the ham would not yield. I tried to cut along the base of the ham to grant it its freedom but only ended up with a few more burns on the back of my hands. The pan had cooled so they weren't as painful as the ones slowly blistering on my fingers.

Frustrated and being carefully watched, I just started stabbing and cutting the ham, careful not to let the pieces fall to the charred bottom of the pan and placing the dry looking pieces on a plate for serving. By the time I was done there were no slices, just chunks and jagged pieces of ham randomly piled up on the plate.

"Dinner is served" I turned and told my audience while gracefully pointing at the plate. The ham looked pathetic on the white plate. It was dried to a dark pink color with white blotches of all the fat being forcefully cooked out of it. I tried grabbing the plate and after a few painful attempts I was able to grip it without the pain making me want to instantly drop it.

I had set the table earlier for three settings and I placed the platter in the middle so that everyone could serve themselves. It wasn't until then that it dawn on me. I hadn't prepared anything to go along with the ham. The table setting, although nice, looked pretty pathetic with three empty plates and one dish with dry ham pieces. I hung my head in defeat and it was Monica's sweet voice that broke the silence.

"Are you ok Gabriel? Let me look at your hands." Pain was radiating through my fingers and I could feel the pounding of my heart in each and every single one of them. I sat down and turned my palms up towards her. She gently grabbed them and her touch made me forget the pain for a second. I looked at her and the concern in her face made me inspect my hands once more. Blisters had formed on my fingertips and were growing and expanding. They had worked themselves half way up my fingers and clear liquid was quickly filling them. All six fingers looked abnormally large and red, like hotdogs expanding over a bonfire.

Monica ordered Bracket to find her a first aid kit and having recently used it he knew exactly where to find it. He placed it on the table and Monica quickly started to dig through it for the right supplies. She pulled out a tube of anti-burn cream and a couple of rolls of sterile gauze. She covered my fingers in the cream and wrapped them with the gauze. I sat in silence and just watched her care for me. Every touch, even though painful, was glorious. And god did she smell incredible. Somehow through the burning stink of the kitchen her sweet perfume was the only thing my nose could smell.

"There, that ought to do it. Are you ok Gabriel?" I smiled and nodded as she still gently rested her hand on my thigh and gave me caring eyes. Bracket sat quietly on his chair letting us have our moment, well me and my moment.

"We should eat." I said and all eyes went to the sad looking plate of ham in the center of the table. Monica dished me and her plate and Bracket, after much prodding, finally found a couple of pieces that met his approval. Bracket pulled some beers for all of us out of the fridge and we sat and ate the dry ham. I couldn't use my freshly wrapped hands so Monica fed me and every bite of the disgusting, chewy and salty pork was heavenly delicious coming from her. The poor girl tried to eat but recoiled at the first few salty dry bites. I learned that night that you are not to salt ham before cooking it, not to grab a hot metal roasting pan with bare hands and that my feelings for Monica were still alive and kicking. We spent the next couple of hours drinking beers, trying to get the disgusting taste of the ham out of our mouths, reminiscing about old times and catching up on our lives.

She never mentioned my naked scamper and no one criticized my ham cooking abilities as we sat at the table, Monica talking and me listening. The night had to end and after giving me a long hug she was off for the night. The door closed and I was on cloud nine. Maybe I was getting my hopes up, maybe life had finally allowed me the chance to be with her, or maybe I was just getting my hopes up over just two old friends catching up. I didn't care to be a fatalist right now and just rode the wave of joy the evening had left me with.

"Smooth Gabriel, that was soooooo smooth." Bracket's jabbing words woke me from my puppy love daydream. He was sitting on the couch sipping on a beer and disapprovingly shaking his head at me. He started to open his mouth to give me some more "constructive criticism" but I beat him to the punch.

"Oh fuck you Bracket, I'm going to bed." I walked away and left him there, his mouth hanging open and his eyes full of disbelief at the words I had slung his way. I made it to my mom's room, shut the door and plopped on the bed. I smiled as I could still smell Monica's perfume on me. I inhaled every last molecule of it as I dozed off with joy in my heart for a change.

Burned Fingers and an Emergency Exit (Bracket)

I don't know for how long I was out but the incessant stampede of elephants outside the door finally woke me up. I could hear Gabriel mumbling in panic as he ran up and down the hard wood floors. I felt refreshed after my cat nap but needed to freshen up before company arrived. I headed for the bathroom and once I opened the door his voice got louder and his footsteps quieter. Gabriel seemed very preoccupied and busy so I snuck into the bathroom, trying not to bother him.

I turned the water as hot as I could stand and plunged into the stream. Steam was already billowing around me and I felt as if I was inside a warm and comforting cloud. The hot droplets stung my skin until it finally relaxed and I had tempered myself to the water. I kept slowly increasing the heat many times, feeling the initial sting only to be quickly followed by the comfortable relaxation. I leaned on the long wall of the bathtub, my hands clutched in front of me, forehead resting on the cold tiles and the water fell on my left side and back. Streams formed over my shoulder and pooled between my chest and the wall. I closed my eyes and let my mind wander and relax.

Thoughts of my old tile shower tried to creep into my head but I quickly pushed them away. There were too many good and lost memories with my love that I did not wish to revisit right now. I focused on the sound of the water racing though the shower head, propelling themselves through the air in a miniature waterfall, and hitting my skin at a million different angles. I breathed, sang my meditation song and felt. I lived in the moment, with no ugly past and no confusing future. I was just there in that particular moment in space and time.

I had kept adjusting the water knobs until the cold water was completely shut and only the last bit of remaining hot water was left to bathe me. It was time to start cleaning myself up and I hurried as the hot water was quickly running out. The door started to rattle and I could hear Gabriel's' muffled screams on the other side of it. I couldn't tell what he was saying but he was definitely in a hurry. I finished up, grabbed the only towel draped over the curtain rod, dried myself partially, wrapped it around my waist and went to the door.

I could finally make out what Gabriel's words were but they didn't reveal anything his frantic knocking hadn't already told me. I opened the door carefully so as to not get punched in the face by a flying knock and stood there giving him a second to collect himself. He was red, sweaty and his eyes open a little too wide. A delicious smoky and meaty smell danced into my nostrils, making my stomach stir with hunger. Gabriel kept urging me to get out, and with me so eager to get dressed and eating, I complied with his request.

I put on one of the other set of clothing we had purchased and headed out to the kitchen and the intoxicating smell. As I walked past the bathroom I could hear Gabriel's yelps and high pitched screams. I was concerned at first but the interwoven curses reassured me he was ok, so I kept on following my nose. I couldn't help but to notice how clean the place looked for a change. I should invite company more often apparently.

The small table in the kitchen had been made up with real plates and silverware. Contrary to what my limited experiences with Gabriel had led me to believe, he wasn't a total pig after all. My nose kept guiding me and my hands soon had opened the over door, revealing the source of the intoxicating molecules. The lovely piece of pink meat sat on a roasting pan, dripping its delicious juices that were soon evaporated into my nose. I carefully reached in and tore a piece of the pre-sliced slices of the ham. The flesh was warm so I quickly placed it in my mouth. The salty delicious meatiness of the ham exploded in my mouth and soon found its way into my stomach.

I had closed the oven door, reminding myself it would have been rude to eat prior to our company arriving. After much debate, my more primal instincts overrode formalities and I had reached in and stolen pieces of ham several times. I would have continued stealing morsel after morsel of the delicious smoked meat but a knock on the door interrupted me. I opened the oven and stole one last slice and quickly chewed it as I made my way to the door.

I opened the wooden threshold and on the other side of it stood a magnificent sight. I had only had the pleasure of seeing Monica in her work uniform and even then she was a very beautiful and striking woman. Dressed up and made up to the nines she was stunning. She wore a knee high blue dress that made her tanned skin radiate. Her gorgeous emerald eyes had been expertly decorated with the right amount of makeup to make them twinkle in her beautiful face. Her lips had been seductively painted and were parted, showing a most exquisite and seductive smile.

The moment she realized it was me her well-practiced expression of seduction and devilishness disappeared and were replaced by a friendly smile. "Hi Bracket, how are you?" I could see her fighting back her blushing face but biology betrayed her. I had caught her trying to impress Gabriel and I had made her waste it on me.

I invited her in and her perfect curves danced in her cobalt dress, accompanied with black high heels and sapphire jewelry, which guided the eye toward her flirtatious cleavage. I tried not to let my eyes wander too much but it was now my biology betraying me. I offered to sit and we each took post in one of the couches facing each other. I faced the outer door as always, in case I had to react to any uninvited intruders or emergency.

We exchanged the expected pleasantries but not being much for small talk I started to ask the question I truly wanted to know. She was my first chance to properly vet Gabriel as an adequate companion. She had known him from his youth, when we start defining who we are and are the most prone to show our poor judgment.

Monica spoke very highly of Gabriel and no matter how sinister or well-conceived my question was; she always had a positive response about him. Seeing how much she thought of him and considering the smile she permanently wore while talking about him, it surprised me that they never became an item back then. Yet here she was tonight all these years later, the universe can work in mysterious ways sometimes.

She was answering me why they never had dated when she stopped midsentence, her eyes widened and her mouth hung open. I thought I had seen her blush prior but her capillaries dilated and her chest, neck and face turned scarlet. She looked at something over my left shoulder so I quickly turned to see what had so violently captivated her attention.

By the time I turned I did not see anything. I could hear heavy footsteps running away from us. I didn't know what Gabriel had done but he had certainly shocked her. We tried to continue the conversation but the flow had been interrupted. What had been a fluid back and forth between Monica and

I, became a muddled mess. We both tried speaking at the same time; there were awkward silences and plenty of nervous laughs. I kept trying but it was obvious that my time to extract information out of her had long passed.

Our awkward exchange was soon interrupted by heavy footsteps, this time coming in our direction. Gabriel stormed by behind us and dove into the kitchen. His behavior was not only strange, but rude as well to our present company. I excused myself from Monica and started to head into the kitchen to confront Gabriel. The clanking and racket coming from inside the kitchen quickly turned into loud and desperate cries. Gabriel was screaming, obviously in pain. I hastened my pace to go check in on him and Monica followed close behind.

We walked in to see Gabriel struggling to hold on to the knife as he cut chunks off the ham and placed them on a clean plate. He was obviously in pain but determined to finish carving the ham. Once done he grabbed the plate which caused him a lot of discomfort and ungracefully plopped it on the table.

"Dinner is served!" He motioned to the plate on the table and we could finally see what had caused him so much pain and discomfort. His fingers had grown giant burn blisters, which made his fingers look like swollen clown balloons. Monica let out a horrified gasp at seeing the fingers and instantly kicked into crisis mode. She sat Gabriel down and started tending to him. She deputized me and made me her gopher, sending me to get her medical supplies and the now very familiar first aid kit.

She was busy tending to him and he looked happier than anyone with severe burns should look. I took a few steps back in panic when she pulled out a round white pill and held it between her delicate fingers. I found myself pushed all the way back with my back against the counter at the other side of the small kitchen. She raised her hand holding the small ivory disc. She slowly moved it towards Gabriel's mouth and handed him a glass of water. I felt instant relief when I realized she wasn't going to try to shove the pill down my throat. Gabriel smiled after he swallowed and I waited for the worst to happen to him. I followed his gaze towards the gentle woman and it was then I realized she would do him no harm and was able to relax a bit.

I left the two of them to their own for now and busied myself inspecting what was left of the burned and butchered ham. The bottom of the roasting pan was covered in a sweet and salty smelling black tar. I tried to grab the ham and wiggle it by the bone that ran through the middle of it and it was securely fixed to the bottom. Gabriel had cut pieces of the ham off as it stood, leaving some of the bone exposed and lots of jagged flesh edge exposed. It looked like a hungry coyote had devoured half of the ham, leaving the other side intact. The salty flesh was pink close to the bone but had turned a dull brown everywhere else. It looked disgusting and smelled terrible, still I found my fingers reaching for it and finding a small piece for me to taste. I carefully tore the bluish grey piece of overcooked ham and brought it to my mouth. The moment my teeth met it, they found more resistance that I had expected. I clenched my jaws hard over and over until I finally broke through the piece of jerky ham. There was no moisture as I chewed and it felt as if I were licking a piece of salt. I had an intense urge to spit it out but being that there was a lady present I toughed it out and had to almost swallow the unchewable piece whole.

Gabriel was all patched up as we sat at the table. It wasn't until then that it dawned on Gabriel that all we had to eat were the chunks he had butchered away from the burnt ham. He looked at me as if it had been my fault but I had provided the ham, he could have figured out the sides. I wasn't sure why he was upset at me; it was obviously his lack of proper planning. Monica quickly got us over the tense silence and we indulged on the dried porcine morsels.

The mood lightened as stories of times past brought ever increasing laugher out of all of us. Gabriel kept asking about what must have been old classmates, and Monica would give him a report of where they were in life now. They seemed to rejoice and elaborate on the ones that had found the greatest misfortunes. I smiled and nodded but didn't understand why the misery of others caused them so much joy. A few times they tried to include me more in the conversation, asking question about my youth. I quickly redirected them with my own questions and was able to avoid talking about the subject. I was pretty sure I could trust Gabriel but Monica's maniacal laughter at other's misfortunes made me distrusts her.

The two old lovebirds enjoyed each other's company way more than they enjoyed dinner. It was getting late and like the lady she was, Monica said she needed to get home. She gave me a quick hug and thanked me for the invitation. Gabriel walked her to the door and they hugged each other very tightly and for longer that I was comfortable watching. They eventually said their final good nights and I was left alone with the smiley large man. His eyes beamed with joy and I could see almost all of his teeth from his oversized smile. I wasn't sure why he was so happy, he was injured and the night had been one chaotic mess.

He walked, well more like he glided past me and I felt compelled to burst his imaginary bubble of success. "Smooth Gabriel, that was soooooo smooth." His joyful eyes held strong and his smile turned into a smirk. He kept floating past me as he left me with his parting words.

"Oh fuck you Bracket, I'm going to bed." I didn't expect to be insulted but found it more amusing than anything. Part of me was happy for him and his unwavering bliss. Another was proud that he had actually stood up to me. Maybe Gabriel had more moxie that I had given him credit for. I sat there on the couch, surprised and proud of the happy man as he closed the bedroom door and disappeared for the night.

The kitchen was a mess and something compelled me to try to clean up, I was a guest, an honored guest, but a guest after all. I picked up the table and cleaned the dishes. After much muscling I was finally able to tear away the ham from the roasting pan. I held the big piece of meat in my hands and tried to figure out how to dispose of it. I didn't want the smell to linger in the kitchen so I walked out to the front porch and heaved the bony, dried ham out into the night. I hoped than an offering to the local wilderness would prevent any future attacks by its inhabitants. I went back to the kitchen, finished cleaning and left the destroyed roasting pan soaking, in hopes that it could be cleaned the next day.

I was tired as well, all the moving around was making my wound ache and my stiches to itch. I retired to Gabriel's old bedroom but as I walked in curiosity drove me to his small bookshelf. As I suspected, I was able to find his old yearbook. I started to look up name after name that I had remembered from tonight's conversation. It was nice to put faces to all the gossip I had heard. Then I ran across the cutest and saddest picture in the whole thin book. It was picture of a bunch of the students huddled together. Some stood on chairs making goofy expressions and dying to be seen. In the middle of the mass of bodies stood two very familiar faces. I thought Gabriel was a large man now but young Gabriel had gargantuan proportions. The very large teenager had his arm draped over the shoulder of a young goddess. Her long dark hair had a slight curl to it, framing her delicate face and disappearing down her back. Her innocent smile pulled you into her from the jubilant chaos around her and her hypnotic big green eyes held you there. Monica was still a beautiful woman, but back then she was the inspiration of a teenager's wet dreams. Gabriel held her close in the photograph as his smile showed his joy and his tense posture how nervous he really was.

Even a blind man could have seen how happy he was with his arm around her and how desperately in love he was with the young beauty. I found myself smiling and a tear rolling down my cheek, as I lay in the bed looking back in time at what pure love truly was. I felt lonely and missed my Michelle more than ever. It had been so long since I had seen her, ever since that ugly and treacherous night. Ugly memories started to creep into my consciousness and I quickly bottled them up. I dried my tear covered face, put the old yearbook on the nightstand and gave in to sleep. Tomorrow would be a new day, filled with opportunities and a chance to start my quest to honor and find my Michelle.

I woke up the next morning dreaming of waterfalls and with a ridiculous urge to go urinate. I got out of the small bed and everything hurt. I hobbled my way towards the bathroom as fast as I could when I heard the voices coming from the front door. I recognized Gabriel's instantly but it took a second to realize he was talking to the Golden Paladin. I looked at the bathroom door next to me with great yearning and need but I had to figure out what the conversation was all about. I silently shuffled my way to the edge of the hallway's wall and attentively listened to the words being exchanged between the two brothers.

They were talking in hushed tones purposely and that made me worried and even more suspicious. I peeked around the corner just to catch Gabriel nervously checking behind him for what could only be me. I quickly hid once more and all I could make out was the last of the conversation in where the Golden Paladin ordered Gabriel to take me for a drive "there" and Gabriel reluctantly agreeing. I had a sinking feeling in my chest and worried about what kind of betrayal they had conjured up for me. I heard them exchange goodbyes and I quickly scattered into the bathroom to take care of my screaming bladder.

I finally relieved myself as goose bumps formed down my back and a happy shiver ran through my body. I washed my hands, face and teeth and clung to the sink looking at my reflection. My tired and concerned eyes looked back at me and we tried to figure out "where" Gabriel was going to take me to. Was he going to return me to the super max prison? What had the Golden Paladin told him about me? I didn't know how truly concerned I should be but my senses were and would remain on high alert until I figured out his next move.

I could hear him stirring outside so I decided it was time to try to extract some information out of him. I left the bathroom behind and headed to the kitchen. I found Gabriel hunkered over a plate of French toast, eggs and bacon. How in the world he got that all ready the few minutes I was in the bathroom perplexed me, but it all smelled delicious.

"Morning Bracket, help yourself there is some of everything on the stove, the bacon is in the oven. There is coffee made too if you want some." I greeted him back and headed to collect my delicious bounty. I filled my plate with as much food as it would hold, made myself a glorious cup of coffee and sat with Gabriel at the table. He passed me the warm maple syrup with which I quickly drowned my French toast. Gabriel might not know how to cook a ham but he can damn well cook an amazing breakfast.

I tried to make small talk but my attention was completely focused on what should be the next delicious bite to dance with my tongue. I scarfed down the plate, and leaned back on the chair very full and even more content. I sipped on my warm sweet coffee and refocused my attention on asking Gabriel some questions.

"I need to go visit my sister today; we should go shopping for some more clothes for you while we are out and about." Even before I could ask him a single question he started to volunteer the information. I had seen the family photos around the house and I knew that the sister did exist; but were we really going to see her? Alerts and sirens were ringing in my head but I knew the only way to find out was to play along. I agreed to go shopping and he went off to get ready.

I was on my last change of clean clothes so there wasn't much getting ready to do. I poured myself another cup of coffee, sat and wondered what mischievous game Gabriel was playing. I was in desperate need of more clothes so I felt compelled to go along. He hadn't led me astray either and

I wanted to trust him. Still, the seed the conversation Gabriel had with the Golden Paladin was growing into a vine of mistrust. I decided I would play along but keep my senses sharp.

Gabriel walked out of the room and I asked him where his sister lived. He walked by me, preoccupied and as if he hadn't heard me. I gave him a few moments of silence to allow his brain to catch up to reality but it never did. "Gabriel!" I raised my voice and startled him even though he knew I was in the small kitchen with him. He finally granted me his attention and he looked worried and concerned.

"Where does your sister live?" I asked again and finally he replied that she lived in Santa Fe. His eyes were a little wide as he spoke but they were truthful, unlike the beads of nervous sweat forming on his forehead. He grabbed a couple bottles of water and we headed out to the Jeep.

It was a gorgeous morning so Gabriel decided to put down the top on the Jeep. I tried to help but he seemed to have it mostly under control. We boarded the square carriage and off we went with the wind blowing through our souls. We headed south and were soon out of the small town, the highway ahead of us framed by the gorgeous red mountains. We were almost to the highway when I realized not a single word had been spoken. I looked over at Gabriel and he looked especially nervous. I had been so busy living in the glorious morning; cutting through the air and admiring the gorgeous landscape that I had forgotten to stay alert.

I cursed at myself silently and sharpened my wits for whatever my gut was telling me was soon to happen. We reached the highway's intersection and the signs pointed to either Santa Fe or Las Vegas. An instant chill ran down my spine as the memories of my escape from Las Vegas, New Mexico ran through my mind. Gabriel had brought the Jeep to a stop and after much hesitation and visual agony he turned the Jeep towards Las Vegas. Fear started to flow through my veins and adrenaline took over from then on.

The vehicle was slowly gaining speed as we made our way through the on ramp. The highway loomed ahead, black and menacing. The gentle breeze that had accompanied us until now was becoming a loud and violent torrent of air. With every second of hesitation my options were becoming fewer. I stared at Gabriel and even though he could see me looking at him, he avoided making eye contact at all cost.

"Where are we going?" The words went ignored and I figured out what the Golden Paladin must have told him. Gabriel was trying to take me back to my prison and I just could not allow that to happen. The meters of the on ramp had almost run out so I took the only option I had left. I opened the Jeep's door and jumped out of the moving beast.

For a moment time slowed down. The violent wind that was beating on the vehicle stopped and I floated in an air of serenity. I could see the red Jeep slowly moving away from me, its door being forcefully closed by the atmosphere. The moment of serenity quickly washed away as I vigorously hit the pavement. I had planned to roll but momentum foiled any plans I had of a graceful landing.

I landed on my right side, the initial hit knocked all the air out of my lungs and sent vicious shocks of pain through my ribcage. I rag dolled, spinning and turning on the pavement a few times and soon ran into the piercing rocks of the gravel. I had survived the hard concrete but the dirt filled with rocks didn't provide any comfort. I lost count at eleven spins and my body was still tumbling. With every revolution a new body part ached and hurt while already injured ones started to go numb.

My body finally stopped tumbling as it came to rest on the hard dirt. My mind still expecting me to twirl, kept moving, washing me over with waves of nausea. I was on my back staring at the infinite blueness of the sky which didn't have a single cloud to interrupt its majesty. I blinked and I knew I was still somehow alive. I heard the screeching tires of the Jeep coming to an urgent stop and I felt compelled to flee once more. I appreciated everything Gabriel had done for me but there was no way on this planet he was dragging me back to that hellhole of a prison.

Unfortunately when my brain ordered my body to move it revolted in anarchy and pain. I tried a couple of more times but each time the pain was more and more intense. By my fourth attempt I started to see spots of lights in my vision and the beautiful indigo sky was starting to turn black. I was about to pass out when Gabriel's large and familiar face gave me something to focus on. I could see his lips moving and his eyes tried to bulge out of his head but I could not hear a single word he was saying. His eyes wandered up and down my body and the look of anger gave way to one of concern.

"What the fuck are you thinking?!" Finally his sound accompanied his moving lips. He sounded as if he were inside of a can, his voice distant and somewhat hollow. He kept talking and every word slowly came into tune, until he finally sounded like himself. He kept asking questions and although I could clearly hear each word he said, none of them made sense. It was like listening to someone talk to you and ask questions in a foreign language. I could clearly understand the words but had no idea of their meaning.

It took me a while but I finally realized why I could not understand him, he was talking in Spanish. The absurdity of the situation made me chuckle, which sent shockwaves of pain through my ribs and made me cough up a little blood. The sight of blood spurting out of my mouth froze Gabriel dead in his tracks. I could see the wheels turning in his head and the concern overwhelming his senses. I knew what he wanted to do.

Tasting the familiar metallic fluid in my mouth I swallowed a big gulp of my own blood so I could get the words that I needed to get out. "No hospital." Each letter hurt as they snuck out of my probably broken jaw. Gabriel's shoulders and head dropped, defeated and full of guilt. He kept talking and I just looked deep into his eyes and slowly turned my head from side to side telling him no. The dirt crunched under my head as I moved it, sounding too loud and making my vision swim. I stopped moving and the French toast stopped trying to erupt out of my stomach.

Gabriel disappeared from my vision and I could hear him start up the Jeep. For a second I thought he might drive off and leave me here for the vultures to clean up, but I soon heard the tires moving towards, instead of away from me. He was still ranting and cursing as I heard him open and slam several doors. I focused on his frantic noises as my vision started to fall into a tunnel. My peripheral vision was completely gone and the big blue sky was nothing but one ever shrinking circle of cobalt.

I could feel my consciousness trying to let go but I fought to hang on. Once again his now sweaty and familiar face filled my field of vision. Focusing on his plump cheeks and kind eyes made my sight come back to some normality. He was speaking real slow, enunciating every word but I was still having trouble understanding.

"Can you move?" After many repetitions I was finally able to make out his question. I tried to respond to him verbally but the connection between my brain and my mouth had been lost. Risking another tidal wave of nausea I nodded my head to give him my answer. I didn't truly know whether I could move or not but I was not going to die here and now in this dusty patch of land.

Gabriel grabbed me in his strong meaty hands and started to move me. Every pull, tug, bend and twist made me see flashes of light of different colors depending on how much pain they caused. I tried to help in the moving of my broken body but I don't think a single muscle fiber reacted as I tried to instruct. Gabriel being stronger than he looked manhandled me into the back of the Jeep. He sat me on the back edge and was talking at me again with no audio. "Are you on ten?" I think I made out from reading his lips. The question was as distressing as the situation so I just gave him the best shrug I could muster.

He visually sighed, frowned and looked incredibly concerned. Sweat just ran down his face carving little paths in the dust that clung onto his skin. He quickly jumped into the back of the Jeep agile like a bear. He somehow held me in place with one hand and he performed the acrobatic maneuver. I felt his strong hands grab me under my armpits and gently pulled me into the back of the Jeep. I was surprised how far he pulled me in but figured it out once he gently secured my head on the armrest between the two front seats.

Pain had become so shattering that my brain refused to let me feel it anymore. I felt numb and an inexplicable coldness was overtaking my body. Gabriel finished folding my legs so that he could close the backdoor of the vehicle. The back door slammed shut and almost instantly the driver's door opened. The coldness kept growing making my body tremble. The Jeep started to move as Gabriel kept talking to me. With every word his voice became more distant and muffled. My eyelids became heavier and heavier, making it almost impossible to keep them open. I could feel my hold on reality slowly slipping away and unconsciousness rapidly creeping in. Before it all faded away I musterded enough strength to remind Gabriel of my wishes. "No hospitals." Then it all went black.

Truth and Roll
(Gabriel)

I opened my eyes and the soft glow of the rising sun was peeking through my window. There was no alarm, no obnoxious noise and no music trying to bring me out of my slumber. I had just opened my eyes and now squirmed around in the bed, stretching and feeling very refreshed. I hadn't woken up feeling this good, well, I honestly couldn't remember. There was no headache, no hang over, no nausea, just the most blissful and rejuvenated feeling.

I could feel a smile plastered all over my face as I sat on the edge of the bed. I raised my arms and leaned from one side to another and enjoyed my final stretch. I quietly got ready for the morning and headed into the kitchen. I wanted to thank Bracket for being such a nosy bastard, and even though it hurt a bit, I made him a breakfast fit for a king. I was about to pour the second batch of pancakes on the griddle when I heard a distinct and familiar knock on the door.

The door rattled for a second time as I hurried towards it. I reached it before Jose could pound on it for a third time. I swung the door open and his fist was hovering in the air ready for his presence to be known once more. There was no "good morning" or exchange of pleasantries, he gave me a disapproving look and went on with what he was there for.

"I looked into your little friend as you asked. His name is Barry Racket and he was reported as escaped from the Las Vegas mental institution. There is a BOLO out for his capture and return to the institution. Here."

He handed me a piece of paper and on it was Bracket's unmistakable picture. The rest of the information on the sheet was what Jose just told me, except for the name of the doctor issuing the report, Dr. Jeff Cross. I started to fold the paper to put it in my pants pocket but Jose quickly grabbed it out of my hands.

"That was a courtesy, which is for the authorities' eyes only." I knew he was full of shit but I let him have it back. I wasn't concerned about the cheap piece of paper, I was worried about Bracket and what the hell I was going to do with him now.

"Where is he? I would like to get him back this morning." Jose started to take a step into the house but I cut him off.

"The hell you are! He is my guest; you are not taking him anywhere." Jose looked down at me and if his eyes could shoot lasers he would have incinerated me on the spot. "I will take care of it." His stare intensified as his jaw muscles visibly flexed on his smooth shaved face. He grunted in disapproval but knew I would not relent. He might have size and physical ability on me but I was relentless. He was not going to change my mind and he knew it. So he did what he always did, pretend it was his idea and take one final jab at me before he left.

"Well, I am very busy today anyways, you should take him. Oh and please Gabriel, don't make me look bad." I hadn't heard him say that to me in a long time and it wasn't long enough. All my life, "Gabriel, don't make me look bad", over and over as if I were such a disappointment and embarrassment for him. It was my time to shoot him a dirty look. Just as I remembered, he gave me this sheepish smile and smug eyes. He turned and started to walk toward his squad car when he turned and shot the final irritating bullet.

"And do it today Gabby, I told Dr. Ross he would be taken back today. Thank you." It was the emptiest thank you ever accompanied with a condescending point of the finger. Even after all these years he still knew how to get under my skin like no one else could. I closed the door and went back to breakfast. I could hear Bracket in the shower and I could not help to wonder why he ended up in a mental institution, and more importantly how the hell did he escape?!

My fabulous mood now gone, I tried to concentrate on the task at hand: pancakes and delicious, salty bacon. The smells were starting to flow out of the kitchen and fill the house. I checked the oven and the bacon was almost done to a perfect juicy but crispy consistency. I sipped on my coffee as I continued to pour and flip the fluffiest pancakes any man had ever known. It was Mom's recipe and no matter where in the world I tried some flap jacks, none were ever able to measure up to hers.

I poured the next batch on the griddle and watched for the minefield of tiny craters to appear. As the once silky surface had become permanently interrupted by small holes I turned the delicious doughy pillows. The batter hissed in protest and small plumes of steam escaped from under the pancakes.

The tops were beautifully crisp and golden. When they were done they would have the crispy exterior walls which held inside of them the fluffiest and softest things to ever touch a human tongue.

Following his nose, Bracket finally walked into the kitchen. His face was turned up as he inhaled all the delicious molecules floating in the air. We exchanged pleasantries and I presented him with a plate full of salty heaven and delicious clouds. His eyes lit up as thoughts and memories rushed behind them. He was happy and I didn't want to pry, especially not now, so I took note but left the questions unasked.

I had to figure out how to convince him to come along with me, back to the mental hospital. I knew damn well he would not come along willingly, so I had devised some sort of mischievous plan. He needed more clothes, and I hadn't visited my sister in Santa Fe. I gave him the pitch and he bought everything I had to sell. I was glad he so happily agreed but was worried sick of how he would react once he figured it out. I panicked, so I excused myself and went to get ready, abandoning on my plate many delicious morsels.

I showered, and thankfully this time Bracket was nice enough to leave me some hot water. Bathed and refreshed, I got ready to head out on our day trip. Millions of question rushed through my head as to why Bracket had been committed. Should I be afraid? He had never shown any true aggression or violence towards me. But what had he done? I stopped torturing myself and started to focus on how to keep a straight face the whole way there. We boarded the Jeep and off we went.

It was a glorious day so I decided to put the top down and enjoy the cool morning air. I thought about playing music to distract myself but my fingers seemed to be fixed on the steering wheel. I drove south and soaked in the rejuvenating breeze and the beautiful mountains in front of us. We were approaching the highway and I really had hoped Bracket would have fallen asleep or been distracted by nature. Instead his eyes were intensely fixated on the road and every passing road sign.

The moment of truth quickly approached. I needed to get Bracket to that mental institution or I knew Jose would come back and next time get his way. Probably get his way forcefully and traumatizing Bracket even more, so I needed to make sure I succeeded. I went under the highway bridge and turned on to the on ramp heading east instead of west towards Santa Fe. I kept hopping Bracket hadn't noticed and I squeezed my fingers until they were pale and devoid of blood on the wheel. I was between a rock and a hard place and I really needed my plan to work. It didn't.

I turned the Jeep on the on ramp and pressed down on the accelerator as far as it would allow me. I felt that once we made it to the highway my chances of getting there would greatly increase. Bracket sat immobile next to me and quiet as could be. We were half way up the ramp when I allowed myself to relax as the impending success of my ruse seemed inevitable. That is when the passenger door swung open and before I could say anything Bracket plunged out of it.

I drove for a second or two mouth agape and arm extended to where he once had been seated. As my brain finally processed what had happened, I steered the Jeep onto the shoulder and slammed on the brakes. I looked back through the rear view mirror just in time to see Bracket take his last tumble and end up lying lifelessly on his back on the warm hard dirt.

My hand instantly reached for the door handle but for some reason I didn't pull it. I kept looking back through the small mirror trying to see if Bracket's chest was moving as he inhaled. If he was still breathing I could not tell. Still my hand would not pull on the door handle. I had grown very fond of Bracket, his idiosyncrasies and totally unique wavelength made him quite entertaining to have around. His personality made putting up with his darker moments tolerable. But this, this was off the scale of fucked up things for a person to do. Never had I seen a man jump out of a vehicle, nevertheless while going at 55mph.

I truly wanted to run back to him and help him but I didn't know if he could be helped. Here I was driving him back to a mental institution and for lack of a better way to explain it he had just attempted to kill himself, rather than go back. Even if he was in fact still alive, what was I supposed to do? I had to take him back otherwise Jose would drive him back in cuffs. He had to be a mess and I had never been too fond of blood.

My hand slowly moved away from the door and back on to the steering wheel. I shifted the Jeep back into gear and methodically removed my left foot from the clutch. The truck started to creep forward as my eyes remained fixated on the rear view mirror. I could feel the truck begging for me to press on the gas when I heard in my head that voice that had guided me all my life.

Her gaze weighed heavily in the eyes of my memory and I knew I had to stop. Chills ran down my spine as I slammed on the brakes, remembering her visit to me.

All doubt dissipated and I was left assured that whatever mess I was about to have to clean up, it was what she would want me to do. The clock was ticking and I needed to make sure I made her proud. I took a deep breath and got out of the Jeep and started to run back to where Bracket laid, looking like road kill. Every hurried step I took made the situation look grimmer. He wasn't moving, not even his chest seemed to be expanding and contracting with his breath. His face, arms, and well, any and all skin that was exposed, was either scratched, bloodied or covered with dirt. Finally reaching him, his eyes were open looking into the infinity of the blue sky. If his insides were as beat up as his outside he was in very critical shape.

I leaned over and started to talk to him trying to get a response. I wanted to touch him but worried I would hurt him no matter how gentle I tried to be. I cautiously extended two fingers to his neck and made sure he had a pulse. The comforting rhythmic percussion under my fingers assured me that death wasn't ready for him yet. I kept talking and slowly the dead glassy eyes, like those of a fish on market display, finally started to focus on me. Bracket tried to talk but it was all moans, groans and gibberish. I kept talking to him as I started to reach for my cellphone in my pocket.

Out of nowhere his incoherent rambles coalesced and he kept repeating the same two words; "No hospitals". He said it over and over and his eyes closed overtaken by the pain. I stood on the hot pavement as the sun beat down on me. The cool morning breeze provided less and less comfort as the sun continued his climb up the indigo sky. I held my phone in my hand and watched the man in front me being taken over by pain and agony. He continued saying "No Hospitals", but it was now a begging whimper more than a command. He had jumped out of the Jeep because of my deception and now was bloodied and broken; lying on the side of the road as the dust increasingly attached itself to sticky liquids covering his skin. I felt guilty and responsible for his current state and debated whether I should betray his trust and take him to the hospital or figure it out on our own once more.

I shoved the phone in my pocket and started walking to the Jeep with a terrible sense of urgency. I backed up to Bracket, careful not to run him over, adding insult to injury. I dropped the back seats and opened the tailgate of the Jeep. Probably breaking every first aid and emergency protocol, I somehow managed to get Bracket to his feet and in to the back of the Jeep. I slid him in as far as the space allowed me and then folded his legs so I could close the back. Bracket's whimpers became penetrating cries of pain as I moved him. I kept starting and stopping but after a while I knew I had to ignore them and just get him in the Jeep. I could feel guilty later, now I had to rip the band aid off no matter how much it hurt him.

I had set his head on the armrest between the seats to protect his neck and head. Trying to mitigate any further damage I might have done while moving him. He had road burn marks on his forehead and right cheek. Tears were streaming down his face, keeping the blood on him bright red and fluid. His eyes were open and once again staring out into the nothingness of space. I checked his neck for a pulse and his heart was racing. At least I knew he was alive, at least for now. I finished reversing my way down the ramp, got back on the road and started heading back to the house.

I drove as carefully as I could while continuously checking on him. His eyes closed soon after we started driving and his breathing became heavier. I hurried as fast as I could and made it to the house. I got out of the Jeep and pondered how the hell I was going to get his unconscious body into the house, getting him in had been difficult enough and he had been semi-conscious then. I paced back and forth up between the house and the Jeep on the dusty gravel driveway. I tried waking Bracket a few times but I got no response.

Finally the light bulb went off in my head, mom's wheelchair. I had seen it tucked away and hidden in my sister's old room. I rushed through the house, opened the door and there it sat, gleaming under the rays of the sun in the excessively pink room. Being the only girl in a house with two brothers, she had embraced her girliness to its fullest extent. Pink walls, pink bed, pink pillows, stuffed animals of every possible pastel color and even a pink desk. It had served her well, we never ventured into the pink palace and certainly never wanted to borrow or use anything of hers.

Posters of the New Kids on the Block and Color Me Bad still adorned the walls. As much as I felt as I was inside of a bottle of Pepto-Bismol, it made me miss her. I had been her favorite doll until I became a stinky boy and even then mom would come home to find me wearing a dress and in full makeup. She was not only my big sister, she had been my second mother, not many kids get to have one good mom and I had two. I had a niece and nephew that I only knew through photographs. I did need to go see her before time ran out, I owed her that, and I owed her the truth.

I grabbed the wheelchair and once I figured out how to disengage the breaks, I rolled it out to the Jeep. Bracket was still lying there just how I had left him a couple of minutes ago. I had left the truck running otherwise he might be half poached by now sitting under the hot sun. I opened the back door and his legs ungracefully plopped out. They hung out of the truck and having no other real means, I grabbed a hold of them and started pulling. Bracket was taller than me but he certainly wasn't heavier. He was a slender man and right now it proved very advantageous.

I heard a loud thud and remembered his head had been elevated on the front seat arm rest. If he wasn't concussed from the jump he probably was now. I cringed, but knew I had to keep going. I had to get him in the house and... well, I didn't know what but first things first, I needed to get him inside. His body kept sliding out of the car like a pizza being slid out of a hot oven. I had him out to his waist and his back was bent in a way that a normal back shouldn't. I sat him on the edge of the trunk, threw his right arm over my shoulder, grabbed a hold of him and lifted him into the wheelchair. Even as light as he was trying to move dead weight like that was quite cumbersome and awkward.

I managed to settle him in the chair, folded down the foot rest and placed his feet on them. His head dangled back at a neck breaking angle, I pushed it forward and he looked like a baby asleep on a car seat. There wasn't really any safe and comfortable way to place his head so I moved on and started to roll him towards the house. As I approached the porch, the three small steps loomed like mountains. I had seen in TV how they would pull people upstairs in wheelchairs backwards, so I turned and started to back up to the steps. What TV doesn't tell you is that pulling those wheels up those six inches with a body sitting in it was a monumental feat of strength.

It took a lot of huffing, puffing and pulling but I managed to get Bracket to the front porch on the wheelchair. I had to take a moment to dry the sweat from my brow and try to bring down my heart rate; otherwise the coyotes might find two unconscious bodies on the porch for them to feast on. The swirls of dizziness dissipated and I finished getting Bracket into the house. I debated whether to take him to the bed or the couch. The couch prevailed. I could keep a better eye on him there plus I didn't have the energy to try to throw him up on the bed. The couch was the perfect height to just, well, plop him on it.

I got him settled as he mumbled nothingness still with his eyes closed. I took that as proof of life and finished moving him. I got some rags and started to clean the mean case of road rash he had acquired on his kamikaze stunt. The blood had started to dry and clung to his skin, brown and crusty. The wet warm towels brought the blood back to its crimson life and revealed tissue where skin should have been. The scratches on his face looked painful but paled in comparison with the ones on his arms and knees. His jeans had provided him some protection but not quite enough. His pants had worn away and both knees lay there naked and chewed up by the hard asphalt. The worst of them all was his left forearm. He must have used it to protect himself as he tumbled and rolled, and it had paid the price. The skin was missing from his wrist half way up his bicep and that was the least of the problems.

After several cleanings his left arm was still peppered with dark brown spots. It wasn't until I touched them with my bare fingers that I realized that they were impaled rocks and pebbles in his flesh. I stopped for a minute, closed my eyes and took several deep breaths. I knew the pebbles could not stay in, it would be impossible for me to truly clean the wounds and God knew what kind of animal shit particles he had incrusted on him. I was going to somehow try to dig all those little rocks out of Bracket's arm and the thought nauseated me.

I gathered the now well used first aid kit and swung by the bathroom to get some tweezers. I came back to the living room and Bracket had not moved from where I had left him. I should really take him to the hospital, if he has a concussion he might never wake up. I took a deep breath and pushed aside all the terrible and disturbing thoughts running through my mind. I held the tweezers in my hands but they seemed to be vibrating between my fingers. My hands were shaking and I could not hold the metal tool steady within my hands.

I tried several times and as I approached Bracket's bloodied arm, my hands would start to tremble more violently. I was at a loss. I couldn't take him to the hospital and I had apparently lost my nerve as his personal nurse. I found myself walking away from his unconscious body and dialing my phone almost on reflex. I held the small device to my ear and after three rings a familiar and friendly voice greeted me with a hello.

I didn't know why I was calling Monica but I did, and now we were talking. I felt seventeen again calling her to vent on problems. It is what we did as friends, supported each other, listened to each other and was always there for the other when they needed us. I told her my quandary, all of it. I told her about Bracket, what he did and his current condition. I told her about what Jose found out to which she said. "Well that explains a lot." Her wit and comedic timing never escaped her. I talked, vented, ranted and raved and her comforting and supporting words coming through the phone slowly calmed me down.

"I'll be there in a few Gabriel, just wait for me." We finished the conversation and I felt a great deal of relief not having to deal with this on my own. I wanted to be there for Bracket, I wanted to honor my mother's wishes, but fuck, this was more than I had bargained for.

I had wandered my way into the kitchen while I talked on the phone and was now standing in front of the fridge digging through it for a cold beer. I cracked the cold bottle open, sat at the table and almost chugged it in one gulp. My hands where still shaky and I kept worrying I was going to have to call my brother to report a dead body later today.

By the time Monica arrived there were six empty beer bottles on the table and I wasn't feeling as stressed anymore. I had run out of beer so had fetched the vodka bottle from the freezer and was now toasting in Russian with myself. She had walked right in through the open front door, briefly stopped to check on Bracket and was now standing at the kitchen entrance with concerned eyes.

"Vashe zrodovye" She didn't seem impressed by my toast and gave me sad concerned eyes. Monica sat across from me at the table, grabbed the vodka bottle out of my hands and took a swig out of it. Her face scrunched into itself, her eyes closing and her mouth making a small snarl. She shivered as the cold but burning liquid made its way down her throat finding its way to her stomach. She let out a "wooooo!" and had never been more adorable to me ever. She handed me the bottle back and all I could do was hold it and smile at her like some deranged lunatic.

"What are you going to do Gabriel?" Her voice was a little horse at first, the liquor still burning in her throat. My smile faded and I seriously thought about the standing question.

I sat at the kitchen table with my phone in my hands as Monica waited for my response. I found myself browsing through my contacts and lingering on Jose's number. I had him listed as "Asshole Big Brother" but I knew if I called him all of this would go away. He would take Bracket, take him back to whatever hellhole he escaped from and I would not have to deal with any of this bullshit anymore. I found my thumb hovering over the smart phone ready to press call. I mean, I had tried; I really tried to help Bracket. I knew there was something off about the guy but I felt that I was in way over my head right now. He could die on my couch for all I knew, I wasn't equipped to deal with all of this. I had enough to worry about myself right now as it was. My finger started to move towards the bright screen, I had to call, for his livelihood and my peace of mind.

On the other hand, I had promised him. My thumb froze once more so close to the screen I could feel the static calling out to me. I had promised Bracket I would not take him to the hospital or doctors. What atrocities make a man jump out of a moving car instead of going back to his captor? Even for a crazy guy that was a very desperate and extreme measure. I couldn't take him back. I couldn't hand him to Jose; he would treat him like a common criminal when what he really needed was help. And as stressful and mind bending as it might be sometimes, I was the only one who could help him now. I could not kick a man in his face while he was down. I thought of my mom and I knew I couldn't turn Bracket over.

"Fuck!" Monica jumped as I broke my silence with the scream of frustration of knowing what I had to do. She stood very stiff, eyes at the ready awaiting what I had to say next. We both pretended she hadn't jumped a good six inches in the air and yelped like a little girl as I began to address her.

"Can you watch him for a while?" Her already wide eyes tried to jump out of her head with surprise and panic.

"What do you mean watch him for a while Gabriel? Where are you going to go?" She asked as sweetly as her concern would allow her. I could see her making a forcible and conscious effort to remain calm instead of telling me to fuck off and leaving me to deal with Bracket on my own. I knew how big of a favor I was truly asking and even for lifelong friends I was pretty sure I was pushing the limits of what was consider an acceptable favor.

"I need to go talk to his doctor. Jose told Dr. Ross, Bracket would be there today. If I don't show up and explain to him what happened, Jose is going to show up SWAT squad style and take Bracket. I know I am asking for a lot and I swear I will hurry as much as I can. You are the only person who can help me, you know I wouldn't ask you otherwise."

She turned and walked away from me. Her head tilted back, hand on her forehead as she disappeared into the living room. I felt the urge to chase after her but years of training came flooding back and I knew I had to give her a few moments to herself to process. I couldn't push her, it never worked, especially the dozens of times I asked her to be more than a friend. I sat and waited as I stared into the black nothingness of the blank phone screen.

"Gabriel." Her tender and measured voiced danced tenderly into my ears. I gently snapped out of the hypnotic trance the phone screen had put me under and stood ready to follow her melodic voice. I found myself standing in the living room as she stood across from me with her arms crossed. She stood looking down at Bracket, her eyes filled with doubt and concern. I knew I was asking a lot and it didn't look like she was going to be willing to meet my request.

I sighed and decided it was time to take her off the hook. "I under...."

"I don't know why you are doing this, what issues you are trying to work through Gabriel. This is crazy." She interrupted me and I felt as if an elephant had been lifted off my back. I rushed to her and hugged her. There weren't any words to show my gratitude and as they say, "actions speak louder than words." I hugged her and I thanked her over and over. Eventually she shooed me away, I left the house and got back on the road that so recently had battered and beaten Bracket.

I had called her twice to check on her before I had even left town. Her sweet tone soured with every call. By the 6th call she threatened to stop answering her phone. By the 7th call, she held steadfast to her promise and after five rings I went to voicemail. I threw down the phone on the empty passenger seat; the damn thing bounced and found its way to the floorboards of the car. I tried to reach it but it was impossible without totally letting go of the wheel. I huffed and puffed as the seatbelt dug into my stomach, leaving me without breath.

I needed the darn thing since it was my navigation system to get to the Mental Health Institute in Las Vegas. Defeated and being mocked by the just out of reach phone, I decided to leave it. I knew Interstate 25 would get me to Las Vegas, it was a short forty minute drive so I just focused on the road and allowed my mind to wander.

Why had Bracket been in the Mental Institution? How did he escape? Question after question ran through my mind as the road flew under the wheels of the Jeep. I kept inching along the highway, closer to finding the answer to some of these questions as I became ever more impatient. I started to fidget, I turned the air conditioning on, then off. I adjusted my rearview mirror at least a hundred times. I rolled the windows down then back up. I played with the radio, changing stations without really listening to any of the songs. If it moved, could be pressed or adjusted inside the Jeep I played with it. I knew my behavior was irrational, and worried that I might get admitted into the mental institution so I stopped messing around and just drove.

As Las Vegas started to show itself in the horizon my stomach started to rumble. I was stressed and nervous, my brain was in overload so my stomach decided to take over as it always did. I pulled out the last piece of gum I had tucked away in the Jeep but it only awakened the hunger even more. My questions and worries disappeared as my mind wondered what delicious treat I would get to savor from the gas station. Thoughts of refreshing sweet sodas, salty, crispy chips and decadent candy bars flooded my mind. So many horrible, unhealthy but delicious choices awaited me.

I spotted a gas station close ahead and without hesitation I exited. I pulled the Jeep up as close to the door and I darted into the store as if I hadn't eaten for days. I stalked the short aisles looking for the perfect combination of heart clogging treats. As I riffled through the candy bars, picking one up just to put it down and grab a different one, I remembered Bracket running naked through my yard with his cash of candy bars. Sadness overwhelmed my heart and I put the candy bars down. I walked out of the gas station with a heavy heart and a bottle of 7Up. The events of the past few days replayed themselves in my head and it reminded me how truly lonely and desperate Bracket was. In that moment I was more scared having to bring him back than anything they might tell me about him.

I moved with a purpose and drove as fast as I could to the institute. I was expecting some scary mansion on the hill but was met with a very standard and boring hospital looking kind of place. I parked in one of the visitor's parking spots and started to make my way towards the entrance. The double glass doors slid open as I approached them and the cold air of the hospital welcomed me inside. There were no guards holding nightsticks as I had envisioned, instead I was welcome by a nice old lady sitting behind the lobby desk.

"How may I help you Sir?" She smiled, her white cotton head bobbing as she spoke. She wore glasses and behind them lived two amazingly beautiful blue eyes. Her smile was welcoming and filled with teeth that were too perfect to be real. She wasn't scary, imposing or any kind of gate keeper. Not at all what I was expecting.

"I am here to see Dr. Ross, my name is Gabriel Moreno." She nodded in acknowledgement, pressed some keys on the keyboard in front of her and read what was displayed on the monitor.

"You are alone?" She looked around me and asked me disapprovingly. Her friendly tone had changed to a chastising one and her lovely blue eyes pierced through mine as she questioned me. Maybe the nice little old lady had a lot more spunk and fight than I had thought.

"Yes Ma'am." I answered her, feeling guilty and not knowing why. She frowned and my discomfort grew. I felt like a little kid being reprimanded by the school's principal.

"Please take a seat, Dr. Ross will be right with you." She motioned me to the comfortable looking couch in what must have been the waiting area.

There were single seat couches and double ones. Already feeling a little awkward, and with nerves quickly rising, I decided not to try to squeeze into the single seaters. I walked past a couple of them, heading straight for the bigger and more comfortable couch. They were red and completely enveloped in the upholstery. They didn't have any sharp edges and had a modern, but comfortable, look. I looked back at the lady behind the desk as she quietly whispered into her phone while keeping a disapproving eye on me.

I could feel the anxiety climbing up my throat, my heart was racing, and my stomach churned. I didn't know why I was so worked up, it wasn't like I was going to get committed. I sat down and my heart dropped. There was a loud snapping sound and the seat bellow me gave. I felt my body wanting to keep going and crash into the ground but mercifully my legs responded in time and I stood up as quickly as I had sat down. I looked back at the damage and could see that the screws holding the piece of furniture together had snapped. They were metal and my ass was lard, and in this case the softness of my butt won.

The little old lady was standing beside me even before I had fully processed what happened. She inspected the seat and her disapproving looks worsened.

"Do not worry about it Sir, please take another seat, Dr. Ross is on his way down." Her words were but empty comforts as she forced herself to remain civil. Her eyes on the other hand told me she was furious and angry over the silly couch. I stepped away from her angry vibration and found a good wall to lean against. I wasn't going to risk sitting again with this obviously flimsy office furniture.

The lady was still fidgeting with the couch when a deep voice greeted me from afar. "Hello Mister Moreno." I thought Darth Vader was summoning me to the dark side for a moment but was relieved; it was a tall, black slender man in a white coat. He approached me serious, formal, yet still friendly. I started to walk to meet him and our hands embraced in a formal greeting.

"Where is Mr. Racket?" Pleasantries completed he got right down to business.

"He is not here, is there anywhere we can talk in private?" I was proud of myself for remaining calm as I answered him. He nodded and led me down the hallway from which he had appeared. We found the elevators and got in for a very quiet and awkward ride. He pressed the button for the top floor and off we went. After wandering through a couple more empty and plain hallways I found myself in a warm and cozy office. There was bookshelf after bookshelf filled with books and trinkets. There were copies of famous paintings decorating the walls. Behind the dark mahogany desk hung various diplomas and certificates all made out to Preston Ross. The big office leather chair rested proudly behind the very well organized desk. Across from his desk there were two matching leather chairs for visitors to sit in. It was all very scholastic, proper and refined. The Doctor apparently liked to flaunt his airs.

"Please take a seat." His voice echoed and resonated inside the small office. His penetrating stare was starting to bore a hole in my soul. I felt uncomfortable in the pretentious little room. I didn't know if I was in for a conversation or an interrogation. I worried that any moment a secret door would open and the torture devices would be rolled into the room to extract information out of me. I wanted to talk but was too busy looking around waiting for some henchmen to come out of the walls.

"Ok Mr. Moreno; where is Mr. Racket?" I could see the frustration and lack of patience ooze out of the doctor. I was trying to help Bracket, it was prudent to use the truth and hoped that help me somehow. I told the impatient doctor the story from the beginning, until the events of this morning. He listened attentively with a very serious and concerned look permanently plastered on his smug face. He kept nodding in acknowledgement and at one point I had to hold back laughter since he looked like a bobble head doll on the dash of a car.

Once I was done he just sat there. He leaned back in his leather chair, crossed his fingers over his stomach, pursed his lips and just stared off into the wall. We sat there in silence, for what seemed like an eternity, while he visually and painfully processed what I just told him. It was now my turn to be impatient, so I cleared my throat, bringing him back to reality and shot at him the first of the many questions I had.

"Why was Bracket committed to this institution?" He snapped out of his trance and he turned to face me. The fingers in his hands remained crossed but were now supported by the wood of the desk, as he had turned to face me once more.

"I see that he got you calling him that. Mr. Racket, was committed to our institution under the orders of the court." That caught my attention and triggered a million new questions. Noticing my inquiring mind Dr. Ross continued after opening the file in front of him and checking the details. "Mr. Racket has been here for now the better part of six years. He was sentenced to spend five years in our mental institution but since he hasn't progressed enough to live on his own and no family member has claimed him he has remained one of our patients."

"What do you mean by sentenced? What did he do?" Witnessing what Bracket had done to himself in the past couple of days I was a little bit horrified to find out what he had done to end up in the loony bin for five years.

The doctor looked at me curiously but proceeded. "Sir, you must have been living in a cave somewhere not to have recognized him by now. Mr. Racket was a very brilliant man and an engineer by trade, working for the defense department. He nearly beat his wife's lover to death seven years ago." He looked at me waiting for something to click or a light bulb to go off, but I just kept giving him the same blank stare so he continued.

"Apparently you have been living under a rock. It was all over the local and national news. He was working on some very sensitive programs so the government tried to sweep the whole incident under the rug but local reporters and his wife's family would not allow the issue to go away." Again he paused, waiting for some sort of response from me but I just eagerly looked at him hoping he would continue. He exasperatedly exhaled while he rolled his eyes and continued.

"As I said Mr. Racket was, well is, a brilliant man. What programs he was working for the government no one really knows, but it is safe to say they were extremely sensitive and highly classified. Along with his great list of achievements, Mr. Racket also had a very personal and in the government's eyes, dangerous secret. He had battled with bi-polar disorder all of his life. He had been able to keep it hidden for many years but during a random background check his secret was discovered. Mr. Racket had been very good at hiding the negative signs of the disease while channeling his manic stages to make great breakthroughs in his research and weapons design. Unfortunately, whichever government branch that he had been working for deemed his disease to be too much of a liability. On June 11th, 2007 he was dismissed from his position and forcefully escorted out of the facility. The government denies that his illness was the cause of his dismissal; instead they claim it was his erratic and unproductive behavior. They might have been able to fool the general public but I could see right through their ruse. It was a clear violation of the law and Mr. Racket's rights but unfortunately what happened next overshadowed all of the government's wrong doing."

Dr. Ross paused for a moment and took a sip out of his silver coffee mug. He was clearly relishing telling the story and making my curiosity wait. "After Mr. Racket was humiliated and thrown out of the facility like some petty criminal he did the only thing he could and went home. When he arrived and entered his home he heard screams coming from his bedroom. Thinking his wife was being attacked and in peril he rushed up the stairs and headed for the bedroom. What he saw happening in that bedroom on top of his dishonorable dismissal from his life long career, caused what is called a psychotic break in Mr. Racket's mind. Mr. Moreno, the mind and the brain still remain a great mystery to both the neurological and psychology world." I didn't know where he was going with this but I felt like a student back in college ready to be lectured to, by some over pretentious professor.

"Whether Mr. Racket was leveled, depressed or manic, I don't think we will ever know. But the combination of his mental state at that time, with his firing and the events with his wife caused his mind to dissociate from reality. We suspect the stress and emotional pain he was suffering caused this "Bracket" persona to surface and in essence take over. I spent many years studying and treating Mr. Racket and I feel I just scratched the surface of what happened in his mind."

"Mr. Racket didn't develop multiple personalities it was more as if this new person took over the controls of his body. Many studies have been done in these subjects but every patient is different, which makes it hard to understand or attempt to cure. I published a study..." For someone who listened for a living Dr. Ross sure liked to talk. I had to interrupt him and get him back of track.

"I am sorry Doctor but you never told me what happened at his house."

"I apologize, I digressed. Yes, yes, Mr. Racket's wife was not expecting him to be home at that time. He was a workaholic after all. She wasn't being attacked or hurt, she was having vigorous and passionate sex with her lover. Mr. Racket was not only fired that day from his job, he also got home to find that his wife was having an affair. What happened next was debated and argued in court to exhaustion. Honestly, I am not sure if any of the three people in that room truly know what happened. What is certain is that the lover was beaten to within an inch of his life and the marriage ended. Mrs. Racket filed for divorce during the trial and had obviously been done with the relationship for many years already. People do grow accustomed to certain standards of living which they are very often reluctant to lose."

"Out of the whole mess and once the very public trial was over, Mr. Racket was found not guilty for reason of insanity. It was a very controversial decision and to this day there are people who argue he just faked the psychotic break to get out of what could have been a 20 year sentence. Instead the judge ordered him to a five year sentence in this mental health institution."

"You said he was here for six years?"

The Doctor continues; "This is all public record Mr. Moreno, you could very well look it up in the periodicals. But yes, after his five year sentence ended there was no one to claim Mr. Racket or to care for him. I find his specific mental state incredibly fascinating and I was saying earlier I have written many well publicized scientific papers on the subject and his specific case. Being that no one else seemed to want to take Mr. Racket off our hands, and the fact that he still needed help with his illness, I decided to keep him housed here for treatment and observation. I have made great progress with him but to be totally honest with you, it might take a few lifetimes to unravel the knot that has become of Mr. Racket's mind."

I didn't know whether to feel sad, scared, worried, relieved or what at that moment, so I pressed on with my questions. "Is he dangerous?" The doctor swung his chair sideways and stared into the wall as he pondered my simple but complex questions. He didn't disappoint and held his chin with his right hand, while he supported his right elbow with his left hand. The only thing he was missing was the pipe and the monocle. Once he was done with his dramatic thinking he turned to me and I was disappointed when he didn't talk with an old English tongue and accent.

"If pushed and stressed Mr. Racket might be capable of some sort of aggressiveness or dangerous behavior...But no, no he is not dangerous. The only person he might constitute a real danger is to himself." I felt an instant relief once the doctor was done with his assertions. With every word of our conversation my concern for Monica had exponentially grown. In my panic of getting this issue straightened out, I might have left her with a dangerous, crazy man. At least now I knew for certain, as certain as you can be with these things that I hadn't left her in imminent peril.

"Why hasn't anyone come to get him? I mean he must have family besides his wife." I can't believe this man had been left here, like an unwanted dog in a pound. It wasn't only sad, it honestly was making me angry to think a family would do that to a person.

"Ex-wife Mr. Moreno. It is reasonable to understand why she never came for him. His family, well his family like many families are just not equipped to deal with a person with this degree of mental illness. They do not know how to cope with, or how to manage him. The sad reality of my profession is that you see this more than you would imagine. Families see the patient as a burden and a wild card in their lives. So they leave them in institutions like this, some visit and stay in contact, in the case of Mr. Racket they never have."

Hearing him say it so matter of fact, like it was such a common thing to happen with people like Bracket broke my heart. Thrown away like garbage and forgotten because they'd be too much work to deal with. "So if someone claimed Bracket he would be free to go?"

"Well yes and no." I could see the hesitation and concern in his face as he was figuring out where I was going with this. "Mr. Racket would be discharged to a family member or to someone capable to properly care for him. The last thing the state wants is for mental patients ending up on the street and becoming a burden to communities or getting in trouble once more. Most people are not equipped to properly care for mental patients so it is in the best interest of the patient and the community for them to remain in institutions like this one." He really liked to hear himself talk. By the time he was done, he was once more confident that his rhetoric would return to him his precious case study. I had other ideas.

"So you are saying that if I were willing and "capable" I could adopt Bracket?" The doctor chuckled at my question and it was so condescending I had to resist the urge to jump over his fancy desk and punch him in the face.

"I am sorry Mr. Moreno but I don't believe you are qualified to care for Mr. Racket or have the capability to do so. You have come here this morning and from what you have told me, it is a miracle he has remained alive under your care." The doctor went from my unlike list to my shit list with his sanctimonious verbiage. I kept my cool as he continued to belittle me. "And no one would be adopting Mr. Racket, he is an adult after all. It just has to be someone capable of caring for him, preferably family." He enunciated "capable" with a mockery and condescension fit for a king. But as he continued to talk, he never said no. He was trying to confuse me with his fancy words and degrees, but I wasn't falling for it.

"So you are saying that if I wanted to I could. I might not be family, and I might have not received years of training to deal with mentally ill people, but if Bracket wanted to come with me, he could. After all he is not a child and is a free man." I used his own words and they stung him. He shifted in his chair as he worried of losing his prized patient.

After a couple of silent moments, a few frowns and one very painfully disgusted look he finally replied. "Yes Mr. Moreno, technically if Mr. Racket wished to go with you, we could fill out all required paperwork and release him into your care. But as I already explained Mr. Racket needs specialized care and constant medication..."

"Thank you Dr. Ross. I would like the necessary forms." I interrupted as he was about to go on once more about the magnificence of the facility and the expertise only he could possibly possess. I had enough of his lecturing, I would be dammed if I was going to bring Bracket back here to be poked, prodded and studied like some sort of weird creature. He was a free man; he was bat shit crazy but free, and deserved to live as such.

"I will get those for you Mr. Moreno." I stood up and the doctor knew our conversation had ended. He left his plush leather chair and went to the metal filing cabinet behind it. He rifled through some of the files and eventually three pieces of paper appeared in his hand. Every step he took to me was slow and methodical, hoping I would run away or change my mind.

"Are you sure you want to do this?" He tried to hand me the papers but held them in his hand tightly, preventing me from taking them away. He looked into my eyes, giving me one last look of defiance which hid his fear of losing his golden goose. I gave the papers one last firm tug and they came free into my hands.

"Yes, I am sure; no one should live their life as some freakish curiosity to be studied in a laboratory. No matter how crazy, broken, disturbed or rare their case might be. This is not healing the sick, this is profiting from their illness." His eyes filled with shame, the doctor could no longer hold my gaze.

I took the papers and walked out of his office promising myself that Bracket would not spend another night here nor be studied by the doctor ever again. I wasn't even half way home when Jose's familiar number displayed on my phone as the thing rang and vibrated.

Promises Kept
(Gabriel)

"What the fuck did you do?!" Oh how many times had I heard him utter that same expression!

"What do you mean?" I talked into the phone while driving and egged him on. I could not see him but I knew the vein on the side of his forehead had to be throbbing by now.

"What do you mean, what do I mean? Have you lost your mind as well? Why am I getting a call from Dr. Ross to tell me, that not only did you not produce your buddy but that you are talking about checking him out of the nuthouse? What in the world are you doing Gabriel?" It had been a long time since I heard Jose so pissed at me and I was trying so hard to keep my chuckles quiet but apparently failed. "Are you fucking laughing?! I ought to arrest your friend and take him back to the nuthouse where he belongs and arrest you for being a dumbass."

My amusement having been discovered, I decided to let out. I started to laugh and giggle as the profanities and shouts continued to come from the other end of the phone. Eventually Jose's verbal attack subsided and I took my opportunity to finally answer him.

"Jose, he is a free man, he served his time and is only there for the amusement and monetary gain of Dr. Ross. I am sorry but I cannot take him back there. It's inhumane. He is a hostage of circumstances and to take him back would be torture. For fucks sake, the man jumped out of a moving vehicle, and almost killed himself in the process, rather than going back there." I could hear him breathing angrily and deep, like a bull ready to charge through the phone.

"Why are you doing this? Are you having some midlife crisis? Is this because of mom?" He had stopped being the disappointed, angry and perfect superhero sheriff and was finally talking to me as a brother. Jose had never been one to share feelings or get up on the sentimentalities of life. So I knew just asking me those questions was a lot for him and it meant even more to me.

"I am not having any sort of crisis Jose. This is about doing the right thing for someone in need; it is what Mom would have done." I heard one last long breath through the phone as I approached the first signs for the Pecos exit.

"OK." Simple, short to the point and the last thing Jose said before he hung up his phone. I looked at the phone to make sure he had hung up and the phone corroborated it with "call ended" flashing on its screen. We should have had a deep conversation about our Mom then instead a simple uttering of agreement and he moved on. I was happy with his consensus but sad about the state of our relationship. He had never been the lovey dovey type but I know I had my fair share of guilt in our estranged relationship. When I left I almost burned down bridges I never had intended to even harm. His was holding on for dear life and almost just a pile of ashes. I feared I had lost my brother and it hurt. He had my back on this decision so at least I had that, for whatever it was worth.

I parked the Jeep and walked up the steps. The smell that hit me as I opened the door was one I hadn't smelled in that house for a long time. It was intoxicating, velvety and made my stomach growl in anticipation. I could see Bracket on the couch, just as I had left him. His arms were covered in bandages as apparently Monica had fixed him up. Not seeing her, I followed my nose into the kitchen to see what the rich delicious smell floating in the air was all about.

I found her stirring a pot with a wooden spoon and the thick and deep smell of chilies dancing around me. It wasn't until then I realized that I hadn't eaten all day. As my mind calmed, realizing everything was as well as it could be at home, my stomach awakened with violent vengeance. I felt nauseous and ill but it was just the overwhelming hunger attacking me.

"What are you making?" I salivated, almost drooling as I asked Monica.

She smiled at me very proud of herself "Chicken Mole, I found your mom's recipe book and could not help myself. I hope you don't mind." Her proud smile was quickly replaced by a look of concern. I knew she was worried it would upset me or make me miss her even more. She was right in part of it and in the other wrong. It did make me miss my mom more but it also made me feel closer to her. I remembered innumerable days of me getting home from school as a kid just to be welcome by the rich and intoxicating smell of my mom's mole. It had been so long and a string of delicious memories flooded my mind. I should have been sad but I felt happy. For the first time since I returned, the house smelled like a home, they way my mom always intended.

"No, no, I don't mind at all, it smells delicious. Can we eat?" The adrenaline that had been carrying me all day long was starting to dissipate. It was almost 7:00PM and I was starting to crash because of hunger.

"So did you meet with the doctor? What happened?" Monica asked me as she started to dish up all of the fantastic food she had prepared for us. We sat at the table and ate and caught up each other with what happened. I told her all about the doctor and Bracket's story. She ate and listened as I tried to talk and eat at the same time. She was patient and listened to every word I said. Once I was done, we both sat there quietly and finished our delicious food. As always, I allowed my tongue to dictate how much I should eat and my stomach was already paying for it. I had gone from empty and hungry to over filled and uncomfortable.

I was expecting her to grill me with questions. Challenge my decision, and tell me I was as crazy as poor Bracket. Instead she just said, "Ok; so how do I help?" That was it, nothing more. I kept waiting for the hammer to drop but it never did. She started filling me in on what she had done while I was gone, besides cook the delicious mole that I still tasted as heartburn was in full effect.

She cleaned up Bracket's wounds, which I had been too squeamish to deal with. I was very grateful for what she did, especially after she elaborated in how many rocks and foreign material she ended up having to dig out of his arms.

All caught up, and Bracket wandering in the world of dreams, Monica decided to head home. I thanked her for everything and right before she walked out the door she gave me a strong, embracing and lingering hug. I melted into her. I was tired, wore out and being in her arms was just pure heaven. Over the next weeks, I would get several more of them.

Every day after her shift was done at the store Monica would show up, bringing me food, and anything she spotted that I needed. I welcomed her face every time as guilt grew. My days were pretty monotonous. I would check on Bracket, help him when he had to go to the bathroom and bring him food the short periods he was awake. He had taken residence on the couch and as he explained it he felt too disconnected hiding in the bedroom. I worried that he was not getting good rest but he insisted. He wasn't conscious for very long, he labored when he walked and had a hard time breathing, probably had bruised if not fractured ribs.

The poor guy was a total mess, but I had to give him credit for toughness and stubbornness. I kept my promise to him and never took him to the hospital as he healed. Monica visiting every night eased the worries of my promise. I don't know if she took more care of me or Bracket during her visits. She would change his dressing and make sure he wasn't getting any infection, but really most of her time and attention was directed towards me. I soaked it up and enjoyed every last drop of it, but a question kept growing in my mind because of it; Why?

After the fourth straight night's visit I insisted she stay home the next day. She surely had things to do at home and all she probably had time for right now was sleeping and bathing. She defied my request and showed up again on the fifth day. The dance continued for the next few days and every time she would show up the next day. Her continuous defiance only made the question grow bigger, big to the point where I finally had to ask her.

"Why do you keep coming back every day? I appreciate it Monica but I don't need it. Why do you keep coming back?" We were standing by the door once more, her ready to leave and having just broken the engage of her heavenly hug. I looked deep into her eyes and I saw a sadness in them which I didn't comprehend.

"Gabriel, you are doing an amazing and wonderful thing for Bracket. It is only just fair that someone at least helps you." I almost bought her answer but I knew it was just a smoke screen. Her smile told me that was all I was going to get out of her so I let her go. She walked past the porch, down the steps and got into her car. The swaying of her hips was intoxicating and every step she took made things deep within inside of me grumble with need. I waved goodbye, closed the door and leaned against it as I composed myself. It had been too long.

I decided to go check on Bracket to help shake away all the dirty thoughts that were running through my mind. Instead of the usual lump of skin and bones sleeping on the couch I was welcomed by a pair of big, blue eyes inquisitively looking at me. He had been up plenty of times over the last week but this was the first time I saw the light on behind the eyes.

"How long have I been out?" He asked.

"Today is night eight buddy. You got banged up pretty good." I didn't know if he remembered what he had done and I didn't know how else to try to explain it to him. He acknowledged my answers and I could see the wheels turning inside of his head as he processed my vague but telling response.

"How come I am not back at the Super Max?" The anger and fear oozed out of his eyes and danced all over his words. I could only assume he meant the mental facility which was as far away from a maximum security facility as you could get. I told him about my conversation with the doctor, being careful to leave out all the details about how he ended up there. I didn't know if it would help him or make him freak out and I didn't want to have to find out right then and there. I told him how all the paperwork had been filed so he could be released to me.

He couldn't understand how I had so much influence on getting him out of such a secure location but he was ecstatic about the news. "You are a devoted and honorable servant; you will not regret pledging you allegiance to me Gabriel." I wanted to be insulted but the joy and gratefulness in his words reassured me. I was pretty certain that was as close to a thank you as I was going to get out of him so I took it.

He asked for some food and after a few more poignant questions about my meeting he was once more tired. I left him with a water bottle and went off to my mom's old bedroom to get some rest myself. I settled in the bed and I realized that I was neither drunk nor tired. It finally dawned on me that I hadn't had a drink for the past eight days. I could not remember the last time I was sober for eight days straight, hell I couldn't remember the last time I was sober for two days straight. Unable to sleep and actually not feeling like total shit, I got down on the floor and started to do push up and sit ups. I didn't get far but after 40 of each I was winded, a little sweaty and starting to feel tired.

I got back on the bed and listened to my racing heart. It was quite sad that I was that physically worked up over 40 push up and sit ups. I had fallen past out of shape and for the first time in a long time I felt like I wanted to do something about it. I remembered Monica's voluptuous hips dancing in the night as she made her way to her car, and I knew I had to do something to look better for myself and for her. My racing heart slowed down as I lay in bed, making plans of the next few days' workouts. My eyes grew heavier with every breath, my heart slowed down and determination gave way to sleep.

Gravel and Sweat
(Bracket)

I woke up in panic, expecting once more to be tied down to a bed. Instead I awoke on Gabriel's now familiar couch. I tried to move and get up but my body protested with great prejudice. Things, body parts burned, hurt or I could not feel them. I settled myself and tried once more to move but the overwhelming pain made the room swim around me. The desperate need to vomit started to press on the back of my throat and I did all I could to hold it back. I wasn't going anywhere so I closed my eyes and focused on my breathing and allowed the numbness to take me.

A stinging sensation woke me up next. I didn't know how long I had been asleep for but I was still immobile on the couch. This time, instead of the room swimming I was greeted by the face of an angel. For a second I thought I might have died, but quickly recognized Monica's beautiful blue eyes fixated on my arm as she poked and prodded it with tweezers. I could barely feel as she dug into my flesh. I could feel the pressure of the movements but the arm felt completely numb. My nerve endings felt destroyed and what should have been excruciating pain was but a distant echo of a feeling. It wasn't until she liberally applied some sort of antiseptic on the raw skin that my arm awoke with an incredible burning sensation. My vision started narrow until I felt as I was looking through a narrow tube. I could hear my lungs struggling for air as my ribs protested with each breath and once more the darkness took me.

I don't know how many days, hours or even weeks for that matter passed. I kept waking up and every time the pain became so overwhelming my body would shut down and I would pass out again. Eventually my bladder beat out unconsciousness and I felt the dire necessity of getting up and going to the bathroom. I tried to yell out for help but my lips were glued shut by saliva. Before I could pry them apart Gabriel was already helping me to stand. I didn't know if I could trust him anymore, but considering he was helping me to the bathroom and not back to slaughter I decided to give him a chance.

With every step something new started to hurt, making the trip to the bathroom for such a simple and natural thing, extremely excruciating. By the time Gabriel had helped me back to the couch I was starting to see spots of lights in my vision because of the pain. I wanted to hold on to consciousness; I had so many questions to ask Gabriel. First and foremost why I was still at his home and I hadn't been turned in. I tried to speak by my mouth still didn't seem to be able to work. Once he laid me back down on the couch exhaustion took over and once more I went back into the land of dreams.

I hadn't remembered any of my dreams until then and how I wish I hadn't. I was walking up a set of stairs. The dark wooden steps felt so familiar under my feet. The only thing preventing the steps from kissing my feet was the thin pair of dress socks that I wore. I had taken my shoes off downstairs as soon as I had entered the large house. I was following my ears as I could hear screams, grunts and moans coming from somewhere upstairs. I had a sickening feeling deep down in my stomach and I could feel my heart wanting to beat out of my chest. I felt a million different things but dread screamed louder than any other of the emotions.

Each step felt as if I were approaching my own execution, I should have been running towards the noises but instead I took one methodical step after another. My trembling hand reached and gripped the cold metal doorknob and the screams and moans only intensified behind the solid wooden door. I remembered and felt the hesitation of wanting to open the door but not really wanting to see what was going on behind it. I turned the knob and slowly began to open the door as the room came into view.

I woke up panting as my heart tried to explode out of my chest. Every detail of the dream was painfully vivid to me still as I sat on the couch covered in sweat. It felt so real even though it was some distant world and life. I forced myself to try to forget the dream but miserably failed. The pain began to help my efforts to erase what I had just dreamed. The adrenaline subsided and I was just left with a beaten and battered body.

Apparently my rude awakening hadn't caught the attention of Gabriel and Monica, who I could hear talking in the kitchen. They spoke in hushed voices but even in their secrecy I could pick up the hints of flirtation between them. Footsteps signaled the end of their verbal dance and Gabriel escorted Monica to the door. It was all awkward and sweet as they couldn't figure out what to do with each other. Gabriel closed the door and just leaned against it as if he could not hold himself up. Once he gathered himself he started to walk in my direction. His eyes looked at me but I could tell his mind was wandering elsewhere. As soon as his eyes focused and almost seemed to recognize me for the first time, I asked the question that had been pressing on my mind since I awoke.

"How long have I been out?" As he answered me with the ridiculous amount of eight days, I thanked my stars that I was still alive. He was patient enough to answer all of my questions and not only had he cared for me all these days, but he had somehow ensured my release from the Super Max Prison. I suspected the Paladin had a lot to do with it, but it was still Gabriel's doing. I didn't know how to thank him and it would take me a while to figure it out and be able to reward him for his great gestures.

Eight days, how could I've been out for eight days? Maybe it was time I reconsidered my line of work and find something that would not push me so close to the edge. Luck had shone on me with Gabriel, but there were no certainties for the future, just promises of danger and probable death. In any case, just because I was conscious didn't mean I was healthy. I could see and much more feel, from my injuries that I was going to need a while to recover. In that time, I was sure to figure out a way to repay Gabriel so I gave him my word that I would care for him as he had for me.

Over the next couple of weeks my body slowly recovered and every day I was able to push myself a bit further. Monica kept coming back and tending to my wounds, which were now protected by a thick layer of dried blood, creating a perfect exoskeleton for me to heal under. The ribs were the hardest to deal with; moving, twisting, laughing, coughing and even breathing made me feel as if I was being stabbed. The more I got to know Gabriel, the more I discovered how utterly hilarious he was, which helped with the spirits but not the ribs.

I needed to learn who Gabriel was and over my recuperation time I did. Every night after Monica left we would sit and talk, at first in the living room and as I felt more up to it, on the front porch. We would rock on the wooden chairs under the stars and sprawling galaxy and I would listen to his stories. I thought I was a well-traveled man but Gabriel more than gave me a run for my money. The exotic places he visited in search for a cure, the memorable people that tried to help him and the tales of the trouble in which only a man with nothing to lose can get into were fascinating. He visited Europe, Asia, Africa, Australia, South America and small island, after small island with the promise of some obscure and magical cure for his cancer. The stories made me laugh, his everlasting search for hope broke my heart.

The saddest part of his journey was the loneliness in it. He never had told anyone and still hadn't. For some reason he decided to confide in me, probably because I was a stranger, but even his mother went to her grave not knowing. I could see the pain carrying such a large load had caused him. It was also the first time I felt like someone knew the pain I felt myself. I didn't dare tell him that, instead I just listened as we grew closer.

As I healed, Monica came over less and less. She tried to get closer to Gabriel but his secret seemed to push everyone away even though he didn't realize it. His drinking became sporadic at best and his clothes were starting to look big on him. I honestly could not tell if it was his illness or if he was trying to get healthier but the big man was looking better. He also had a pep in his step and a twinkle in his eye. Being that we both were in high spirits, I asked if his sister really existed in Santa Fe and he assured me she did.

My next question, which even I was surprised that it came out of my lips, but with great surprise and bewilderment, Gabriel confirmed that there was a mall we could visit in Santa Fe. I didn't know where that yearning for centralized shopping had come from but I blurted the question out before I could process what I was saying. We made plans and decided to head to Santa Fe the next morning. I was full of excitement and anxiety. I had just barely grown accustomed to Gabriel's house after so many years locked up and the thought of leaving it was making my throat tighten, my stomach swirl and my jaw to clench. The fear of being recaptured always loomed big in the back of my mind, but so far Gabriel's promises held steadfast and no one had shown up to collect me, not even the Paladin.

I decided to continue to trust my reinvigorated friend and follow the other voice in my head screaming to get out, discover and live. I would like to say I could barely sleep with the nervousness and excitement of the next day's travels but in reality once my head hit the pillow I was out for the night. I did wake up earlier than usual and with a surprising burst of energy. I was ready to leave the small house, dusty yard and small town. As much as I liked Gabriel I was ready to see other places and newer faces. The mall called to me and I still didn't understand why but I was definitely going to find out.

I was already in the kitchen enjoying some coffee along with some buttered toast when a sleepy bear decided to wander into the small room. Gabriel's eyes looked closed but must have been open since he didn't run into any wall or obstacle. He lumbered forward, his feet shuffling on the linoleum while his arms dangled ungracefully from his torso. He rubbed his eyes as his aimless wandering finally delivered him in front of the coffee pot. He somehow managed to concoct his caffeinated elixir without spilling a drop or making a mess and quickly shuffled his way to the chair adjacent to me at the kitchen table.

He looked at me and I could finally see his pupils through his barely open eyes. He raised an eyebrow and looked at me as if I had sprouted a second head.

"Well you seem all excited and ready to go." His voice was deep with the growl of half-asleep vocal cords. I hadn't realized it was that obviously painted all across my face. Feeling caught, I just smiled and nodded to the sleepy, grumpy bear sitting there enjoying some coffee with me. He didn't linger long as he picked up his cup and disappeared. Not too much later I heard the toilet flush and the shower turn on soon after that.

About a half hour later he finally reemerged into the kitchen, looking a lot more presentable and awake. After four cups of coffee I was ready to go and starting to wonder if I was one of those few people that could actually see sound. We were soon in the Jeep and on the road. The seatbelt felt even more confining that usual as it clicked and jerked me back into place after every one of my involuntary coffee driven movements. We were soon approaching the familiar overpass and the excitement of the trip was soon replaced with fear and anxiety.

I knew this trip was mostly my idea and Gabriel had no reason to try to take me back to the prison: still a small voice inside of me was screaming in terror and urging me to jump out of the car. I had listened to that voice before, it had been right at the time, but the physical price I paid had been steep. My hands were clinched around the seatbelt as if I were trying to compress the nylon strip into a singular strand. I was ready to jump out of the truck once more when Gabriel mercifully took the Santa Fe exit. The world didn't come off my shoulders; I think the whole galaxy did. I felt like a balloon being set free, all its air rushing out alleviating the stretching pressure and returning it to it calm shrunken state. The crash from the disappearing tension triggered an impromptu traveling nap.

I awoke as my body lunged forward and it felt as if a python was trying to squeeze me to death. I soon realized the Jeep was quickly decelerating and the seatbelt was just trying to keep me inside of it. What had once been a beautiful sunny morning had turned into a grey and wet day. Rain steadily fell in gentle waves making the roof of the truck sing like distant drums. The noise was relaxing unlike the view out of the front windshield. The fat droplets accumulated and hung on to the glass faster than the two small wipers could clear them. I had assumed our slowing was due to our arrival but it was in fact caused by the lack of visibility ahead of us.

Gabriel was holding on to the steering wheel as if his life depended on it, and maybe it did. His knuckles had turned whiter than his brown skin should have allowed and his forearms strained and flexed like an arm wrestler ready to battle. He was leaning forward on his seat and squinting out towards the road past the curtain of water. Even in the desert water finds its way and apparently monsoon season had arrived.

I wasn't sure how long we had traveled but I was no longer sleepy and was hoping we were close to getting off the highway. Gabriel continued with his accelerating and breaking dance as we carved our way through the water, which was now coming down with all the force of the ancient gods. It didn't take long until the next large green road sign blurrily appeared. The next exit was ours and a bit of the tension that had been growing deep in my shoulders and back evaporated. Just a couple more miles of this close to underwater excursion and we would at least be off the highway.

As we finally took the exit after two very long miles, Gabriel sat back on his seat and looked like a deflating balloon. Whatever tension I had been carrying had to pale in comparison with the stress he had just released. The rain continued to beat down and the puddles to fly as we drove through them, making the drive fun rather than stressful. We ran out of puddles to cut through as we arrived at the mall.

The large cube structure loomed ahead of us and reminded me of some of the spaceships I had seen back in my day. It felt as if at any moment the earth would tremble from the firing engines and the whole mall would lift and disappear into the cosmos. Instead it just sat there, mostly plain except from a few colorful signs spelling out what stores the structure contained. We drove around for a bit up and down aisles filled with cars trying to find a spot close to one of the entrance doors. The universe had decided we needed to get cleansed by the rain as the only available spots were as far back as you could get.

Defeated and tired of searching for that one elusive close spot, we parked and readied ourselves to brave the liquid bullets. I started to run following Gabriel's lead but soon my long strides shortened to a slow walk. The clean pure water felt amazing hitting my head and face and I could not help myself but to stop and enjoy them. I found myself looking up at the grey skies and tracking the droplets as they found their way to my face. A smile had appeared on my face as I could feel my cheeks straining in joy. Gabriel didn't notice my change of pace as he continued to run towards the doors of the mall like a penguin trying to escape a walrus.

By the time my slow stroll through the falling skies had delivered me to the mall's entrance where Gabriel awaited, I was completely soaked down to the underwear that I wasn't wearing. Gabriel's mouth started to open as if to ask me something as his perplexed eyes studied my current state. Before a sound could come out he closed his mouth, started shaking his head and changing his mind, he turned and started to walk into the well-lit space.

A multitude of small stores lined each side of the oversized hallway as we walked through; each of them inviting me to go in and explore them with their colorful and well placed merchandise. My eyes, becoming overwhelmed, were quickly rescued by my hungry nose. I could smell the delicious food court off in the distance, which was the reason I had wanted to visit such a trivial place. I followed my olfactory appendage as I squeaked and left watery footprints throughout the mall.

The smell intensified and as I turned one last corner around a piercing and earrings store; the magnificence of the food court sprawled in front of me. Pizza, Asian food, pretzels, burgers, tacos a true cornucopia for my taste buds. I didn't know if Gabriel was in tow anymore or not and I truly didn't care. I wanted to explore and study each stall and the goodies the Plexiglas hid behind it.

As I walked up and down the store fronts a nice young lady offered me a delicious treat of some sort of Asian chicken. I grabbed one of the toothpicks and kept walking as I delivered the delicious morsel into my mouth. The tender chicken gave way under my teeth and the delicious sauce coated my tongue, activating all of its sensors and providing me a great deal of pleasure. I did a quick turn about and went hunting for another one of the tiny savory and sweet samples.

By the third time I had grabbed a sample the young blonde girl's smile had turned from polite to amused. At the seventh fly by she became concerned and on the eleventh time I walked past her grabbing what was now the last sample she had become irritated. She retreated behind the counter with her empty tray quickly reporting of her experience to one of her coworkers. She scowled as she spoke in hushed tones, making her look older than she was, looking and pointing in my direction. It was obvious she was not going to be coming back with any more delicious treats for me to enjoy so I decided to move along and find my next prize.

After much wondering and debating, I found myself standing in front of a pizza place. The metal industrial oven hid in the fake stone walls was like drawers hiding delicious treasures. Behind the curved Plexiglas display was circle after circle with different savory colorful toppings. I stood there for a minute and soaked it all in while I decided which triangle I wanted to consume. I started to approach the counter and the young smiling man behind it when I realized I didn't have any money. I panicked and frantically started to look around just to find my trusty companion standing right next to me. I don't know for how long he had been with me, or if any at all, but when I needed him he was right there.

Before I could ask he handed me a crisp twenty dollar bill and let me go procure my bounty. I ended up with five different slices of pizza, one of them stuffed, and one oversized soda. I handed Gabriel the seventeen cents the young man gave back to me as change and I went on my way to find an open table to begin my feast. Gabriel soon joined me with his own single slice of pepperoni and a small cup of soda. I thanked him for his generosity and wished him a good meal and quickly dug into the first one of my slices.

The first greasy bite of crispy dough, silky cheese and tangy sauce exploded in my mouth. As I closed my eyes to savor the true experience of the pizza my mind exploded as well. Nonsensical image after image flew through my brain like a bad slideshow on overdrive. My mouth stopped chewing as I sat there paralyzed by the avalanche of memories and pictures running through my mind, none of which seemed to be mine. I didn't know whose subconscious I was taking an accelerated tour through but I wanted, no I needed it to stop. When what I though was a never ending barrage of moments that had played in my head stopped, I opened my eyes to find that I was still holding the slice of pizza inches from my mouth; a piece missing from it and still resting on my tongue. Tears were running down my face, falling onto the paper plates and being absorbed into them like the pizza grease.

Gabriel sat there looking more confounded than usual, eyes open wide as he took a drink through his straw. For once I felt as confused as he looked. I didn't know why I was crying and I couldn't control it either. The tears just streamed down my face and I knew somewhere in that kaleidoscope of memories hid the reason for my tears. I put the greasy slice down and reached for a different one. Again I took one bite and a world of memories fast forwarded too fast in my mind for me to keep up. The tears kept pouring out and a pit started to form deep in my stomach.

"Are you ok?" The large man asked looking around to see if anyone else had noticed the deluge pouring out of my eyes. I wanted to answer yes but honestly didn't know if I was truly ok. Unable to give him a concrete answer I shrugged and kept eating. It took me almost ten minutes to devour every last piece of greasy, cheesy crust and throughout the whole time tears unstoppably flowed down my cheeks. Once finished, we started our trek back to the car and onwards to Gabriel's sister's house.

It was a quiet drive as neither of us could explain or understand what had just happened. The welcoming to Gabriel's sister's house was not much less confounding. Gabriel parked the car and our shoes resonated as we made our way to the front door on the hard and wet pavement. The rain clouds had long passed but their muggy evidence remained. Every step we took made Gabriel tenser. By the time we had reached the door I could feel the nervous energy flying out of him and sticking to me. I had never met this woman and I was anxious by association.

Gabriel reached for the colorful red door to knock but his fist froze a few inches from it. He lowered his hand and looked at me in hopes of rescue. I met his gaze and without saying a word and with a quick movement of my head, told him to go ahead and knock. He hung his head in defeat as the tension overwhelmed me. The door started to tremble as it was forcefully being knocked. I was glad the suspense was over but was surprised that the fist knocking on it was mine. The whites of Gabriel eyes had grown so much in surprise that his pupils looked like small brown buttons inside of them. I embraced my proactive hand and continued to knock. It didn't take long for the door to open and a very annoyed looking short woman to fill some of the space the door had once occupied.

"What?!" Came out violently and angry from whom could only be Gabriel's sister. She was short and by short I mean fun sized. Her skin was caramel color with very dark freckles and birthmarks scattered through it. Even in her anger I could see the incredible resemblance between her and Gabriel. She was quite beautiful even though her brown eyes were shooting daggers in our direction. The scowl on her forehead teetered between scary and adorable and her petite figure hung to the door, blocking us access.

Her eyes darted from my still raised fist to Gabriel and after muttering a few words in Spanish she slammed the door on us. It was certainly not the kind of welcome I was expecting. Gabriel's defeated look became pathetic as he hung his head once more and shook it negatively. I didn't like seeing my companion in such poor spirits, so my over eager fist was once more shaking the red front door.

The door opened once more, and the small woman's right hand hung on to it, ready to slam it once more. Her hips, neck and head were all tilted in awkward angles of annoyance and sassiness. She ignored me and stared intensely at Gabriel with pain and anger in her eyes. Her big brown eyes glimmered as she held back tears from running down them. She hid her pain with anger and attitude, and was doing a pretty good job at it. Cutting daggers, or words, finally broke the silence.

"Oh didn't recognize you there the first time. To what do I owe this honor your grand world traveler?" The words visibly stung Gabriel as he recoiled with every angry syllable. He stood there refusing to meet her gaze and taking all of her rage like a willing victim. I knew she was family but I felt compelled to step in for Gabriel's sake.

"Hello, I am Bracket. May we come in?" Her poisonous eyes slowly shifted in my direction and I met them without fear or hesitation. Her mouth slowly shifted from angry to disapproving as I didn't cower under her impos-

ing glare. It was actually quite humorous, like a tiny barking Pomeranian trying to intimidate a German Shepard. The hilarity of the situation crept up on
me and before I knew I was smiling and giggling.

Her now indignant eyes switched back to Gabriel with a quick snap of
her head. "Who... quien es este pendejo?!" I didn't know what she was yelling
at him but I could make out from her tone it wasn't anything good. This only
contributed to my impromptu case of the giggles. It was now time for Gabriel
to save the situation and thankfully he snapped out of his cowardly state and
spoke up for both of us.

"Can we come in? I would like to see Madison and Lucas. This is my
friend Bracket, please excuse him." It wasn't quite what I would have said
but in the particular situation it worked. She rolled her eyes, took in a deep
breath which she released with her shoulders and stepped aside so we could
enter. Once in the clean but modest house I was finally properly introduced
to Rosa. I extended my hand and Gabriel's sister reluctantly took it and shook
it. Progress I guess.

It wasn't long before a stampede of footsteps started to approach us. I
readied myself to fight whatever hoard of animals were charging us. We had
walked into an ambush and served up to slaughter by Rosa. To my dismay,
Gabriel's smile widened as the thundering rumbling steps grew louder. He fell
to one knee and I was quickly at his side to help him back to his feet. The
noise was having a hypnotic effect on him, leaving him powerless and offering
himself for sacrifice. I could and would not allow that to happen. I tugged on
him trying to get him to stand but it was too late.

Two small and vicious creatures broke the threshold of the small living
room in which we stood and were making a direct and urgent route towards
Gabriel. Before I could do anything they closed the distance on him and fe-
rociously jumped on him. He braced himself for the impact but was almost
knocked to the ground. He held both creatures, one in each arm as they made
high pitched noises. Noticing my panic his eyes met mine and he mouthed a
reassuring "It's ok". His blissful smile and gentle eyes guided mine towards the
ferocious creatures who to my surprise were only two very excited and happy
kids.

Gabriel hugged and kissed them as they buried themselves deeper in his
chest with tiny arms reaching around to hug him around his back. The shrills

of excitement made even Rosa crack a smile behind crossed and angry arms. I relaxed but gave them some distance, as I didn't want to become their next victim. Gabriel rejoiced in the embrace and allowed it to last for as long as the children decided. Eventually the hug ended and was replaced by wide and excited eyes accompanied with bouncing feet. As if on cue, Gabriel reached into the lower pocket of his Bermuda shorts and produced a thumb sized object.

He held it in his hand as if presenting it to the children and they obliged with the ooh's and aah's of amazement. Their eyes followed the object through the air as Gabriel did his elaborate presentation of it. My eyes followed his fingers as well and between them he held some sort of treasure, which was a Matryoshka doll. With his other hand he reached over and unnested the first of the Russian dolls. This prompted more noises of surprise and wonder from the children. He repeated the process a few times until the kids were driven into a frenzy.

Knowing that the children could not contain their excitement anymore, he replaced all the tops he had removed and handed the doll to the small girl. Her eyes impossibly widened as she held it, her smile showing the gap of a missing tooth and her body visibly trembling with joy. The young boy's eyes followed the movement of the doll into his sister's hands and with every inch his joy was replaced by a pout and despair. The Russian doll firmly secured in his sister's tiny hands, his eyes fluttered back and forth between her and Gabriel.

His pouty lip and concerned brows showed his utter disappointment but his eyes yet held onto hope. Gabriel quickly produced another nesting doll, this one painted like a soldier. The boy exploded with excitement and quickly grabbed the small toy out of Gabriel's fingers. They both vibrated with joy and embraced their uncle once more. They bathed him with thank yous, kisses and hugs. And as fast as the stampede had happened they retreated to their lair to play with their new toys.

As the rambunctious pair disappeared into the house, so did Rosa's smile. Gabriel was back on his feet and faced his sister, reinvigorated and looking a little braver. His air of confidence was quickly deflated by more piercing words from the small, angry but beautiful lady.

"So to what do we owe this great honor?" Her words stung even me as they were filled with sarcasm and contempt. Her expression had mellowed but I could see that it stung Gabriel. I wanted to rescue him from her but I knew this was one battle that only he could fight. When I thought he might crumble under her venom, Gabriel surprised me, worked up some courage and answered his small big sister.

"I wanted to see you and the kids. Make sure you didn't need anything." Rosa instantly rolled her eyes and her nails dug into her arms as she still held them folded over each other.

"Well a nice debt free house in a much nicer neighborhood would be nice." I hadn't realized until then what was the cause of all the angst and it sadden me to think it was all about the house and money. My oversimplified conclusion was quickly destroyed as Rosa kept talking.

"How long has it been Gabriel? Seriously, you don't even make it back for Mom's funeral and you expect me to receive you like some prodigal son and with open arms? How long have you been in town? The kids have been asking about you nonstop since the funeral. All the gifts, postcards and trinkets you send them... Arg!!! They idolize you and you have kept them waiting to see you. And for what?! To make new friends? For what?!"

Her words were charged with sadness and pain. She spoke in hushed tones, trying to keep her words out of the ears of her children. She pointed at me when she said "new friend" and said it with disgust. I should have been offended but I could not help but to feel as guilty as Gabriel looked. Every word she uttered made him nod in agreement and visibly broke him. He had no response, no words and no response for his sister's hurtful but yet honest words. I had knocked on her door as he had hesitated so it was my duty to help and protect my loyal companion.

"It is not his fault madam. It is mine. Gabriel saved me from the wilderness and angry villagers and has been tending many of my wounds for the past couple of weeks. I must apologize for having kept him from such beautiful children and even more beautiful sister. He is a good man, in fact, a very good and selfless man. Without him I would probably have died more than once. He is here now and I know he wants nothing more than to be of service and support to you and your brilliant children."

With every compliment and kind word about her brother, Rosa's face softened, making her even more beautiful. By the time I was done, most of the anger had flushed out of her as she prompted Gabriel with one more question. "Is this true?"

Humbly and quietly, Gabriel answered her with repeated nods of assertion while still averting his eyes. She took in one deep sigh and her strong features softened as she slowly approached the large sad man and embraced him in a hug of her own. She cradled him and held him as she most probably had when they were younger and he much smaller than her. His head found her shoulder, his arms wrapped around her and he melted into his big sister. She gently said "Oh Gabo" as she stroked his hair and head. My eloquent words had resolved what seemed like an impossible situation and had quickly reconciled the two siblings. I had negotiated intergalactic cease fires before, a little scuff between a brother and a sister was truly nothing for me. I will say that seeing that embrace was much more rewarding than anything else I had witnessed before.

From then on the tone and energy changed. We were invited to sit and visit and soon snacks and drinks were littering the glass coffee table. The two little creatures reemerged from their den and were a pair of balls of electric energy. I was stuffed but could not pass on the pastries and salty snacks sprawled in front of me. One, I didn't want to be rude and two, my tongue forced me to.

The little girl, and her enormous almond shaped brown eyes, seemed to take a special curious interest on me. She would hide behind the furniture only to jump out smiling from ear to ear. Her million dollar smile was accompanied by squeals and giggles of pure joy. I played along and eventually was rewarded with a hug. The young but older boy found his way into Gabriel's lap and listened and hung to every word he had to say with all of his attention and focus. We had gone from getting the door slammed on our faces to a warm welcome and even I was starting to feel like part of the family.

Madison abandoned her shy and coy game and was now sprinting towards me, leaping and having me pick her up in the air. The inhuman noises of joy that emanated out of her little body forced me to smile and giggle every time. During one of the anti-gravitational lifts my stomach gave me the first sign of distress. With every impending lift my smile faded as the sharp pains invaded my lower abdomen. It felt as if a serpent was dancing and twirling inside my stomach, moving organs and chewing its way through. The sharp pains and audible gurgling noises told me I needed to find a bathroom, and urgently.

I politely interrupted Gabriel and Rosa's conversation and secured the location of the nearest powder room. I tried to walk calmly and inconspicuously towards it but I could feel the fire trying to push its way out of my entrails. All that pizza and chicken samples were making a comeback with vengeance. I followed the instruction and was soon rewarded with the great relief of finding the bathroom. I slammed the door shut behind me and made a bee line for the toilet.

After the much needed relief I was left in a quandary. Where there should have been a big fluffy roll of toilet paper, stood but a sad hard brown tube of cardboard. I frantically looked under the medicine cabinet and every possible place within reach where I could possibly find some toilet paper but to no avail. I sat there for what seemed like an eternity, until my legs started to tingle from being asleep. I consider carefully all my options as I looked around the bathroom. That was until there were forceful knocks on the door accompanied by shouting and chaos.

"We have to go now!" I had never heard Gabriel sound so authoritative and angry ever. I nearly fell off the toilet as I jumped in shock and surprise. Besides him I could hear that Rosa's calm and comforting mood had evaporated. Instead the shouting went back and forth and whatever truce I had brokered between them was now broken. I wanted to feel bad for them and help them once more but I had more pressing matters at hand. Gabriel knocked once more this time urging me to go with some colorful words.

I looked around once more in desperation and reached for the only thing within grasp and that could serve the purpose of cleaning me, the hand towel. I carefully thought through my plan of attack with the small blue towel and proceeded to clean myself with it. Once I was done all evidence of my usage was carefully folded and hidden while I felt clean and fresh. Out of reflexes I almost threw the towel into the toilet but that would have caused a whole other bucket of problems. With more pounding and screaming coming from the other side of the door, I wisely or foolishly decided to hang it back up on the rack.

I washed my hands, dried them on my pants and opened the door to an almost purple Gabriel. To say he was angry was an understatement and I could see why. Rosa was barking at him like some angry little dog, spewing poison about the house and how she deserved it. Either the temporary peace had been all an act or a nerve had been forcefully pushed. In any case, it was obvious that our visit was done, so I headed towards the front door and hoped that my evidence in the hand towel would never be found.

Rosa yelled at Gabriel all the way until we got in the Jeep, as he pulled out in a hurry he almost ran over her small feet. I thought she had been pissed, but that near miss pushed her into a new and more intense level of madness. We drove off and even as we increase the distance from the house I could still hear the small woman screaming and barking obscenities at us. The drive back to Pecos was silent and tense. There wasn't much I could say to console my companion, so I sat quietly looking at the window and allowed him to process and deal with what just had happened. It was a sad thing, but sometimes that is the reality of life.

We made it back without a word. We entered the house and it was Gabriel's turn to disappear into the bathroom. I settled on my couch and contemplated what I could do to help him. I could hear him sobbing in the bathroom through the thin walls and decided to give him some privacy. I headed out to the front porch and was met with a blazing orange and pink sunset. The sun had just started to hide and the sky had exploded with warm colors. I enjoyed the view and allowed my mind to keep working to help my broken friend.

I opened my eyes, which I hadn't realized had closed, to find the beautiful sunset gone and the chill and darkness of the night having replaced it. I wasn't sure for how long I had been out but the sky was now ablaze with stars and a crescent moon. I felt chilled to the core and my neck hurt from being hung in some unnatural position while I slept. I slowly got out of the deceivingly comfortable rocking chair and ventured back into the house to see where Gabriel was. I searched the whole house for Gabriel, but for the closed door to the bathroom. I didn't think to check in there, he could not possibly still be in there. I tried to turn the knob but the door was locked. I knocked and called out for him but received no response. A sick feeling crept into the depth of my stomach and my brain yelled at me to open the door at any cost.

I tried to unlock it but nothing worked. Out of options and always having wanting to do it I decided to kick the door in. I wound up and gave the door my best kick as my right foot hit near the lock. I leapt into the kick and soon find my way to the ground. I unceremoniously bounced off the door and fell to the floor, landing forcefully on my ass. I got up and looked around to make sure no one saw me. I knew I was alone in the house but I still had the urge to make sure there were no witnesses to my foolishness. Seeing that the door was stronger than my leg I decided to throw my whole body into it. There wasn't much room in the hallway for me to get a running start but after four attempts and once very sore right shoulder I was finally in the bathroom.

I was hoping I would break in and find the room empty. That Gabriel had snuck out the window like I once did and had gone for a walk or drive. I really wished that had been the case. On the cold tiled floor of the bathroom laid the large man. He was sprawled out like a starfish and if his stomach hadn't been rising with each breath I would have been convinced he was dead. I quickly rushed to his side and not even my well delivered slaps made him regain consciousness. He had a pulse, was breathing and had no visible injuries but was gone to another world. I searched through the pile of dirty clothes on the floor and found his cell phone, opened it and dialed the three digits no one ever wants to have to dial on a phone, nine, one and one.

Got to love family; or do you? (Gabriel)

Bracket kept getting a little better every day. He would stay up longer and longer each time and seemed to really enjoy Monica's company. I enjoyed her as well but her constant looks of pity and guilt towards me were starting to get to me. I needed to get away; being that Bracket was unconscious and she was there I decided to go for a drive. Before I knew it I was entering the Vista Grande public library with a mission burning between my eyebrows.

I searched the periodicals, public records and anything I could find on the internet about Bracket and his case. Every tidbit I found made his story sadder and more gut wrenching. I also figured out that the good ol' pompous ass Dr. Ross shared way more than what was on the public records. He could not help himself when it came to proclaiming his own perceived accomplishment. I should report him but I didn't know to whom and honestly didn't give a shit.

I did care about Bracket and I was surprised how much I actually cared for the walking mess sleeping on my couch. Reading the sensational headlines and the true height of his fall was excruciating. The first result on the search engine was "Genius not so smart, leaves trail of evidence after attempted murder." One after the other just got more decadent and sensational. Bracket has been quite a prodigious professional and child. Once I had worked my way through all the garbage, I found photos of a young Bracket tying a game against a chess playing computer. He was 13 when he was accepted into MIT and looked like someone's little kid brother in the research team's picture. His wedding announcement pictures were baffling and made me jealous. I mean, not that he was an ugly guy but he wasn't any prized catch either, when it came to the looks department. His wife on the other hand, was movie star beautiful and sexy. She must have had a thing for big brains because otherwise I could not justify the union.

My already aching heart sank to new depths of sadness when I stumble upon a picture of Bracket, his gorgeous wife and his two beautiful girls. The older one looked six, while the younger one could not be any older than three. They both wore pigtails and sundresses and were adorable enough for

147

television. The older one was missing one of her front teeth, which made her cuteness factor increase exponentially. The younger one's big blue eyes were intense enough to make the most savage beast want to adopt her and take care of her. They both took after their mother thankfully, but they were obviously his pride and joy.

Seeing him as a family man shocked me more than I had expected. His life, his family, his accomplishments and his meteoric fall from grace was all very well documented. I went back and finally clicked on all the sensational newspaper articles about the incident. The reports said he had been fired from his job. The reasons provided by the different media outlets were diverse, some very plausible while other ridiculously sensational. Even Dr. Ross' explanation about him being dismissed for being bi-polar was reported on a few of them. Regardless of the cause, the reports about what happened when he got home that late morning were pretty consistent.

Bracket had returned home early after being fired, just to find his wife in the middle of having sex with her lover on his bed. Bracket's mind snapped and threw him into an unstoppable rage. Some reports said he beat the man within an inch of his death, others that he just assaulted him. The verdict as the mouthy doctor had said was aggravated assault. That day Barry Racket died and Bracket was born. His brilliant mind broke and in trying to heal itself, a new persona arose. I didn't know how much Bracket remembered or how much he wanted to remember. I know if it was me I would not want to recall a single second of what happened to him. His madness was the only thing keeping him sane.

I had enough of memory lane and decided to go back to the house. Any fears or concerns I had about Bracket blew away as I drove back with the top down on the Jeep. He was not a dangerous man. He was a broken human and his unique mind did the only thing it could to keep him from exploding and mentally dying. I didn't completely understand his illness but I understood what it was to truly be alone, to survive just to encounter more obstacles in life, to want to just give up but refusing to stop fighting. Doubts of my decision to take him in evaporated under the hot afternoon sun and I could not wait to get home and help this once amazing man.

Over the next few weeks, Bracket slowly healed and we got to know each other much better. I was careful in the questions I asked him, not wanting to trigger some avalanche of painful memories. But I needed to know how much he remembered. I did my best at sorting through his fantastical tales of missions, aliens, spies and intergalactic wars to decipher how much he recalled. Sadly, it appeared he remember quite a bit, his mind had just twisted and transformed that information into incredible tales to protect him from himself. I felt tempted to probe and push him and the few times that I did he became agitated and isolated himself. I apologized through the bathroom door a few times as he shouted at me for questioning him and not believing his stories. It was just too much pain for him to ever go back, so like him I decided to burry Barry Racket and just move forward with the greatly eccentric Bracket.

I don't know if Monica started to feel like the third wheel but as Bracket and I bonded and spent more time together, she started to show up less and less. I assured her it was ok, even though I missed her I knew it was for the best. Finally feeling better and suffering from a severe case of cabin fever, Bracket asked if we could go for a trip. I agreed before we had chosen a destination and was unable to back out once he suggested my sister's and the mall in Santa Fe. I had been back just over a month and had been able to avoid her until now. Apparently my luck had run out and it was time to face the angry wolverine.

As soon as I opened my eyes the next morning, Rosa popped in my head. I wondered if there was any way to convince Bracket to cancel our day trip or choose another destination. He had been more interested in going to a mall than seeing her so maybe we could go to any other mall, in the United States, North America and possibly South America.

I walked out into the kitchen following the intoxicating smell of coffee just to find Bracket sitting at the kitchen table all ready to go. He was cheerier than I had ever seen him and knew right then that I was not going to be able to weasel out of the trip. I sat down with him, ate some food, drank my warm elixir and made small talk. He was like a kid on Christmas Day and even in my morning grumpiness it was infectious. I decided to stop stalling and left the over eager Bracket in the kitchen while I showered and got ready.

Once ready I headed back out in the living room where Bracket sat like a dog waiting to be let out. I put aside any plans of getting out of it and got into the Jeep with him. I could tell Bracket was tense but I was too deep in thought on how to deal with my sister to tend to his current neurosis. I loved my sister but life had made her an angry and bitter woman. She was now divorced and raising her two kids and acted as if the world owed her something. So many times I had been so close to telling her about my ailment just in hopes of shutting up her whining about life. I wasn't looking forward to seeing her, but I did miss the kids.

The whole drive I pondered what the conversation would be like, what to say to avoid a huge fight as Bracket's snores accompanied me. The vocal lumberjack awoke as the Jeep slowed down on the off ramp. He tried to look all cool and collected as he got his bearings but no one ever does. His excitement was visible as we approached the mall. I had never seen anyone get so excited about a shitty mall, but Bracket wasn't anyone after all.

I ran into the mall trying to escape the rain. Bracket kept up with me, until he didn't. I stood under the safety of the entrance canopy as Bracket slowly walked; almost dancing with the rain as he stared into the dark clouds. By the time he reached me he was completely soaked. We walked into the mall and he stood, hands on his hips, soaking in the view of what he was seeing. He looked like a Spanish conquistador surveying the new lands he was about to pillage and rape for god and country. Once I finally caught up, I could see what Bracket was looking at so voraciously and satisfied, the food court.

I had the money out before he could even ask for it. He quickly grabbed it from my hands and off he went to hunt some paper plate delicacy. Feeling a bit hungry myself, I grabbed some pizza and found us a table. There were plenty of open tables but I made sure to find one as far away from other people; who knew what Bracket might pull once he sat down with his food. Eventually, and with a wide grin, Bracket found and joined me at the isolated table. I was surprised at the amount of food on his tray as the white, green and red plates filled with pizza were barely hanging on.

Bracket kept smiling as he sat and started to dig into the first of the many slices he had bought with my money. I wanted to be pissed, I knew there was no way he could eat all of it and would just waste half of it, but the pure look of joy on his face prevented me from getting angry. He ate like a man that hadn't eaten in weeks and as he savored each bite, tears started to stream down his face. I looked back and forth between his happy but teary face and the four plates on his tray. My mind instantly flashed to the pictures I had seen of him and his family, the four of them. I wanted to say something, as some part of him obviously remembered, but could not bring myself to saying anything. I just sat there and watched him as he ate his way through repressed memories that were fighting to get out.

To my surprise, only but a few pieces of crust were left on his plate once he was done eating. Finished, he started to lead and we ended up back in my Jeep. All the fuss about going to the mall and just for that? I started driving and took the very, very, very long way to my sister's. We pretty much toured the whole town before I finally parked in her driveway. I did a slow zombie shuffle to the front door as Bracket watched me, confused, already at the door. For some reason I could not work up the courage to knock on the door and noticing my infinite hesitation, Bracket's knuckles rasped on the wooden door. I didn't know whether to be thankful or to kick him, but the deed was now done.

The door opened to a short angry woman who slammed the door on us quickly after sharing a few choice words. I was ready to turn and retreat when Bracket's anxious fist pounded on the door again. We were finally reluctantly invited in to what had to be the most bi-polar family visit in the history of mankind. I had to almost drag Bracket out of the bathroom as what seemed like possible reconciliation turned into a nuclear argument with my sister Rosa. I could hear her screams all the way down the street as I left plenty of rubber on her driveway as I peeled out in the Jeep.

I didn't know why I tried with her anymore. It was heartbreaking but it was the truth, our relationship would never be salvaged. At least I got to see my niece and nephew; they had grown so much but were still so innocent and full of joy. The drive back was just as quiet and thankfully Bracket gave me my space, I truly needed it. I had traveled so much, looking for a cure to extend a life that didn't exist anymore. In my search to escape death I had killed myself already. That thought broke me inside and it didn't' matter how I tried to rationalize it or explain it away, it held true. Mom was dead, my siblings held nothing but contempt and anger towards me, I had found no cure and all I had now was an empty house full of memories just to rub salt into my emotional wounds.

So lost in thought I was that I didn't remember how I had found my way back to the house, but there we were pulling into the driveway. Back in the house, I wanted to hide and my favorite place was the shower. I made sure Bracket didn't need to use the facility and he said he was fine with a very guilty look on his face. I didn't have the energy to try to figure out what that was all about right now, so I went in the shower turned, the water as hot as my skin would tolerate and disappeared into the stream of droplets. I felt angry, sad, lonely, frustrated and defeated. My tears joined the avalanche of water that was beating against my head and I wondered what the point of fighting was anymore. I knew I was fighting an impossible battle but, I don't know, I hoped there was some sort of reward, some prize, something to tell me I had fought a good fight. Instead, I was more alone now than I was traveling the world and my only friend was a broken, crazy man child who I had to babysit through his delusions of grandeur. All the thoughts swirled around in my head and the water kept falling.

It wasn't until I opened my eyes that I realized I was dizzy. I turned down the temperature of the water, worrying that the hot air was getting to me but the swimming visual sensation persisted. My chest got heavier by the second as my once blurry vision began to close up on itself. All of the sudden I was traveling through a tunnel and everything around me slowly got enveloped by a circle of darkness. I turned the water as cold as I could, hoping to snap myself out of whatever was happening to me, but to no avail. My vision kept closing in on itself until all I could see was one point of light. I could feel my body falling through the air towards the hard tile but before I could feel the impact everything went black.

Partners in Crime
(Bracket)

The woman on the other side of the telephone line insisted on talking with me. I just wanted them to send an ambulance to get Gabriel. I was so worried about his current condition that I didn't even care about his rotund nudity. His breaths were shallow and I was getting absolutely no response from any of my methods to wake him. Even slapping extensively wasn't doing the trick. She kept asking me where I was and Gabriel's house in Pecos was not enough for her. She kept asking for an address and I had to run outside the house to figure out the address..

All the meanwhile, Gabriel lay motionless. Once I was able to cobble an address for the mystery woman I tried to hang up but she insisted I keep talking with her. I didn't see the point of it and demanded to know how long until the ambulance would arrive. She informed me it would be another twenty minutes and the absurdity of the number made me want to puke. The woman calmly listened as I screamed and yelled about their poor and untimely service, while for some reason she kept trying to calm me. After a while I just sat there in silence with the phone up to my ear just saying "Yep" every time she asked if I was still with her.

Eventually the distant cry of the sirens reached my desperate ears. All the meanwhile, I had been sitting on the bathroom floor next to Gabriel rubbing his head gently, urging and begging him to wake up. I had covered his body with a towel, not for me but for him so the paramedics would not find him naked. The noise of the sirens grew, letting me know it was neither the wind nor my imagination. The noise of the sirens grew until it was deafening, only to mercifully shut off. Soon after, a friendly female voice announced her presence through the open front door. I called to them directing them to the bathroom.

The pair hurriedly walked into the bathroom wearing their white shirts and toting bags in their gloved hands. They started to ask me questions and I think I answered, but I was suddenly overwhelmed with a feeling of numbness. Before too long they had Gabriel strapped onto a gurney and we were all walking towards the ambulance. The male EMT kept asking me a question but I could not hear him. All I could see, hear or process was seeing my friend in the back of an ambulance, unconscious, being strapped up to oxygen and the possibility of never seeing him again.

The EMT grabbed me by both shoulders and moved his head around until we made eye contact. "Is he your partner?" I didn't know why he was asking me that and in the blur of the moment I answered him; "Yes". Before I knew I was sitting in the back of the ambulance ridding along with the female paramedic. She informed me we were heading to Santa Fe after I queried her about our destination. Apparently the universe really wanted us both in Santa Fe today. The ambulance could not move fast enough for my liking and I just sat there looking at my only friend, really hoping he would wake up.

We reached the hospital after what felt like an endless eternity. They unloaded Gabriel and I followed in tow. Hoses, straps and clamps were all over his body trying to monitor if he was still with us. Nurses in colorful scrubs joined the procession and began to converse with the paramedics in unintelligible words. I looked back and forth between them trying to decipher what they were saying but it was a completely alien language to me.

We raced down the hallway and at the third double doors a very polite and sweet nurse with kind eyes told me I could go no further. I tried to protest but she assured me I could go back once he was stabilized. I knew I could not win this quarrel so I found residence in a pink Pepto-Bismol chair and waited. For the first time and only for a moment, my concern shifted from Gabriel to me. He was in good hands; probably the best hands to handle whatever mysterious ailment had overtaken him. I, on the other hand was alone, in a strange town and in an unknown hospital. I had no idea how I had gotten there and more importantly no clue in how to get back to the house. If Gabriel never were to wake up, I feared I would once more be completely helpless, lost and alone. The thought of it frightened me so I decided to bottle it up and worry about Gabriel's health first and only for now.

There was a small TV in the waiting room to distract future patients and anxious family members from their current shitty reality. Worn faces and fearful eyes were glued to the small noiseless screen. Subtitles scrolled at the bottom of the picture, always two seconds too late for things to make sense. I found my comfort studying my fellow prisoners of the unknown. The mother, comforting her child, and holding their awkwardly bent and probably broken arm. The daughter in her fifties who looked exhausted, sitting next to her wheelchair ridden elderly mother. Her look of desperation and entrapment, which only the painful departure of her mother could ever really comfort. The construction worker holding a blood soaked rag against his arm, impatiently waiting to be helped, hopefully before he bled to death. And then there was me.

The adrenaline slowly abandoned me leaving me worn and fighting to keep my eyes open. I awoke a couple of times from the violent jerking of my head as I had temporarily fallen asleep. The merciful touch of a nurse's hand on my shoulder snapped me out of my zombie like state. Even though she tried to be gentle I could not help to jump in my seat.

"Is Mister Gabriel Moreno your partner Sir?" She asked while giving me a comforting yet curious smile. I didn't know why they kept asking me that question and my frustration leaked out as I answered.

"He is more of my loyal servant but yes, yes he is my partner." Her eyes opened with surprise at my words as her body tensed from head to toes. She averted my eyes and found refuge looking for something in the papers her clipboard held.

"Ok then, come with me Sir." Her once sweet tone disappeared and was replaced by a dry and official one. She turned and without checking if I was following took down the hallway. I did my best to catch up, but one of my legs had fallen asleep from my lengthy wait. Electric needles engulfed my right leg as I awkwardly planted it to propel me forward. Every step racked my senses with pain and a unique tickling sensation. The nurse, unaware or uncaring of my present situation, continued to lead me at a neck breaking pace. We weaved back and forth through a labyrinth of double doors and hallways.

Her pace finally slowed as we were approaching a particular room. I could already see Gabriel inside of it and all the machinery he was attached to. The nurse delivered me into the room and ran away as fast as she could. I stood at the doorway not knowing what to do. He was still unconscious but the recurring beeping of the machines let me know he was indeed alive. We were alone in the room and besides the bed he rested in and the machine, the only other thing inside of the small hospital room was a lonely chair. The chair was right next to the bed and taking the hint from the furniture I put one foot in front of the other and found my butt a home in the chair.

I grabbed Gabriel's left hand in my left and was patting it with my right, in hope of waking him up. The cuff around his arm beeped and started inflating, startling me. The thing kept growing until the Velcro that held it shut protested under its expansive powers. The machine that the cuff was hooked up to made clicking noises and the device started to deflate at jerky intervals. Once it had gathered whatever information it was looking for, all of the air was let out and the cuff returned to its original size.

"Excuse me Mr....?" The voice coming from the door startled me once more. I guessed that if they kept scaring me and I had a heart attack, at least I was in the right place. The polite greeting was an exploratory question as well, so I decided to satisfy the gentleman's curiosity.

"Bracket". The man wearing black scrubs jotted down what could only be my name on his chart and let me know the doctor would be in soon to talk to me about my partner, again with the damn partner. I was starting to feel insulted. Even though I held Gabriel under great esteem, I was the commander of this operation and he was at best an apprentice, but in reality my loyal servant. To call him my partner insinuated even rank and it was really starting to get under my skin.

I worried that I was in for another lengthy wait but it didn't take long for there to be a knock on the open door and a lady wearing a white lab coat walked in. "I'm Dr. Angerer, Mr. Bracket, I am the treating physician for your partner Mr. Moreno." Her hand extended out towards me holding long skinny fingers, I took it and shook. I really wanted to say something about our ranks but I could tell the very serious blonde lady had a lot of information to share with me. So instead I held my complaint for later and decided to listen and learn what, if anything, they knew about what happened to Gabriel.

"As you must know your partner's condition has advanced to its last stages." I wasn't sure if she was asking me or telling me so I tried my best to look as if I knew what she was talking about. Satisfied with my assured response she continued. "At this stage there is not much more we can do but make him comfortable for whatever time he has. To be honest with you Mr. Bracket I am surprised he was still functioning with as much as the cancer had spread in Mr. Moreno. Again, rest assured we will make him comfortable and make sure he is not in any pain."

To say a pile of bricks hit me would be a gross understatement, it was more like a whole house got dropped on me. I knew Gabriel was sick, we had talked about it but it never clicked how seriously sick he truly was. The moment she left the room a million questions popped into my head out of nowhere. How much time did he have? How much pain? What could I do? All of them would have helped satisfy my curiosity but none truly mattered. My trusty companion was on his last gasp. I wanted to feel bad for him but the first fears that exploded in my head were about me. What was I going to do if he went away? I felt an overwhelming feeling of being lost and powerless. I shook aside those thoughts, I was a highly trained operative and I would figure it out. Certainly, I would.... Or would I?

Seeing the concern and desperation in my face the doctor led me away from the room. She guided me through the maze of hallways until we were in a small room with a pair of round tables and a counter filled with boring treats. I followed my nose, finding my way to the old, bitter and slightly burned coffee. I served up some of the dark tar looking liquid into a small white Styrofoam cup and doctored it with some of the packets of sugar and dry creamer. I grabbed a chair at one of the tables, there was a box of donuts on it and I helped myself to a very dry and stale pastry. I sat there staring out the window, sipping on the undrinkable coffee and eating the un-chewable donut.

I don't know for how long I had been there, but where the serious lady doctor had once been, a friendly looking nurse was now standing, obviously waiting for me. I followed her long black braid all the way back to Gabriel's room. She motioned me in towards the door as if I had won a brand new car on some TV gameshow, but I truly didn't want the prize that awaited me inside. I hesitantly walked through the oversized doorway as I thanked the kind nurse.

You always expect hospital rooms to be dark and gloomy, especially when the person residing in it is dying. That is never the case, instead the room is lit with a sterile white light which makes it feel cold and uncaring. The beeping of the machines welcomed me first, along with rhythmic pumping of the oxygen machine. Gabriel welcomed me next with a soft smile and concerned eyes. It felt as if I was the one sick and he was the concerned friend the way he was looking at me. We both knew that wasn't the case and I needed to stop worrying about my future and instead worry about my friend's present.

"How you doing buddy?" I didn't know how to answer the large man. It should have been me asking him how he was doing, but I couldn't even muster a single word. Unable to respond I found myself hugging Gabriel, but more than just hugging, I was holding on to him for dear life. I started to feel the sudden urge to shed tears, but determined not to allow my servant to see me like that, I broke the embrace, turned around and left the room. I didn't know where I was going but I knew I could not stay in that cold stale room for another second right now.

I wandered up and down the over cleansed and busy hallways but even the hospital was feeling claustrophobic. I had no means to get back to Pecos so right as I exited the front doors of the hospital I did a 180 degree turn and walked right back in to ask the front desk lady for some assistance. Her cotton ball hair and wrinkled smile welcomed me right back in to that place of death. I explained my quandary to her and before I knew it there was a taxi awaiting me out in front of the hospital.

The ride back was longer than I remembered and quiet. The cab driver tried to indulge me in the customary cabbie small talk but noticing my disinterest he stopped trying to converse. That was until we arrived at Gabriel's house in Pecos, then the conversation got quite heated and interesting. The cabbie kept demanding monetary payment, which I didn't have on me. Gabriel was the one that usually carried the funny colored pieces of paper. Why they were valuable on this planet still confounded me. I offered and gave the taxi driver quite a few forms of verbal payment in advice and secrets but none seem to satisfy him.

What I thought was a friendly negotiation turned into ugly threats and the possibility of incarceration. I hid in the house and soon enough an authoritative knock rattled the door. I recognized it right away and knew the Golden Paladin awaited me on the other side of the thin wooden door. I knew the flimsy door could never hold back someone of such power. Escape from Gabriel had proven futile, so there was no chance to escape the Golden Paladin. My options being nonexistent, I opened the door and hoped I could talk my way out of this one.

Shinning Knight
(Bracket)

I slowly opened the door and awaited my fate. I was smiling, ready to use my wit and charm to defeat the Golden Paladin. It was after all my only chance against him. A game of wits. The smile quickly evaporated under the desert's heat and was replaced by confusion. The Paladin was standing in front of the door, filling the frame with his immensity, but the ugly yellow cab was gone. I had expected the cab driver to be right behind him yelling and egging him on to destroy me like some fight promoter, instead he had vanished.

"Where is Gabriel and what happened to him?" The voice thundered and echoed through the house and the Golden Paladin's eyes tried to burn through my skull. My problems with the disgruntled cab driver now seemed minuscule compared to the powerful giant problem currently interrogating me. Intimidated, and probably a little scared, I caught a case of diarrhea of the mouth. My lips and tongue took over for the sake of my self-preservation and I told the Golden Paladin everything that had happened.

With every word he shrunk a little, although his armor remained just as golden and brilliant. By the time I was done telling him not only about the events, what the doctor had told me and what Gabriel had confided in me he had shrunken to large but normal human size. He was still a strong menacing presence but as he removed his helmet his kind eyes reminded me of Gabriel's. The resemblance was uncanny between the two of them. The Golden Paladin's face was thinner and looked somehow more muscular than Gabriel's but they were almost identical. He somehow became more human in that instant in front of my eyes and his paladin's armor disappeared and was replaced by a policeman's uniform and badge.

He didn't speak a word but his eyes told everything that needed to be said. I could see him processing and his expression would change from anger to crippling sadness. Remaining silent, he stood up from the couch where we had sat down for our conversation and exited the house. For a moment I thought he was just going to get back in his cruiser and leave but his footsteps pacing up and down the wooden porch told me otherwise. It was obvious he needed space so I didn't dare go chasing after him. Even in his "human" state I knew he could slice me in half at any second.

My stomach started grumbling and I couldn't remember the last time I had eaten. I left the Paladin pacing and I wandered into the kitchen to look for something to eat. As I was coming out of the kitchen in mid bite of the delicious sandwich I had prepared I heard his voice out on the porch. Not sure if he was talking to me or himself I stopped chewing with a mouthful of bread, ham, cheese and mayonnaise. His voice was somewhat muted and sounded more like grumbles than words. I walked carefully and quietly towards the entryway and finally spotted him murmuring words into his cell phone. I finally finished chewing the food in my mouth and took residence on the couch knowing he wasn't summoning me.

Footsteps and a clear "Good Bye" and the Golden Paladin was standing at the doorway, back to normal size, shinning like the sun and pointing his finger at me.

"You are coming with me." He was calm and authoritative and he enunciated every word carefully slow. It was clear that it wasn't a request and it would have been foolish for me to argue. Finished with my sandwich, and with a full stomach, I left the plate on the coffee table and started walking towards him. Satisfied that I was going to obey and follow, he turned and started walking towards his car. I didn't wish to disappoint so I followed him all the way to it. He had already entered and taken his seat behind the wheel; I walked around to the passenger side, opened the rear door and entered the vehicle.

"What are you doing?" He asked me frowning through the rear view mirror. I looked around the backseat trying to figure out what I had done wrong but had no answer for him.

"You are not under arrest and I am no one's chauffer, get your ass in the front seat." I did not wish to anger him, my life certainly would be of no consequence to him if he felt the need to take it. I hurriedly tried opening the door from which I had entered the vehicle but it denied me access to the outdoors. Panicking, I quickly scootched over to the other door and once more was denied exit. The Golden Paladin let out a grunt and mumbled incomprehensible curses as he got out of the cruiser and opened the rear driver side door. Terrified of what he was planning to do to me, I scooted back towards the other door as far as the interior would allow me to scoot.

More angry mumbling and the Golden Paladin took imposing steps through the dirt driveway towards the door by which I cowered. I consider bolting out of the open door on the other side, but before I could decide what to do in my peril, he opened the door and I tumbled down on to the dirt. I hadn't realized the only thing that had been holding me inside the car was the closed door. I didn't know whether to feel foolish or terrified and the Golden Paladin's next command assured me I was just an ass.

"Get in the front seat I said. I don't have time for your crazy!" I scrambled to my feet, patted away as much dirt as I could and got in the front seat as he had instructed. He slammed all the doors shut, including his, after he had gotten back into the car. This left me time to start admiring the front seat. This wasn't any regular front passenger seat; it felt more like the cockpit of an airplane or a rocket. There were buttons, knobs, displays, switches and cables everywhere. He threw the car into gear and we peeled out in the dirt, sliding and twisting as we went. For a second I thought we had joined some high speed chase but soon I realized it was just us. I didn't know if he was trying to scare me or if he was just driving angry, but I stopped looking at the little orange needle on the speedometer once it passed one hundred miles per hour.

The seatbelt that had been hanging from its reel, quickly found its way around my chest and waist. The needle kept following the numbers up as the scenery zoomed past us. I had no idea where we were going and why we were driving so ridiculously fast. I considered for a mere instant jumping out of the car but at these speeds, even with my training, I would not stand a chance. I was in it for the long haul and had to trust the Golden Paladin not to crash us to death. I noticed a green road sign in the distance and it zoomed past us before I could barely read "Santa Fe" on it. Apparently we were heading back to the hospital yet again today.

What once had felt like a long, boring, trip became a short terrifying one but once more we were exiting the highway into Santa Fe. I thought we would be pulling up to the hospital, but to my mortifying dismay we pulled up in front of Gabriel's sister's house. There was no way Rosa hadn't found the towel I left yet and I did not want to have to face that angry little woman. The Golden Paladin quickly exited the car and as he slammed the door once more he screamed at me to get out. I took a deep breath and prepared to face even more of a hell in which I was in. I reluctantly exited the vehicle and took one after another step towards the front door and my impending doom.

I didn't have to knock this time as the Golden Paladin was already knocking by the time I reached the stoop. The door opened as I took my last step, trying to hide behind him. My attempts at stealth failed miserably as the small woman ran around the Paladin and started to hit me repeatedly with both open hands. I covered myself as the hail of tiny hands kept swatting at me as if I were some pesky fly. I kept waiting for the Paladin to rescue me, but instead I was met with his deep rolling laughter.

The barrage of insults and avalanche of hits started to hurt because of frequency not because of strength. Fully amused the Golden Paladin finally decided to pull Rosa off of me. After lifting and moving the small woman to a safe distance from me, he asked her what had instigated her fury. She obliged and told him how she discovered the towel I left soiled while she tried to dry her hands. The Golden Paladin was rendered incapacitated as he was bent over laughing to and past the edge of tears. This allowed Rosa to once more escape his guard and rain on me an avalanche of small angry hands.

Defenseless and feeling guilty, I let Rosa get her anger out on me. Thankfully the Golden Paladin came to my rescue once he saw I wasn't even blocking her strikes. He told her a few stern words and she reluctantly stopped hitting me, crossed her arms, stomped on the ground and stormed off into the house. He looked at me and appeared to be ready to say something. Laughter overtook him once more as he disappeared through the doorway, shaking his head.

The door stayed open, inviting me in. I didn't really want to break its threshold and follow the other two but I knew that I had to. I peaked in first, making sure the coast was clear and another tornado of small angry hands wasn't going to meet my face once more. Hearing voices up ahead and away from my view I reluctantly entered, one slow foot step after another. I followed the voices and they led me into the dining room. Inside the dining room was a table where both Rosa and The Golden Paladin sat. Her angry frown had vanished as the Paladin appraised her of Gabriel's current condition. As if feeling me and without looking, he ordered me to tell her what I had told him. I wasn't much for following orders, but I had enough abuse for a day and didn't want to have to fend off the Golden Paladin. Rosa might had gotten a few decent slaps in, my cheeks were still burning from them but I didn't think I could withstand a barrage like that from him.

I sat down after being invited to sit by a now much calmer Rosa and began to tell her. I told her about his disease. About him leaving, desperately searching for a cure after doctors had told him they could no longer do anything for him. I told her every single bit I knew, in so violating Gabriel's confidence but I was pretty sure we were past the point of secrets. Every word of my long tale softened her tough expression until a tear broke the threshold of her left eye and gently rolled down her beautiful cheek. For the first time, I felt sad for the small woman and contemplated stopping. As much as I wanted, I knew I could not stop now and her wide eager eyes confirmed it for me.

When I was finally finished she instantly looked over to the Golden Paladin. "Is this true Jose?" Without a word he puckered his lips and gently nodded, now in his human form. Rosa stood and started to pace up and down the adjacent kitchen, her eyes searching for something that wasn't there and answering her own mumbled question before we could even understand to answer. Finally she stood in front of the table and both of us, nodding with a resigned look in her eyes and keys in her hand. I didn't know where she produced them from but she was obviously ready to go and there could only be one destination for this trip.

The Golden Paladin and I followed behind her for the short drive to the hospital. Once there, her short legs made it hard for me to keep up with her pace. The nurse at the main desk of his floor greeted us and asked for us to identify ourselves. Both Rosa and the Golden Paladin did, when it was my turn I did not know how to answer. Sensing my awkwardness she looked down on the notes on her files, gave me a wink and allowed us to proceed to his room.

A much younger nurse was walking out of his room with her colorful paisley scrubs. She brightened up at the sight of us three and informed us that he was awake and alert. I could see him through the open door, sitting on the bed, eyes fixated on the television on the wall. Hearing the voices of his sister and brother converse with the nurse he brightened up and shut off the television. Both of them started to go in but I couldn't force myself to follow. Instead, I cowered back into the hallway and found a waiting room. I didn't know what they were going to talk about but I knew it didn't involve me. Actually soon, nothing would involve me and that more than frightened me.

One Last Curtain Call
(Gabriel)

I awoke to rhythmic electronic beating of my heart. My vision was blurry for a few moments but soon the room came into focus. There were cables and hoses wrapped around me, some of them even going in and out of me. The beeping became louder and reassured me my heart was still beating. I wasn't sure what had happened, but I was obviously in a hospital room. I knew this day would come eventually, but I had hoped it wouldn't come quite just yet.

The reality of the situation, and the numerous machines monitoring my every bodily function, told me that I must be in pretty bad shape. A blond woman wearing kaleidoscopic scrubs entered the room and instantly smiled at seeing me conscious. She quickly approached the bed, reading all the instruments and writing down on her clipboard whatever information they gave her.

"How are you feeling Mr. Moreno?" Her voice was young and sweet as she almost spoke to me as if I were a child. I didn't mind, she was quite easy on the eyes and her scrubs accentuated her heavenly curves. Distracted by her blue eyes and wide smile, I forgot to answer so she queried me once more, this time raising her a voice a little to make sure I heard her.

"I am not sure, why don't you tell me?" I snapped out of my momentary trance and answered the kind lady.

"I will go get the doctor so he can explain everything to you." She started to turn to walk away and I grabbed her by the wrist.

"I know I am in bad shape, I have for a long time and honestly I am in no mood to hear more medical jargon from some know-it-all doctor. I much rather hear it in simple terms from someone as beautiful as you." She blushed at my brash compliment, her cheeks turning red first, then the red pigment shooting down her neck and upper chest. I didn't know what had gotten into me, maybe I just didn't care anymore or maybe Bracket had rubbed off on me. But it felt wonderful just letting my thoughts freely exit through my mouth without my brain wrestling to edit them. Compliments will really get you anywhere. The nurse looked back to the door one more time and decided to fulfill my request.

What the pretty lady told me was not very beautiful. She kept it simple for me, which I appreciated, especially since the news perplexed me. My liver had decided to work when it wanted and my energy levels plummeted to unconsciousness. After further inquiry, and discussion between the two of us, my lack of drinking was most probably to blame. In her opinion, which she made clear a million times that is was just "her opinion", and by no means any kind of diagnosis. Here I thought I was doing something good for my body and it almost killed me. My search for a healthy today left me with a giant goose egg on the back of my head and lying in a hospital bed. I needed a drink...

I thanked her for her honesty and as she was about to exit the room, she turned and said; "Oh your partner just left, if I may say, you two make an adorable couple." I didn't know who she was referring to and then I remembered Bracket. I could shake my head and giggle about it; I could only imagine what he must be thinking about being called my "partner".

The day drug on so I found refuge in the crappy and outdated television hanging from the wall in the corner. Nurses and doctors kept coming in and out to check my vitals and talk to me. There was nothing they told me that the beautiful, kind nurse hadn't already. I sat there and pretended to listen to them as they impressed themselves with big and technical words. I didn't once give them the satisfaction of asking what they meant so they repeatedly left unfulfilled and disappointed. I wasn't there to boost their self-esteem; I was there to be treated.

Eventually, a normal human being wearing a white coat entered my room. He spoke to me like a human and sat at the side of my bed as we conversed. The head of oncology confirmed what the nurse had told me, but also gave me great insight into the big picture. As it was, the big picture was that there wasn't one. I wasn't leaving, this was it. The only reason I was feeling so cheery and watching television, is because I was being pumped full of pain killers. My bottles of alcohol had been replaced by a bag and a drip of legal narcotics. Like I said, I had been waiting for this day for a long time but now that is was here, how I wished it wasn't.

I thanked him for his time, and he left me alone to my thoughts. The thoughts and ponderings were short lived as my nurse returned only to be followed by Jose and Rosa. I didn't know how they knew or how they got there, although I did have one guess. Rosa threw herself on me and hugged as mightily as she possibly could. Jose tried to remain stoic as always but the severity of the situation betrayed him and his emotions started to leak out. Before I knew it we were all siting on the bed together our bodies in contact, supporting each other like scared little kids once more.

I told them what the oncologist had just told me and it was down Jose's face that the tears began to roll. Rosa just held my hand in her left and gently petted it with her right. We talked and talked for what must have been hours, being tired and at the end of my road, for once I spoke and told them everything. There were quick flare-ups of anger and frustration about my decision to keep it secret until now. Fortunately, we quickly moved on and focused on the now and what little future we had together.

I honestly could not remember the last time all three of us were together like this, just talking, catching up and being brothers and sisters. It was truly bittersweet, I had to wait so long to live it but it was almost the end of the movie. Jose finally let his guard down and even told us about his love interest, an EMT out of Santa Fe. Apparently they had been dating now for a while. I was glad to hear he had finally found someone. He was the definition of an impenetrable fortress, so this girl had to be quite the catch.

Rosa tried her best to keep things positive and catch me up on her life, but playing the victim was so ingrained in her that it was almost impossible not to. Didn't seem like there was any man ready to take on that bee's nest, no matter how sweet the honey might turn out to be. It was nice to talk and hear about the kids while not being guilted about them.

Over the next few days and weeks the visits continued and the conversation deepened. We eventually were able to talk about Mom and the conversation was filled with tears and left us with great relief and peace. I made sure I said everything I ever wanted to say and straightened every last detail.

On a particular sunny morning, the blinding rays of the sun awoke me, shining through my eyelids. I quickly realized I wasn't alone in the now, very familiar, hospital room. Sitting next to me staring out into the glorious sunrise was Monica. She held my hand in hers while she sat on a chair right next to my bed. I remained motionless so I would not alert her of my waking. The rays of the sun were bounding off her copper skin, making her truly shine. I laid there quietly soaking in every inch, freckle, wrinkle and beautiful detail that made her, her.

After my eyes explored and wondered to my heart's content, I broke the silence. "Are you supposed to be in here Ma'am?" The peaceful silence interrupted, Monica jumped on her seat, her startled eyes quickly meeting mine. Her surprised expression quickly gave way to a warm smile that melted me as it always did. She quickly rose to her feet and came in closer for what I thought would be a hugging embrace. Instead her tender, soft lips met mine as her eyes closed, giving herself to the kiss. She tasted better than I had ever imagined and after all these years, my dream of feeling those succulent lips on mine was finally happening.

I answered the kiss and lost myself in her. So many years, had I waited, so many other lips I had kissed wishing it were hers, so much longing for her and as our lips danced with each other my heart filled with joy. After a few seconds of blissful eternity the embrace broke and Monica instantly looked embarrassed. She tried to sit back down and turn away but I held her hand and reassured her it was ok. She fought at first but after a few tender words she graced me with the beautiful brown eyes, coy smile and blushing cheeks.

"How are you feeling?" Her voice was trembling with nerves and her grin betrayed her attempts at composure.

"Well I am much better now." The words turned her pinkish cheeks into beat red morsels. I wanted to continue to razz her but a sadness showed in her eyes that broke mine. She started to say something but I interrupted her before she could bare her soul to me.

"Don't." The word sounded harsh even to me and her broken eyes begun to well up with tears. I repeated it but this time much more tenderly and softly. I squeezed her hand between mine and continued as she stood next to me, a little hurt and shocked.

"Don't say it. Please don't." Her eyes filled with puzzlement, she opened her mouth to protest but I once more continued. "You have known all your life and I now know also. I just don't want to hear it, here, like this."

"But I need to, Gabriel. I have been a fool for too long, I need to set things right before..." She couldn't say it. I knew, she knew, but saying it out loud made it real, and she was not ready to accept that grim reality.

"Did you mean it? The kiss." She nodded as fat tears formed in her eyes and tried to escape down her beautiful face. "Then I want you to do me a favor."

"Anything" she answered without any hesitation.

I didn't know how to say it without sounding heartless so I just said it. "I want you to leave, I want you to leave and never come back." The tears that she had been so valiantly holding back started to stream down her face. I continued to hurt her because I cared.

"I want you to leave this place of death, I want you to pack your things up and leave this place all together. I want you to pack your car with as much as you can, drive and never look back. I hate still seeing you here. So many dreams, so many travel plans so many adventures that never happened and just got lost in the desert. I don't care if you only make it to San Diego or if you finally make it to Barcelona. But I want you to leave and never come back. I need you to live and wake up from this daze you have been lost in all your life. I want to you stop being afraid and live your dreams."

I could see her getting ready to protest and before she could I finished. "There is nothing left here for you but sadness and loneliness. Please, for me, go and be, go and bloom into the beautiful flower I always knew you were."

I wasn't sure what made her understand, but the pain and sorrow left her eyes and was replaced by hope and determination. She got it, she smiled down at me, her eyes gleaming with love. She gifted me one more kiss. It was long and gentle. Her lips danced over mine, plump and moist. She held my face between her hands as she lost herself in me.

The kiss ended and as I asked her she left. I watched her take every painful step away from me and towards, hopefully her new life. She never looked back and part of me wished I could have seen those eyes just one more time. The rest of the day flew by in slow motion. All I could do was stare out my window while nurses periodically wandered in. I couldn't eat, my insides were in knots and it wasn't because of my sickness.

Night came and the blue sky outside the window slowly disappeared. The tall parking lot lights came ablaze as darkness rolled in. There was one I could clearly see from my bed and its orange glow had attracted a swarm of moths. They flew around spastically, desperate to reach the light, briefly landing on it just to take up and fly some more around it. They danced in the night, desperate to reach their goal, most never coming close and the few that did burning up in its miraculous glow. I felt bad for the live ones, for the dead ones got to touch and feel the warm glowing embrace of what they wanted and loved the most, even if in the end it killed them.

The only person I didn't get to talk to was Bracket. I would see him peeking in and quickly disappearing. I could tell he thought he was stealthy but it was more like a little kid clumsily checking on their parents to see if they were awake. I even tried to call out for him when I saw him, but he never entered the room. I knew he would never enter the room, just hover around. I just hoped he wasn't creating chaos in the cafeteria, running around naked or pretending to be a doctor and attempting surgery. I really couldn't help him from the hospital bed so I could only trust he would keep himself out of trouble.

The days eventually started to become shorter and dreams more convoluted. I would wake up and ask what day it was and sometimes I was informed that I had slept for two, three and even four days without waking. The hoses and cables stayed firmly attached to my skin and it was becoming obvious they were the only things keeping me alive. On a brighter note, I finally got to lose all that weight I had been fighting all my life and the cute nurses gave me sponge baths. So life wasn't completely terrible.

My crash diet and quick descent took from my best estimations a month. There were days I would open my eyes and just listen. My body was shutting down with me trapped inside of it. The four white walls of the room slowly began to close on me and every day that passed it felt like less of a room and more of a coffin. My only distraction became the small television on the wall that somehow became more distant and quieter each day. The visits helped but were becoming more frustrating than pleasant. Some days I could converse and feel like myself, others even and mighty as I tried, not a single word would come out from my lips. I would send well-constructed sentences from my brain to my lips and only moans and mumbles would come out.

On one of the better days I asked Rosa for several favors and asked her where Bracket was. I had imagined he had become a mangy bearded man hiding in the basement and closets of the hospital, periodically venturing out for food and quickly peek through my door. Thankfully Rosa had "adopted" him and the kids were enjoying playing with him. He was a third kid in the house, as she explained it, but knew that I would not want him alone. I made her a list of everything I needed and told her to ask Jose if she needed help. We spoke on great detail on what I was trying to accomplish with it and she did her best at playing devil's advocate for me. We went around and around a few times but with the help and advice only she could provide, we came to a finished and polished plan.

I remember her kissing me on the forehead before she left, telling me she loved me and how proud Mom would have been. She knew how much it meant to me and my chest filled with pride and joy. I was tired, very tired, I don't know how long we had been talking for, but it had zapped the energy out of me. I slowly moved my hands over my thighs and it surprised me how skinny they were. I had enjoyed being skinny for once in my life but feared I was past the point of handsome and quickly reaching grim. As it was now, customary darkness took over and the weird timeless dreams began. The cocktail of drugs and impending mortality birthed the most amazing and disturbing dreams I had ever had.

I don't know how much time had passed, it might have been a couple of hours or days, but at this point everything I had asked Rosa for was stacked neatly on the small night table next to me. My brother thought it was hilarious and had brought me a large pink pansies plant. The bright flowers kept guard of the stack of photos and papers Rosa had left. Energized by it I felt alive, the most alive I have felt in weeks. As I was frantically writing, Rosa walked in the room and her face lit up with a smile. She helped me finish and left, taking it with her.

For the first time in what seemed like an eternity, I felt a sense of complete accomplishment. My chest became swollen with pride and tears of joy rolled down my face. I could hear the silent splat they made as the small, aqueous orbs hit the pillow.

I must tell you my friends that this is the end of our journey together. From that day on the blur became the norm, and I could not distinguish between dream and reality anymore. I had fulfilled my task and my malfunctioning body embraced the chaos and madness that raged within it. I don't know if I went silently into the good night, went out with a bang or if some shadow of me still lingers on. Whichever the case, I am no more, so I can't tell you anymore. I will tell you that I am at peace and wherever I finally get to see my mother again, whether it is in heaven, the cosmos or the heart of an exploding supernova, I know when I see her she will be proud and her arms will embrace and hold me once more.

The gift of sand
(Bracket)

I successfully hid for three days in the hospital. Hospital food is not the most appetizing thing in the world, especially cold and half eaten. I was able to feed myself by plundering waiting room after waiting room of their crackers and coffee, as well as picking through the leftovers left on the room trays. I would periodically check on Gabriel but could not bring myself to enter the room. Searching for better and more secure accommodation, I allowed myself to be detected by Rosa. My only other option was the Golden Paladin, and he didn't strike me as the charitable kind.

I had expected her to swarm on me once more and attack relentlessly. Instead, she kindly greeted and even thanked me for bringing Gabriel's reality to light. She offered me her home, and I quickly accepted. The ride was short and awkward. Her attempts at making conversation failed miserably. I tried my best to remain courteous and gracious but small talk had never been my strong suit.

"It is not much but you are welcome to stay here until we figure things out." I found her apologetic tone to be unnecessary. Her house, although small, was well kept and immaculate. She guided me through the hallway, introducing each room we passed as a family member. I could not help but to cringe as she pointed where the bathroom was. Thankfully the tour kept moving along until I was delivered and introduced into the spare bedroom. She excused herself and left me alone in a sea of flowers.

The room was plastered, decorated and completely covered with flowers. Not the happy go lucky kind but the dramatic rose bed sheets and horrible fake tulips on a vase. I considered for a second abandoning the room, it was cruel and unusual punishment. Sadly, my option was the old lady flower room or back to the hospital's custodian's closet. I settled in and thankfully the bed, although hideous, was quite comfortable.

The next morning, I was once more introduced to the children over breakfast. Soon after I became their toy, friend and nanny. I solemnly swore to protect them the first time Rosa left me watching them, but I soon found out that, I was the one who needed protection. The two creatures climbed all over me, constantly requested my attention, needing to be fed and insisted on particular kinds of juice boxes when I would fetch them for them. By the time Rosa finally returned I was exhausted, I excused myself and welcomed the sea of tacky flowers that awaited me in my room.

She was only gone for one hour that first time. The times left alone with them increased with each assignment. Fortunately, I was able to devise some tactics to deal with the two little monsters. After a few weeks, I found that I was actually enjoying the time I got to spend with the kids alone. We would play games, they would help me make their snacks and even clean up around the house to help Rosa.

Once a week I would tag along with either Rosa or the Golden Paladin and try to go see Gabriel. I would peek in time and time again but the room would not allow me to enter it. He was getting thin, so very thin. By the 12th week he looked nothing like the man I had met. I wasn't a doctor but I could tell time was winning and what he had left of it was short. I was lucky to have found some refuge with Rosa, but I knew that could not be permanent. Entering that room and seeing Gabriel in that state only intensified my anxiety about my impending despair. Surviving would not be an issue for me, but he was..., well he was my friend. The only friend I've had according to my damaged memory banks. And I did not wish to lose him.

On a hot Thursday evening, Rosa returned from her daily post-work visit to Gabriel. There was something odd in her eyes and I feared my partner had passed. I quickly queried her about it and she assured me that he was fine. Right behind her walked in Jose, he gave me his customary nod and went off to summon the children with the pizzas he carried in his strong arms. He had left his armor in his car since Rosa wasn't to kind about it around the kids.

"Let's go for a drive." It was more of a command but she was kind enough to present it as a pseudo request. Still suspicious of the worst, I followed the small woman into her car. She held her car keys ready to open the door of the old Volvo station wagon she drove, from the moment we left the house. The patrol car was parked out on the street and knowing the kids were safe with Jose she didn't even bother to lock the door.

I sat down on the old cracked brown leather seats and felt my skin trying to burn even through my clothes. I shifted from side to side, allowing one piece of flesh to temporarily cool before it was attacked by the burning leather. The air in the car wasn't much better. It was heavy and scalding as it punished my lungs, making it hard to breathe. Rosa had rode with the Golden Paladin to the hospital today so the old blue Volvo just sat under the day sun, boiling and blistering, preparing itself to attack defenseless asses and lungs.

Rosa slid in and without hesitation she turned the engine, cranked the air conditioning to max and rolled down the windows. She also danced, her curvaceous butt wiggling from side to side on her worn out seat. We were quickly rolling down the street and the breeze flushed out the boiling air. We rolled up the windows and rejoiced in the cooling powers of the loud air conditioner.

As she silently drove, I feared a return to the Super Max prison and as we mounted the interstate my anxiety intensified. We were heading towards Las Vegas, New Mexico, as indicated by the green sign with white letters. I knew I had probably overstayed my welcome at her house but I had even learned how to change the toilet paper roll. I would think my continuous strides for improvement and my help with the kids would have granted me some sort of amnesty. The road ahead was long so all I could do was contemplate my reactions to every possible action and enjoy the ride.

Accustomed to each other's company, there were no uncomfortable attempts at small talk. Instead, the ride was filled with comfortable silence. That was until Rosa decided to meddle with the radio. After fiddling through several stations she settled on some ranchero music with an overexcited tuba player. I wanted to protest but it wasn't my vehicle nor did I have a clue of what was going on. I endured the barrage of yelps, screams, out of tune singing and damn tuba.

My heart finally slowed as Rosa let off the gas as we approached the Pecos exit. My hands relaxed the death grip I had been subjecting my thighs to. The list of possibilities for this mysterious trip was quickly erased and a new one started to be compiled by my brain. I would admit relief in so that most of them were benign. We weaved through the familiar streets and once more I was facing the old familiar house. It looked just how I had left it, besides the small mounds of dust and sand forming on the front porch.

Rosa led the way into her childhood home, opening the door and turning on the lights. As I followed her short and careful footsteps I noticed a large yellow envelope clasped in her hands. The envelope triggered a whole new set of possibilities in my brain. It was one of those large legal sized ones which usually hold documents the recipient never wants to receive. I had the sinking feeling I was the recipient, and even though I didn't know what was in it, I did want it in my hands.

We settled in the house and Rosa disappeared into the kitchen while asking me if I wanted something to drink. The tension was steadily mounting and I almost asked for one of Gabriel's beers. Somehow I filtered my response and asked for water instead. Rosa's trip to the kitchen took longer that it should for the two single glasses of water she brought out of it. The ever looming envelope now resided under her arm, tightly clasped against her torso. She was obviously stalling and hesitating to explain to me why we were there. This just pushed me further and wound me tighter. Whatever hammer she was about to drop on me, I begged it happen quickly and put me out of my misery swiftly.

She sat down on the couch, which had been my bed for many nights, and placed the cups of water on the coffee table. I followed her lead and sat on the loveseat in which Gabriel enjoyed getting intoxicated in and waking up the next day wondering how he ended up there. I know those days were quite self-destructive for both of us, but part of me held great nostalgia for them. I could see her eyes searching inside her brain for the right words to say and the agony of the wait overtook me.

"What? What?! What is going on? What's in the envelope, for fucks sake, what the hell is in the envelope?!" She could not help but to break a smile and giggle at my outburst, finding my cursing amusing, even though it was strictly forbidden in her house and around the kids. I learned that the hard way. Nothing like a 6 year old saying "fuck" to receive the full ire of the mother. I made sure to use my adjective and adverbs a lot more carefully in her house since that explosive day.

I wasn't very amused, but had made my point. Now I just sat there and awaited her response. She put me out of my misery by finally breaking the silence.

"I am still not sure if this is the right thing to do or not. But I promised Gabriel; so here you go." She extended her arm and handed me the dreaded yellow envelope. It had to be filled with anthrax, or some other biological agent. I had no doubt in my mind about it. She continued:

"Please don't' open it until I leave. Read it and study it carefully, if you need anything you know how to get a hold of me." She stood, and not having taken a single sip from her water, she lovingly kissed my forehead and left the house, closing the door after herself.

The words "Don't open it until I leave" kept echoing in my mind. It had to be some biological agent, maybe some radioactive isotope; that would explain her not drinking the water. I was probably already infected and whatever was inside was just going to detail my painful, agonizing and excruciating death. They would probably come back at some point and just burn down the house with me in it. Get rid of the evidence and cleanse the area. I was for certain already dead, so I opened the yellow envelope to discover how painful my fate would be and the reason for the betrayal. They prepared us for this sort of incident but I never expect the treason to come from Rosa and the Golden Paladin.

My finger explored the flap of the secret-holding yellow envelope and soon found a small wedge where to cram my pointer finger. I slowly wiggled it in and gently pried the flap from the main body of the envelope. The glue and paper softly moaned and protested and I broke the bond a wet tongue once forged. Once opened, I peeked inside and didn't identify any powder or mysterious substances. Just a small stack of papers and a set of keys at the bottom. Radioactive isotope without a doubt. This was going to be a long and agonizing death.

I pulled the papers out and gently placed them on top of the coffee table. The top item was another envelope, this one regular letter sized, white and with "Bracket" written in big letters on it. I was the only Bracket I knew so it must have been meant for me. I grabbed it and it was fat with the many pieces of folded paper inside of it. I readied myself to break another glue bond but the envelope was open. I pulled out the folded letter and gently expanded it.

Between my fingers rested four pages of paper, hand written and from what I could quickly scan filled from top to bottom. At the top of the first page it said. "Dear Bracket," Letters that start that way are never a good sign.

The two words did bring me some peace as although fatal, my fate was no longer uncertain. I took a drink of the water, filled my lungs with a deep breath and started to read the cursive words that adorned the white sheets.

"Dear Bracket,

If you are reading this it means that things have taken a swift turn for the worst. There are several things I wished I had the time to share and tell you but life didn't allow it. I wished many a time that you had wandered into my room instead of just peeking in. Instead, I write you this letter to tell you everything I have wanted to tell you.

I have long debated whether to and how to tell you all of this. I now know deep in my heart you not only deserve to but need to hear it. My wonderful friend Bracket, your true and forgotten identity is Barry Racket, as you can see from the first documents and pictures included in the envelope..."

I looked over the letter my eyes burning into the stack of papers on the coffee table. I reached for the first and it was a birth certificate corroborating the name Gabriel had just indicated was mine. Clipped to it were numerous pictures from an infant to a young man which I could identify as myself. The last picture had my name written under it and appeared to be from a year-book because of my overanalyzed pose. I set the birth certificate and pictures to the left of the stack and continued with the letter.

"... I want to make sure you understand that you are a good man, a noble man and a special man. The events I will describe, and you will see that news clipping don't define you, but they did change you.

Like many brilliant minds, your gift of intellect is directly interwoven with some challenges. Life always finds an equilibrium, even if in some cases it is chaotic, such as your case..."

I looked through the news clipping and court documents, all with the name Barry Racket scattered all over them. Some even had a picture of a man in a suit that I must admit looked strikingly similar to me. I looked at them over and over, reading each word carefully. "aggravated assault, Genius Snaps, five year sentence, mental institution..." It all seemed legitimate but it didn't make sense. I threw the papers down and they scattered and floated all over the table and floor. I just couldn't look at them anymore. It was a trick, some sort of sick joke. Why would Gabriel be doing that to me? This had to be a joke.

I abandoned the letter and papers and went searching through the house for Gabriel. I looked through bedrooms, the bathroom and finally found my way into the kitchen. I opened the fridge in desperation and expected him to somehow jump out of it and tell me this was all but an elaborate joke. The fridge door remained firmly clasped in my left hand, and inside the fridge the only thing I found was a half empty jar of pickles with three slices gently floating in the brine and a bottle of ketchup which rattled as I slammed the fridge door shut.

There was no Gabriel and the pain deep inside my head somehow told me this was not a joke. I looked out on the mess of sheets all over the living room but could not bring myself to leave the kitchen. An invisible barrier had formed and would not allow me to exit the kitchen. I plotted a way to escape and the front door kept catching my eyes. I wanted to go and be anywhere, anywhere would be better than thumbing through those pages full of pain and lies.

I paced back and forth in the small narrow kitchen, searching for answers and peace. I knew I wouldn't find either in there so filled with Gabriel's courage, I ventured back into the living room and started to reluctantly pick up the pages. Once organized, I turned back to the letter in hope of the elusive answers. The words on the paper continued to explain truths that I didn't understand and it wasn't until the last page that I finally believed the message the flowing letters were giving me.

"I don't know if this is reaching you or making any sense. I do hope there is peace and hope in the words I am telling you and the things I am showing you. Even if they are painful right now, I promise you my friend they will bring you joy.

There is one last picture I want you to look at. It should be the only large one and at the end of the stack..."

I looked at the coffee table and only one piece of paper remained on top of it. It was a full page photograph which my eyes had refused to look at. Having almost finished the letter and painful journey Gabriel had sent me through, I picked it up and carefully looked at it as I continued reading.

"...The one on the left is Megan, she is three in the picture and nine now. The one on the right is Sophia, she was five at the time of the picture, now a young lady of eleven. Look closely my friend, the smiling man in the middle is, YOU. I have seen many of your smiles but never a smile like that..."

The two little girls in the picture were huddled into me with my arms wrapped around them. I ran my hand through the picture and I could feel the touch of the hair under my fingertips. Nights of me reading bedtime stories, botched braids and gentle kisses flooded into my mind. Even if everything else in the letter was a lie, I knew in that instance that my two princesses were real. Megan, scared of thunder, and my Sophia, the ballerina. I remembered, I remembered so much and with every memory a tear accompanied. I re-read the letter, six years had passed without me seeing my girls.

I wasn't dying a painful death but my eyes, my throat, my stomach all screamed in agony as I sobbed, looking at the picture. I remembered what I had done that took me away from them and how I was left, abandoned as some ugly memory to be forgotten.

"I really hope you remember my friend. I really do hope with all my heart you remember them. I fear our time together is over now and I must thank you for every day I got the joy and frustration to spend with you. I have done my good deed, I hope. I hope these words do you some good. I can die vindicated and having made my Mom proud.

It is time now for you to vindicate yourself my good friend. Inside the envelope is a set of keys. My Mom left me the house but it was never meant for me. It is yours. The Jeep as well. Jose has arranged for you to visit your girls. Sophia and Megan are waiting for you. There are years to be made up, many wounds to heal and the time for a smart and wonderful father to start again.

Oh my wonderful and loved friend Barry, it is time for you to grab those keys and drive. Drive to your girls, drive to your future; it waits for you. You will always be my Bracket and I your loyal companion, but it is time for you to be Barry and more importantly, Dad to your precious girls.

Thank you for entering my life, being my friend and my salvation. One day we will ride again through the cosmos together, but for now good bye my friend.

Forever and loyally yours,
Gabriel Moreno"

Fin

Special Thanks to:

Editors:
Rita Dragoni
Nicole Straker
Darren Bass

Cover Artist:
Scott Norem

Connect with Ricky Dragoni at:

www.rickydragoni.com[1]
Twitter : @RickyDragoni
Instagram: ricky_dragoni
Facebook: rickydragoni

Don't miss out!

Click the button below and you can sign up to receive emails whenever Ricky Dragoni publishes a new book. There's no charge and no obligation.

https://books2read.com/r/B-A-HRGE-QHCO

Connecting independent readers to independent writers.

Also by Ricky Dragoni

Prime Infinity
Ripples
The Angel of a Madman

26162790R00107

Made in the USA
Columbia, SC
06 September 2018